She was halfway into her car when she noticed the book on the back seat. . .

"Crap!" Grabbing it with one hand, Cassie pulled out her cell phone with the other. "Maybe she hasn't left yet...she's probably fixing her face in the mirror." She hit the speed dial number for Solange and rushed for the stairs.

She was on the third floor landing when she heard the scream, followed by several horribly loud cracks.

Gunshots.

Echoes reverberated in the garage and in Cassie's head as she stood paralyzed for a moment. Swallowing the shock, the panic, and the fear, she ran down the next flight of stairs, missing the last step and slamming down on her right knee. The pain helped clear out the last of the shock as she scrambled up and lurched towards the body she could see lying on the cement floor.

Solange.

Dead to Writes

Cathy Wiley

Upcoming books in the Cassandra Ellis series
Two Wrongs Don't Make a Right (available winter of 2010/2011)
Write of Passage (available in 2011)

More Zapstone Books
~~~~
Science Fiction/Action
T. M. Roy
*Convergence – Journey to Nyorfias*, Book 1 (available now)
*Gravity – Journey to Nyorfias*, Book 2 (Coming Soon!)
*Stratagem – Journey to Nyorfias*, Book 3 (TBA)
~~~~
T.M. Roy and Sara V. Olds
Casualties of Treachery – The Ukasir's Own, Unit One
(check website for details)
~~~~
Sff-Romance
T.M. Roy
*Discovery – A Far Out Romance* (available now)
~~~~
Middle Reader/Historical
Sara V. Olds
Anna – A Farewell to Juarez (available now)
~~~~

Visit
www.zapstone.com
for the latest releases, updates, sneak previews, and more!

To contact, please email:
publisher@zapstone.com

Please write with any comments, concerns, or questions
~~~~

Dead to Writes

A Cassandra Ellis Mystery

Cathy Wiley

A Zapstone Production

This novel is a work of fiction. Names, characters, places, and incidents are the products of the author's imagination or are used fictitiously. Any resemblance to actual persons, living or dead, or events, incidents, or organizations is entirely coincidental.

ISBN 10: 0-971543303-X
ISBN 13: 978-0-9715433-3-1

Trade Paperback Edition
Published by Zapstone Productions LLC

Library of Congress Catalog Number (LCCN): 2010934798

For my dad.

Acknowledgements

Like Cassie, I have consulted various subject matter experts to try and get details correct (any factual errors, however, are my own.) For their suggestions and input, I want to thank Austin C., James C., Bryan E., Rachael G., Arlene J., Christa K., Don M., Laura T., Colin W., Terry W., Beverly M./BiZee Bird Store, and Dean and Sharon C. And thanks to Sharon, for her encouragement throughout the years.

Throughout the various renditions of this book, I have been fortunate to have a wonderful critique group to offer suggestions and comments. I wish the best of luck in their own writing efforts to the Ink and Quill crowd, especially Dana, Mary, MaryN, Ronda, Ryl, Susan, Trish, and Vivian.

Thanks to Shari H., Mary N., and Jenn S., for the beta reviews and enthusiastic comments.

A big thank you to Steve W. for his thorough edits and commentary.

A special shout-out to those who participated in the "Name the Parrots" contest, especially winners Diane, Christa, and Spot D' Bird.

Of course, I appreciate all the support from my friends throughout the years, especially Amy and David M., Alison and David M., Tina and Andy P., Aleta B., Mal H., Donna K., and the other members of Jix.

I wouldn't have been able to do this without my wonderful family, especially my mom; David, for constantly badgering—I mean, encouraging me to write; Lynette; and nieces Allie, Aubree, Alyssa, and Ashlynn. Aubree, now it's your turn.

Finally, I have to grab the opportunity to thank T.M. Roy, editor/designer/talent extraordinaire, for walking with me through all the blood, sweat, and tears as I looked to have my first book published. This book is now much, much better than when I first started the process, thanks to you.

Cathy Wiley

DEAD TO WRITES

A Cassandra Ellis Mystery

zapstone productions LLC

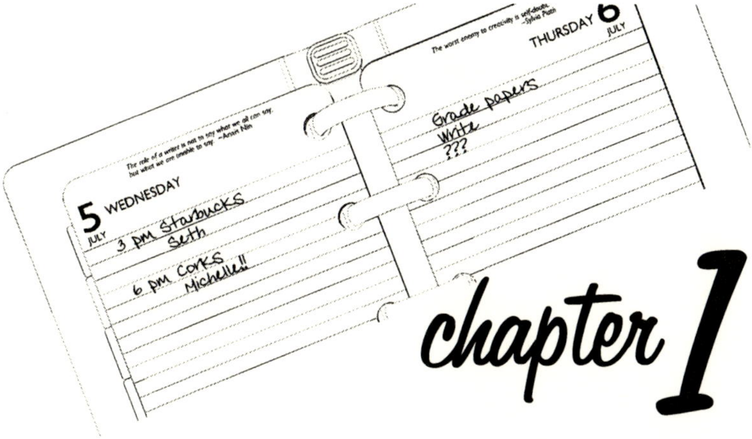

chapter 1

One day, she was going to kill her best friend for always being late.

In the meantime, she would just kill someone else. As Cassie Ellis looked around the upscale restaurant, she barely noticed the sleek design, the contemporary furniture, or the exposed brick walls. She concentrated on the people. Waiting, watching, for that perfect moment, that perfect mark.

Her eyes fell on a distinguished older gentleman sitting in a back corner. She smirked when she saw him glance over to the considerably younger—and considerably more attractive—blonde with him. Clearly, he was checking to see if his date was impressed by the ambiance of the restaurant.

Just as clearly, he was her perfect victim.

Still, she was a fair sport. If he didn't order wine, he'd be fine. If he did order wine—at least a particular bottle—then he'd die.

He ordered wine. He had to show off for the blonde, after all. Cassie wasn't surprised to hear him order the most expensive Merlot on the menu; she had him pegged as a Merlot drinker. A pretentious one, she thought, staring at him like her cat stared at a doomed mouse. She knew something about that particular wine, that specific bottle.

The waiter unknowingly acted out his part of the drama. He took the bottle from behind the bar, walked over, presented it, and waited until the man nodded his approval before wielding the opener. He then handed the cork over to the man for inspection.

She let out a sigh of relief when the man nodded again. The fool didn't notice anything.

The waiter poured a small portion into the man's glass. Even with the dim lighting, she was able to see the rich, deep ruby color. She approved of the man's technique as he raised the balloon-shaped glass and swirled. Rivulets of liquid flowed down the sides of the glass, showing off the legs of the wine just like the blonde was showing off hers in a beaded black dress.

The man brought the glass to his lips. He sipped delicately, inhaled to aerate the liquid, and swished it around in his mouth. Finally, after the wine passed all those tests, he swallowed.

And all hell broke loose.

He lurched out of his chair, sputtering and clutching at his throat as his face took on a dark red color that rivaled the wine. The blonde screeched as he dropped the glass on the table, destroying the pristine whiteness of the linen tablecloth with shattered crystal and splattered Merlot.

Cassie didn't blink as she watched the man—no longer so distinguished looking—crash into the next table. The guests screamed as the victim thrashed about, sending whipped potatoes, baby field carrots, and black truffle meatloaf all over the restaurant. She could hardly blame them, she'd scream too at the loss of such a delicious—

"Are you okay?"

She blinked a couple of times and brought her mind back to the real world. Her waiter stood next to her table with a concerned frown on his handsome face.

"Is everything all right, Cassie? I kept saying your name, but you didn't answer."

"Oh sorry, Drew. My mind was...well, elsewhere. Hazard of the writing profession." She looked over at the table in the corner, where another waiter was just now bringing out a bottle of wine for the distinguished gentleman and the blonde. "I'll wait to order until Michelle gets here, but could you prep a bottle of the Schramsberg Blanc de Blancs?"

The waiter raised one sandy eyebrow. "Bubbly, Cassie? Do we have something to celebrate?" He paused a moment and grinned. "Let me guess, your book's being pub—

"Don't say it," she interrupted, and held up a hand. "I want to tell Michelle first. I promise I'll tell you afterward. Anyway, I want to surprise her. Can you bring out the bottle about five minutes after she arrives?"

"Of course. Shall I open it with a big flourish?"

She smiled her approval. When Drew left, she turned back to the couple in the corner. Just like in her fantasy, the man went through the entire tasting process, including distributing the liquid in his mouth. Even with her love of wines and appreciation of the tasting ritual, she never liked swishing wine around her mouth. It reminded her too much of gargling mouthwash.

She watched as he swallowed. The results were much less dramatic than the story in her head. She had to laugh at herself when she heard the blonde ask about the wine and refer to the man as "Dad"; she'd read that scene wrong, that was for sure. But, in her humble opinion, her version of the story was more interesting.

Cassie bent down to snag a notebook and mechanical pencil out of her purse. Tucking a curl behind her ear, she made a note to check out the efficacy and speed of cyanide poisoning. She tapped the pencil against her lips and wondered how the poison could be added to the bottle without any evidence of tampering. If she could figure it out, it would make a fascinating murder method for her next book. And the older gentleman's choice of wine would make the perfect title: *The Merlot Murders,* which would continue the "M" alliteration pattern she'd started with her books.

Her *books.* Drew had been right, but more right than he knew. Than anyone knew. She couldn't believe she had managed to keep the secret for this long, but she wanted to be certain it really was going to happen. So she had waited. And waited. And now...

As she put away her notebook—something on her "never leave home without" list—a flash of red from the depths of her cavernous bag brought a mixed surge of butterflies and pride. She wasn't nervous telling Michelle the news; she knew her best friend would be excited. But her temperamental friend might get upset that she had withheld the information for so long. Well, she'd find out soon.

She grabbed the salt shaker from the center of the table and slid it back and forth while she resumed observing those around her. This time, she decided to forgo her usual diversion of imagining murders. Not that she felt animosity towards her fellow diners; she just was fascinated by mystery stories, especially murder mysteries. Since childhood, she had enjoyed following along with the clues, outwitting the villain, and cheering on the detective. Later, she enjoyed writing new and different ways to commit and solve such crimes. Now, the stories she created were going to pay off. Literally.

That would be good, since she didn't make that much teaching online writing courses. She was fortunate to have a trust fund from her grandmother that she used to buy a house seven years ago when she turned twenty-one. She didn't have to worry about a mortgage, and the writing courses paid the rest of her expenses. Mostly. She still had tons of student loans. If she sold enough books, she might even be able to pay them off before she turned forty.

The advance would help with that. Of course, she was putting most of it towards promoting her book. It wasn't cheap to send out postcards, advertise online, and attend conferences and book signings. But it was going to be worth it. Her Great American Novel was getting published. She hoped it would even sell.

She popped up from her chair as a petite brunette scurried into the room, breathless with apology for being late. Seeing Michelle Edwards in her work clothes, Cassie was glad she had changed into a nice outfit. Her emerald silk shirt and black pants weren't as nice as Michelle's navy blue suit, but at least she wouldn't embarrass herself. She gripped her best friend in an enthusiastic hug.

As they sat down, Cassie reflected on how much they both had grown and changed over the years. She had known Michelle since they were in elementary school. They met through a book, naturally, a book both of them had wanted to read at the same time. When they fought over *Trixie Belden and the Mystery off Glen Road,* the teacher told them to share and read alternate chapters to each other. Mr. Baldwin probably regretted that action as the two girls became best friends and giggled and whispered back and forth throughout the school day.

Back then, Michelle had been a shy, nerdy girl with messy braids, broken glasses, and a buck-toothed grin. Several years of wearing braces had corrected the overbite. And now, her long, chestnut brown hair was smooth, her glasses stylishly bohemian.

Cassie liked to think that the years had improved her as well. Her carrot-red hair had darkened down to a burnished copper, although the curls were wild as ever. Her skinny, gangly body had morphed into a tall, athletic one. Not a graceful one though, unless she was on a bike. Then she could almost fly.

"So…tell me. Why are we here? We only come to Corks to celebrate, so tell me, tell me, tell me."

Cassie had to laugh. That very impatience was the reason they had fought over that book all those years ago. Michelle refused to wait until she was done.

Of course, she was just as impatient. So rather than the long speech she had rehearsed, Cassie took a deep breath and blurted it out. "I'm being published."

Michelle leaped out of the chair with a squeal and grabbed her in a choking hug. "That's incredible, Cassie! Which book? *Mailbox Murders*? *Matchbox Murders*? Who's publishing it? When? How can I buy tons of copies?"

She chose the safest questions to answer. "Both books, actually. I have a three-book contact with DSG."

The name of one of New York's largest publishers brought out another squeal from Michelle. "Oh my God! That's so awesome. When will the first book be out? This year, oh no, probably not, publishing takes forever. Next year?" She sat back down, bouncing in her seat.

"Actually..." Cassie bit her lip as she reached into her bag. "July 8th."

"Of next year?"

"No, this year. As in Saturday." She pulled out *Mailbox Murders* in all of its beautiful glossiness. Caressing the red and black cover, she passed it to Michelle, who was sitting there with her mouth open.

Snapping her jaw shut, Michelle narrowed her eyes as she grabbed the book out of Cassie's hand. "How long have you known about this, Cassandra Ellis? It usually takes years to publish a book."

"Um, well, this has been in the works since last January."

"You've known about this for over a *year*?" Michelle's hazel eyes flashed in anger. "And you never told me? I thought I was your best—"

"Don't even go there," Cassie interrupted. "You *are* my best friend. And as my best friend, you know how I am, how I think. I was afraid I might jinx it if I told anyone."

"You didn't tell anyone? Not even your dad?"

"Not even my dad. No one knows yet. Well, Aaron, of course, since he's the one who negotiated the contract with DSG. And he sent it out to various people for reviews. But I, personally, didn't tell anyone. I didn't want to mess it up."

"You and your superstitions. This shouldn't surprise me." Michelle's frown became a delighted smile as she examined the cover. "Oh, I'm so proud of you for getting published. Even if you didn't tell me."

"You're the first I told, Chelle." Cassie pointed at the book. "Read the dedication."

Opening it up, Michelle's smile trembled as she read the fifth page. "Aww. *'To my best friend and editor. I couldn't have done it without you.'* Okay, now I really forgive you. And you dedicated it to your dad too. And..." Michelle teared up and reached across the table to squeeze Cassie's hand. "And to your mom. I still miss her."

"I miss her too, especially now. I wish she could see my childhood dream come true. Of course I had to dedicate this book to her. After all, as an English teacher, she was the one who got me interested in books in the first place. And in Trixie Belden."

Michelle sniffled once and tossed her head in defiance. "I still say I got to that book first."

They both jumped at a loud popping noise. Cassie laughed at their reaction as Drew walked over with an open bottle and glasses.

"I don't have to ask now," Drew said, pouring the sparkling wine. "I could hear Michelle across the room. Not that that's unusual or anything." He laughed when Michelle stuck her tongue out at him. He placed the first glass in front of Cassie. "For our newest and soon-to-be greatest author."

Her face was going to hurt if she kept smiling so much. "Thanks, Drew. You want to join us for a toast?"

"I would, but I'd get in trouble with the boss." He nodded at the open kitchen. "But I'll toast to you later when I'm off shift. Got a hot date tonight." Waggling his eyebrows, he sauntered off to take care of his other tables.

They watched him go. Shaking her head, Michelle sighed. "All the good ones are either priests, married, or gay. But never mind that." She raised her glass high. "To DSG, for recognizing the awesomeness that is Cassandra Lynn Ellis."

After the traditional clink and sip, Cassie raised her glass again. "And to Aaron Kaufman, the world's best agent, for negotiating the contract."

"Hear, hear," Michelle said and took another drink. "And the world's sexiest agent at that."

"Agreed. It was hard enough talking to him the first time, knowing he was an agent and the source of my future happiness. Then I had to get over the talking-to-a-really-cute guy nerves too. I was tongue-tied."

"I'd love to be tongue-tied with Aaron," Michelle said with a snort. "He's not a priest, married, or gay, is he? You should go after him."

Cassie tried to visualize herself dating Aaron, but even her imagination wasn't up to that task. "Oh, please, he's out of my league."

Michelle sputtered in dismay. "That is so not true."

"I know, I know, I'm gorgeous and sexy and could get any man I want, " Cassie interrupted, rolling her eyes as she saw Michelle take a deep breath to say similar words. They'd argued about this for years.

Michelle released her breath on a long-suffering sigh. "Some day you'll realize how beautiful you are. Beautiful and talented. I'm so freaking proud of you. I love everything you've written."

"Even my thesis on the prevalence of psychopaths in Elizabethan literature?" Cassie grinned wickedly.

"Okay, not so much. But I've loved all your articles and short stories. Even when you were seven and your main character was Kerfluffel, the purple unicorn. But *Mailbox Murders* and *Matchbox Murders* are your best so far. Especially *Mailbox Murders*, you've worked so hard on it. You've been writing, and rewriting, and re-rewriting that story for ages now."

"And re-re-rewriting." Cassie frowned into her glass. "I hope to never again hear the phrase, 'That concept's been overdone' as long as I live."

"Well, now you're going to hear things like 'Cassandra Ellis brings a fresh and unique perspective to the world of mystery. The best new mystery writer since Agatha Christie. Buy her book.' Or something like that."

Laughing, Cassie picked up the menu. "It sounded good until that last sentence. Though the Christie comparison was probably over the top. What do you want for dinner? My treat."

Michelle raised her eyebrows at that. "Do you have your wallet? With your credit card?"

Cassie hunched in her chair. She had, on more than one occasion, forgotten to bring some essential payment method when they went out to dinner. "I checked it before I got here, and again when I sat down."

"Caviar and surf-and-turf then."

"That's fine. It's a celebration. Besides, I happen to know that you hate caviar. Nor does the chef have surf-and-turf on the menu."

Michelle shook her head. "No. Caviar's too salty. But I am going to have the filet mignon. The boursin mashed potatoes sound divine."

"There you go, choosing your entrée by the side items again."

"I've never gotten a bad meal that way yet." Michelle closed the menu. "Not that we've ever gotten a bad meal at Corks, period."

Corks had been their favorite restaurant for years. After all, any restaurant that focused on food *and* wine had to be a good thing. Cassie had even managed to convince Michelle to join her for some of the cooking classes taught by the executive chef. She adored cooking; her friend just liked the eating part.

"So, does having a book contract mean you can quit teaching?" Michelle wanted to know.

Cassie shook her head. "No, the advance was good, but not that big. Unless it goes best seller, I still need to teach. At least I do so online, so I can stay home and write when I'm not instructing or grading." She switched her concentration to the menu. After deciding on potato-crusted salmon, she closed the menu with a snap and again grabbed the salt shaker for fidgeting purposes. "So, how was your day? Any new horror stories from the land of human resources?"

"It was pretty quiet. Fired someone, but they really deserved it, so I'm okay with that. How about you? What did you do, besides glory in your success? And gimme that." Michelle grabbed the salt shaker mid slide. "Oh good, Drew's coming back, that should distract you."

Cassie gave her order after Michelle, all the while looking for something else to fidget with. After Drew left, she answered her friend's question. "Well, I graded some papers. Some were good, some sucked, but at least I didn't catch anyone plagiarizing this time. Then I met with Seth Montgomery at Starbucks."

"The arsonist? The one you said reminds you of Alan Rickman? Like Snape, but slimier?" Michelle grimaced. "I really wish you wouldn't meet up with those weirdos, Cassie."

"Look, I've gone over and over this with my Dad, and Paul, *and* Liam," Cassie said, rolling her eyes. Paul Larson and Liam Brody were paramedics who gave her advice on medical matters. "Don't *you* start. Most of my sources are good guys like cops and paramedics. But this time, I had to meet with Seth. I needed to get info from him, since he was my resource for *Matchbox Murders.* The editor at DSG had questions about some of the arson methods in the book."

"So that book is in production now?" Michelle asked.

"Yeah, it'll be the second book in the series, comes out next February. And today I came up with a good idea for the third one." Cassie glanced over at the couple who had starred in her imagined murder scene. They seemed to be enjoying their dinner…and their wine. She told Michelle about her idea for *Merlot Murders.*

"That one sounds cool. But I still think you should have gone with my idea."

"Which idea? *The Marshmallow Murders* with the poisoned 'smores idea? Or *The Methane Murders*?"

Michelle grinned. "Hey, flatulent cows can be dangerous. But no, I meant *Menopause Murders.* That's a good one, right? Hot flashes and mood swings are great motives to kill people."

"And the book would have a built-in target audience," Cassie agreed with an answering smile. "Still, I think I'll go with *The Merlot Murders.*"

"You just want to write about wine. Not that I'm saying that's a bad thing. If you need help picking out the perfect wine, include me in the taste tests."

"Before or after I add the poison?"

"Funny, Cassie." Her friend took a deliberate sip of her wine. "I'm just glad I know this one is safe. Talking about safe, is this at least your last meeting with the arsonist?"

Cassie nodded. "As far as I know. I hope so. I think that's the last questions from DSG. They wanted to know more about that rat tail arson method."

"Oh, don't bring that up again," Michelle pressed a hand to her stomach. "It makes me sick."

But when the plates came over a few seconds later, they both dug in.

"Enough about arson," Michelle said around a mouthful of mashed potatoes. "Tell me more about the book deal. You said you're getting a good advance?"

Cassie took a bite of the salmon and savored the taste before she replied. "Aaron says it's a decent amount for a first-time author. I'm happy with it. And it's going straight into promo costs, so don't get any ideas."

Michelle looked up with a gleam in her eyes. "I personally think new shoes, a makeover, and a new outfit or two or five would fit nicely into promo costs. You have to look good when you're on *Oprah*, after all."

Cassie rolled her eyes. "I wish. I'll look just fine for the local cable shows. Actually, I'll be going on Christine Schmidt's show next Wednesday."

"Christine? From your writer's group?"

"That's the one. I've been sort of romancing her…no, not that way, pervert. She's been an active member of the Baltimore Writer's Group for years, even longer than I have, and she said she'd be happy to interview me when the time came. Oh, and since she does reviews, she came over earlier this week and interviewed me. She'll post the review online on her blog tomorrow. And it'll be in the Book Review in *The Baltimore Dispatch* on Sunday."

Sipping her wine, Michelle arched an eyebrow. "So, when you said you told no one about this…"

Cassie stared at the plate as she sliced her asparagus. "Well, outside of professional contacts, I told no one."

"Fine. Talking about professional, I still say you need to look professional for any television show. So we have to glam you up some."

"Please, the show has maybe ten viewers. It's a local cable show." She sighed at Michelle's steely stare. "Fine, I'll get the new outfit and shoes, but do I have to do the makeover?" She hated going to a make-up artist. It seemed like she always left the place $250 poorer, sometimes looking even worse. But Michelle swore by them.

"Absolutely." Michelle waved a potato-covered fork. "It'll be my treat to celebrate your success."

"Well, at least I won't have to pay for it."

As always, Cassie finished her meal ahead of Michelle. She picked up the decorative parsley from her plate and began to twirl it. Glancing around the restaurant again, she studied the people. She had dressed up for dinner, but she still felt outclassed by the other customers in their trendy designer clothes. While she didn't understand the need to pay outrageous amounts for a brand name, there were times she wished she could afford it. Maybe if the book sold well, she could start to pick up a few pieces.

Her idle thoughts vanished when she looked towards the front of the restaurant. Two men entered and strode directly to Drew at the host stand.

"Cops," Cassie said. "Homicide."

Michelle ignored her hiss to be subtle and turned around to stare for a moment. "Okay, I'll grant you that you have some magic cop radar now and can tell one from ten paces. But how do you know they're homicide cops?"

Cassie continued to study the new arrivals at the front of the restaurant. "Homicide is the best dressed department."

She admired more than the dark gray suit on the one man. He was at least four inches taller than she was, putting him at about six feet tall. Well built too. She loved broad shoulders on a man. He even had a full head of thick, dark hair. Hair seemed to be a rare commodity whenever her friends set her up on blind dates. So much so that Cassie had taken to calling them bald dates instead.

She had to admit; there was something in the tall man's bearing that drew her attention, especially since she had spent time researching the police and their procedures. The police played a large role in her novels and short stories, and she'd become fascinated by their culture. She wondered why the police were here. Cops didn't normally frequent Corks for dinner.

Maybe someone here was a murderer.

She tore her attention from the cops to rake the room with her gaze. Which of the customers was the killer? Probably the man eating alone at the bar; he looked suspicious with his—

Her fascination died when Drew turned to point straight at her. The taller cop she had admired turned shrewd eyes in her direction.

"Me? Oh my God, they're coming here. Who's dead?" Cassie's stomach clenched as she worried about her dad. Anyone but him, she prayed.

Michelle didn't get a chance to even hazard a guess before the men walked up to the table. All of a sudden Cassie found herself staring into cool gray eyes the same color as the cop's well-tailored suit. The flash of his badge focused her attention away from his eyes.

"Excuse me, Ms. Ellis?" At her nod, he continued in a deep, serious tone. "Detective Whittaker. Detective Freeman." He nodded towards the shorter black man next to him. "Since you appear to be done with your dinner, I hope you'll agree to accompany us to the police station. We have some questions regarding the death of Seth Montgomery."

"Seth Montgomery?" Although Cassie was relieved to hear it wasn't someone she had known and loved, she was still shocked. She had just seen him—alive and well. She turned, dumbfounded, toward her best friend, who seemed just as stunned. Cassie had to give her credit for recovering first.

Michelle closed her mouth before clearing her throat. "So, I guess I'm getting the check then?"

chapter 2

As Cassie followed the two detectives outside, she shook her head to clear the confusion. Seth Montgomery. Dead. Murdered. Wait, had the detectives even said he was murdered? He must have been, she thought, since the detectives wouldn't have chased her down if Seth had died of natural causes. Did they think she had something to do with it?

"Am I being charged with anything?" she blurted out.

The shorter detective shook his head. "No, Ms. Ellis. We just want to ask you a few questions regarding your meeting with Mr. Montgomery in order to establish a timeline of his day."

"Um. Okay," she said, then stared at the uniformed police officer waiting outside. She thought she'd be riding with the detectives, but that was a stupid assumption. She wasn't thinking straight. After all, she'd spent time researching police procedures.

She glanced around to see if there was anyone she knew in the area before she slid into the back of the patrol car. Then she considered the irony of her current situation.

For months, she had fought with the Baltimore Police Department's PR people to allow her to do a ride-along with homicide detectives. They had balked at letting an untrained, unknown, and unpublished author tag along. They hadn't even let her tour the more interesting places in the police station.

Now she was going to see it all. She twirled a curl around her finger, getting nervous now that she was going to the station under these circumstances. Maybe she should have asked Michelle to call a lawyer. Not that she had one. Well…there was Solange Gavreau, a college friend. More acquaintance than friend, really. No, she didn't need a lawyer. Especially not Ms. know-it-all, drop-dead gorgeous, oh-so-French Solange. Solange was annoying enough when Cassie had to call her to verify the legality of something. She was not calling the woman for this.

Besides, she hadn't done anything. Okay, so maybe she did think about murder often and came up with creative ways to kill people. But that didn't mean she'd actually *do* it. Although if she had killed Seth, she would definitely have gone for some type of fitting justice, something with fire and—

She shook her head and wondered what was wrong with her. Her friends always told her she was morbid, but she was taking it too far this time. This was not a fictional novel. This poor man was really dead.

She tried to remember if he had any close family who would grieve. He hadn't mentioned any that she could recall, but then again, they hadn't talked about such matters. Just arson.

As they passed the red light district on the way to Police Headquarters, she tried to find the humor. It normally amused her that Baltimore's police headquarters was located right next to prostitutes, strip clubs, and bars. This time, she felt nothing but worry and sadness as the gray, blocky building came into sight.

Her stomach clenched as she realized she was going in there, not for research, but as a potential suspect. She wasn't buying what Detective Whatshisname, the one who wasn't Whittaker, had said. Police didn't pull people into the station just to establish a timeline. She wondered when Seth had died. Maybe she'd been the last person to see him alive. How the hell did the police know she had met with him that day anyway? Seth obviously hadn't been the one to tell them.

After they pulled into a parking space, she took a few deep breaths to steady her nerves. Again, she wondered whether or not she needed a lawyer, then dismissed the idea. Even with the book advance, she couldn't afford lawyer fees. She could handle this. Her research into police procedures should protect her against trickery, as long as she remembered them.

Whittaker opened the car door for her. When Cassie stepped out, she accidentally brushed against him. Her stomach clenched again, but not from nerves this time. He was cute…and well built. But when she looked up at him, those stern gray eyes dispelled any superficial thoughts. She had read about someone having "cop's eyes." Now she understood.

The other detective, a black man who was probably fifteen years older than Whittaker, seemed friendlier. Laugh lines wrinkled his face, making him look more like someone's favorite grandfather than an imposing cop, even in his stark brown suit. There was a calmness in his deep brown eyes. He made her feel reassured, as if she had nothing to worry about. Not at all like his taller companion. She wasn't sure how to identify what Detective Whittaker made her feel, on any count.

Mixed emotions went through her as they got onto the elevator. She wondered if the men were going to play good cop/bad cop with her. Her police contacts had told her that didn't work in real life, since the witness or suspect would clam up if a detective came on too strong. But if these two did use that technique, she was certain Whittaker would be the bad cop.

She watched the floor numbers count up to five and stepped out behind Detective Freeman, very conscious of Whittaker's presence behind her. With every step, they left the loud but somehow organized chaos of the homicide division and entered a dark, gloomy area that smelled of sweat…and fear. All it needed was dripping water somewhere and the screams of tortured souls to make it resemble a medieval dungeon.

"In here," said Freeman, ushering her through a door into a dank, ill-lit room that was the size a broom closet.

She swallowed. She could see why the scare tactics she'd read about worked so well. What with the three of them, a cigarette-scarred table, and several plastic chairs, there was hardly room to breathe. Not that she really want to breathe in too deeply considering the odor. And then they left her. Just like that. Walked out, without a word, closing the door behind them and leaving her in this moldering dungeon to contemplate her guilt.

She felt like kicking something. She wasn't guilty. So what did they expect now? For her to start crying? Not in this lifetime. She would sit down and wait for them, nice and calm and—

She jumped as a rumbling sound rattled the walls, the table, and her chair. What was that? If it was the air conditioning, it wasn't working. The waft of air that fanned her damp forehead was warm and smelled stale, like burnt dust on a heating element. She watched her reflection shiver on the bouncing wall and become still as the rumble died away.

They were back there, on the other side, watching her. She imagined she could see them through the two way mirror, watching and analyzing everything she did.

She was tempted to stick out her tongue at the mirror, but that was probably not the right way to start off this interview. Instead, she stared at her reflection and tried her best to appear relaxed and innocent. At the moment, she looked neither. Her face, already naturally pale, was ghostly white. Her eyes looked glassy. She took some breaths to settle down and was glad to see some color come back into her cheeks. She tried to smooth down her hair, but as usual, it was fruitless. Looking at her purse, she thought about refreshing her makeup, but decided against it. That seemed a bit vain.

As the minutes ticked off, her panic faded and her curiosity came back. After all, this would make a great scene for her next book and now she was getting firsthand knowledge. Not that her main character, Dr. Martina McCallister, spent a lot of time in interview rooms. Marty wasn't a cop, but an intelligent and feisty university professor. Perhaps she could write a scene where Marty would be pulled into an interview room in conjunction with the poisoned wine story she had been thinking about earlier.

Cassie imagined it now—how brash and bold her character would act going up against police questioning. Marty wouldn't be scrunched in her seat feeling like an animal at a zoo exhibit. She'd be indignant.

Now that she thought about it, Cassie was indignant as well. Not that she'd ever have Marty's chutzpah. She wasn't as confident as her main character. Confident in her knowledge and research, yes, but not in her day-to-day life. She prayed she'd hold her own when the police came back. Maybe she should call a lawyer.

No, she was innocent. She had nothing to fear.

Right?

* * *

On the other side of the glass, Whittaker frowned. "Okay, how many emotions did she just go through?"

Freeman shrugged. "Many."

"She has a very expressive face." Whittaker leaned against the back wall, watching the woman and trying to gauge her guilt.

Freeman turned around. "Definitely looks a bit nervous. However, one expression is missing. That would be guilt."

"Yeah, I noticed." Whittaker frowned again, this time at the evidence bag in his hand. "I thought the day planner was a bit too easy. Most murderers aren't going to kill someone, coldly shoot them in their own home, and then oops—leave her day planner in the house. A day planner that not only conveniently had the victim's name marked for one hour prior to time of death, but also lets us know exactly where the killer would be next."

Freeman nodded. "A little too easy, huh? It would be really stupid to leave evidence there. Or really smart. She might be that clever—planting evidence to incriminate her so we would think it's too obvious."

"That would be pretty ballsy of her, especially since we'd still pull her in for questioning," agreed Whittaker. "And we'd nail her…unless she's faking how expressive her face is. Which would be, in fact, very clever. But I think she's probably a bad liar. And if she's a good liar, we'll still nail her."

"Damn straight. We should get in there and see if she's really stupid or really clever. Or hell, she might be able to help us establish the vic's timeline. That's why we're questioning her, right?" Freeman laughed before turning back to look at their subject again. "What's she getting out of that suitcase?"

Following Freeman's line of sight, Whittaker was amused to see his current—although unlikely—suspect pull out a notebook and pen from her huge purse and start scribbling. She looked around the room and scribbled again. "A notebook. She's taking notes. I think she's a writer or something."

At Freeman's raised eyebrow, he nodded at the day planner in the evidence bag. "She had written 'BWG 7:00 P.M.' on Monday night. I looked that up online and found the Baltimore Writer's Group had a meeting that day at that time." He placed the evidence bag in the folder.

"How did you look it up online?" Freeman demanded. "You haven't been near a computer yet."

Whittaker pulled his smartphone out of his pocket. "Magic, Freeman."

Freeman scowled at the phone. "Do you go anywhere without that Blueberry thing?"

"No, not really," Whittaker answered dryly, not bothering to correct his partner. Freeman was aware of the true name. "I sleep with it, even shower with it."

Snorting, Freeman headed towards the door. "I don't doubt it. Well, let's go interrupt her before she writes a novel about us. Although for the reader's sake, I hope she makes you better looking."

* * *

Cassie looked up from her notes when the two men walked back in. They were followed by a female uniformed police officer who went over and sat in a chair in the corner. Cassie realized that since both detectives were male, the officer must be there to make certain another female was in the room with them.

She turned and caught Whittaker standing over her, blatantly reading what she had written. Closing the book, she refused to respond to his raised eyebrows. She was certain most people didn't react to being left in an interview room by pulling out a notebook and filling several pages with notes. Hopefully, they'd realize that meant she wasn't guilty. It was annoying to be treated like she had done something. What happened to innocent until proven guilty?

Then again, it was the detectives' job to find the killer. So, if innocent people were made to feel uncomfortable, it was all in the pursuit of justice. She'd suck it up and enjoy the opportunity for first-person research. Trying to channel a bit of her character's bravado, she remained composed as the detectives sat down, even when they crowded in on her.

Then Whittaker looked up and pinned her with such an intense stare, she had to fight not to look away. When he wrote down and stated the date, time, and their names, she saw in the mirror that whatever color she had regained was now gone. She swallowed hard and struggled to breathe normally.

"Ms. Ellis," began Detective Whittaker without further ado, "thank you for taking the time to answer a few of our questions tonight. We appreciate you coming in on your own volition. I'd like to give you our cards, in case you come up with anything important later of which we need to be made aware. If you need to contact us, the numbers are at the bottom left corner."

He handed her two business cards. The first card bore a large, intimidating gold shield embossed on top and "Detective James A. Whittaker, Homicide Division" in bold type. The other card read "Detective Arthur R. Freeman" in the same bold font.

She slid the cards into her notebook, although she doubted she would need them. She knew nothing about Seth's murder, but the cards would be good reference material later.

"I'm more than willing to answer your questions," Cassie said, taking a cue from Whittaker's formality. "But I'm not sure I'll be able to help. I barely knew Mr. Montgomery."

"Well, perhaps you know more than you think," Freeman said, then led her through a few easy questions about herself that she figured were a warm-up. When Whittaker cleared his throat, she suspected it was about to get harder.

"When was the last time you saw Mr. Montgomery?" Whittaker asked.

"I met with him this afternoon, which I assume you know, or I wouldn't be here. But he was alive and well when he left the Starbucks." She hesitated. "How did he die?"

"That information hasn't been released," Whittaker said. "Why don't you walk me through your day then, including before your meeting?"

Cassie gulped. That didn't sound like establishing Seth's timeline. "My day? Um...let's see, I woke up at seven, had breakfast, and spent time online grading papers until about eleven. I teach creative and technical writing for several colleges. Then I worked on my next novel, skipping lunch actually, I tend to do that a lot, until about two-thirty, oh wait, you use military time. Um, so that would be 1430."

She noticed the slightest sneer on Whittaker's face. *Well, excuse me for trying to be accurate,* she thought. She straightened her posture; she was not going to let him get to her. "Then I had to take a quick shower and rush over to meet with Mr. Montgomery."

"When and where did you meet him?"

She caught herself tapping a foot and stilled it. "I met him today at 1500 at the Starbucks on Pratt and Third."

"Why did you meet him?"

"For information."

"Information?"

"Well, as you probably already know, Mr. Montgomery is...*was* a convicted arsonist."

Whittaker raised an eyebrow. "Why would you need information from him? Planning on burning something?"

Instant heat rushed up her throat and into her face. She didn't need the mirror to know she was turning as red as her hair. "No!" She nipped back the uncomplimentary label she wanted to insert. "I'm an author." *You idiot.* "It was research."

"Hmm," was all Whittaker said before writing something in his book. She wanted to kick the table leg and make him mess up when she saw he was writing *"Claims to be an author."*

Fisting her hands under the table, she leaned forward. "I *am* an author," she insisted. "My first book comes out this Saturday."

"Did I say otherwise?" Whittaker asked, leaning back in his chair and sending her a bland look.

She stared at him and resisted the urge to point at the notebook, all the while annoyed that she had fallen for that bait: hook, line, and sinker. Damn, he was good at this.

Freeman took over. "How long have you been using Mr. Montgomery as a resource for information? What type of information?"

"I suppose I've known him for about two years now." Thank God, the heat was leaving her face, but not as fast as she would've preferred. She made sure she was taking regular breaths. "The killer in my second book, *Matchbox Murders*, commits the murders via arson. Mr. Montgomery gave me some insights into arson, and into an arsonist's mind. Since I want to make my stories both realistic and unique, I do a lot of research. I pride myself on research. I culled articles and police reports, interviewed paramedics and police officers, read true crime stories, and reviewed a number of different resources on police procedure." She ticked off the different methods on her fingers.

"Realistic, you said. Just how realistic?" Whittaker leaned forward.

She arched back in surprise as he crossed into her personal bubble. Then his words registered.

"Not that realistic! I don't go out killing people, for God's sake." *Deep breaths. Calm down.* Her attempts to restore some balance flew out of the non-existent window when Detective Whittaker removed an evidence bag from his folder.

A bag containing a very familiar-looking day planner.

Grabbing her purse off the floor, she rifled through the cavernous interior and its many side pockets, but soon resigned herself to the truth. She looked back at the evidence bag, then at the detectives and realized that every cop in the room had tensed when she had gone for her purse. She was lucky not to have gotten shot.

"Well, I assume you recognize the day planner," Freeman stated quietly. "Do you confirm that this is yours?"

"Since it has my initials on it, and mine appears to be missing, I guess I do. Although, what's that stain? Oh." She sucked in a breath as she realized the dark blots on the cover were blood. Seth's blood. Swallowing hard, she gave up on trying to remain calm and worked instead to avoid throwing up. "Where did you find it?"

"When do you last remember seeing it?" Whittaker countered.

She scowled at him for avoiding her question, but at least he didn't say anything trite like "We'll ask the questions here."

"I always hated it when my dad asked that question. You know, when you'd say you lost something and someone asks where you last remembered seeing it. Obviously, if I could remember that, it wouldn't be lost." She sat back and thought. "I really can't remember when I saw it last. I've gone in and out of that purse many times today and don't remember seeing the day planner…or not seeing it for that matter."

"Why don't we continue with your activities today?"

This was from Freeman. Cassie had to admire the detectives. Although it wasn't quite a bad cop/good cop routine, the partners had a pattern.

Whittaker would ask the hard questions, and Freeman would get her to relax again with his comfortable attitude and quieter tone.

She waved at the evidence bag. "Well, you know I had plans to meet with my best friend, Michelle Edwards, at six…sorry, 1800, at Corks."

"You don't have to use military time, Ms. Ellis," Whittaker interrupted before she could continue.

She frowned. It wasn't that hard to do the military time, and it made her feel more official. But whatever. "Okay. I left Mr. Montgomery—alive and well—and we went our separate ways about three-thirty. I wrote for a while, then went home to get ready for dinner. Michelle and I were supposed to meet at six, but as always, she was late."

"Where did you go to write?" Freeman wanted to know.

"Since it was a nice day, I left the Starbucks and walked over to Federal Hill and wrote there."

"So you left Seth Montgomery at the Starbucks?" Whittaker asked, leaning in again.

"Yes." She suddenly realized why he was asking these questions. "Why, where was he killed? Where did you find my day planner?"

Again, Whittaker avoided her questions. "Have you ever been to Mr. Montgomery's house?"

"No! I'm not stupid enough to meet up with a criminal at his house. Nor do I allow one in mine."

"Just stupid enough to meet up with one at all?" Whittaker asked, settling back again and pulling what appeared to be one of the hottest new smartphones out of his pocket. Cassie had coveted one of those ever since she saw her agent with one.

At the same time she envied him the gadget, she was annoyed he was no longer looking at her. She liked to multi-task herself, but it felt rather wrong for him to be texting or looking something up on the Internet when he was supposed to be interrogating her. "It's not stupid to meet up with someone in a public place, Detective Whittaker. Listen, I hear about this from others. I'm careful. I meet them at a neutral location. I don't allow them to know personal information about me."

"Like your address?" Whittaker set the phone down on the table and swiveled it around so she could see her home address on the screen.

She stared. "Okay, maybe I need to be more careful. I thought I'd removed that from public sites. Is that some special police site?"

He shook his head. "No, completely public. Did Montgomery follow you to the park?"

"What?" She stopped worrying about her address being public and focused on the detectives. "No, I told you. I left him at Starbucks."

"He didn't follow you home? You didn't have words?" Whittaker leaned closer.

"No...and honestly, I doubt he could have looked up my information anyway. I don't think I gave him my full name. And he probably doesn't even have a computer."

"Why do you say that? I thought you hadn't been to his house."

She gritted her teeth. "I haven't. But he's old-fashioned...and not that smart, either. I just assume, since you keep talking about his house, that's where he was killed. I know you can't confirm that, so I'll just go with that assumption." Leaning back in her chair, she looked down at the table in deep concentration. "So my day planner was at his house? How did it get there?"

"What makes you think—"

She waved away Whittaker's question and pointed at the day planner. "It has blood on it. I can assure you it didn't have blood on it this morning...or whenever I saw the stupid thing last. Therefore, basic deduction, it was at the scene of the crime. How was he killed?"

"Unfortunately, I cannot—"

"Right, right, you can't release that information at this time and blah, blah, blah." She looked over at Freeman when he coughed, although it sounded more like he was covering up a laugh. She resisted the urge to grin at him when she noticed Whittaker looking annoyed.

"Sorry, I tend to interrupt." Now curiosity replaced her initial disgust and dismay, and she reached for the evidence bag, inching it closer. "Well, I don't know how close the day planner was to...um...the victim. But looking at the spatter, it looks like a mist pattern. I know it could be from another source, but typically, that's from a bullet wound. Especially since there seems to be two areas of convergence, so, two bullets then? We can't be certain unless there is gunshot residue as well, of course, but..."

She looked up to see both detectives staring at her; one grim and the other vaguely amused. She fumbled for something to say. "Sorry, I studied spatter patterns during my research."

"Did you also fire guns during your research?" Whittaker asked.

Cassie hesitated before answering. "Yes. Yes I did."

"Do you own a gun?"

She shook her head. "No, I don't actually like them in my house."

"Worried about children accessing them?" Freeman asked.

"No. I don't have kids. Just a cat. And although he gets into everything, he probably wouldn't—" She stopped, she was babbling. They didn't want to hear about her cat. She took a breath and got herself back on track. "I just...I don't want one in my house. But I've shot them at the range, for research."

Whittaker made notes in his book again. "What kind of guns have you fired?"

"Well, for *Mailbox Murders*, the killer used a shotgun, so I had a friend take me out hunting. Well, shooting, really, since I refuse to kill anything." She made sure to get that in there. Besides, the pattern wasn't from a shotgun, so she was safe stating that much, right? As long as Whittaker didn't press her—

"Have you used any other types of firearms?"

She hesitated again. Unless the gun was left at the crime scene, they hadn't completed ballistics analysis and wouldn't know the murder weapon. Even so, she worried about appearing guilty if she admitted to firing the same type of gun.

"Ms. Ellis?"

She was taking too long to answer. That couldn't look good for her innocence. And darn it, she was innocent, so she went for the truth. Fact was, no matter what type of gun had been used for Seth's murder, she had probably tried it out—and on record, at a firing range.

"Yes, I've fired a number of them, actually. The final scene in the book involves a gun battle of sorts, and I wanted it to be realistic. So I fired the 9mm Glock and the 40-caliber Glock, knowing those weapons were often used by Baltimore City Police. I've also shot several SIG handguns, including the P210. Several Rugers and Lugers, including the Luger Parabellum—that one was sweet." She smiled in remembrance. "A number of Smith and Wessons, Berettas, including a Beretta 418—James Bond's original gun—so then I had to try the Walther PPK, of course. Oh, and some revolvers too. But I preferred the semi-automatics really since they..."

She suddenly stopped and realized she was babbling again. She cursed at herself when she saw Whittaker was furiously writing down each word while Freeman sat and stared at her, looking as if he couldn't decide whether to laugh at her or arrest her.

She scowled. "If I had killed him, I'd hardly admit to having used a similar weapon now, would I? That would be really stupid."

Whittaker looked up from his notebook. "Or really clever."

She didn't have an answer for that. Not that Whittaker waited very long for one.

"Where have you shot these guns? Some of the ones you listed are rare."

"Again, I like to do my research. So I went to On Target near Fort Meade and took a class, which included time on the range to practice the stance they recommended. Afterward, I started asking questions, like I always do, and this gun collector wandered over to contribute his opinion. He's got plenty of opinions, trust me. Anyway, he invited me to join him on the range so he could show me other shooting stances. Then we became friends and went out shooting several other times. I got to see and shoot a lot of the guns in his collection."

"That would be Mark Griffin."

"Yes," she said in surprise. "How did you know—" She stopped. "Of course. The day planner." Damn it, the cops had access to almost her entire life with that thing.

He tapped the book through its protective plastic cover. "Correct. Just like I know that you had Seth Montgomery's address."

Cassie stared at the day planner in shock. Hell, Seth had given her his address, hadn't he?

"So, this gives you means and opportunity," Whittaker said. He leaned forward, an intense edge in his smoky eyes. "So, tell me, Ms. Ellis, just what was your motive for killing Mr. Montgomery?"

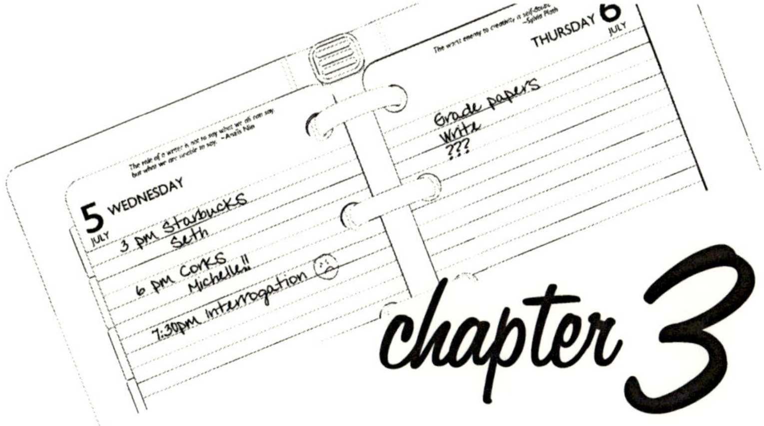

chapter 3

"Motive?" Cassie sputtered in disbelief. "I don't have a motive. I didn't kill him."

"Then why do you have his address?"

"I don't know." She considered it, struggling to get her thoughts in order. It happened again—she'd let him get to her. Evidently knowing the techniques cops used to fluster suspects didn't give her any actual defense against those methods. She supposed it was like a job interview: no matter how much one studied and practiced, nothing could compare to the real thing. "I believe he gave it to me the first time we met, so I could send him a copy of my next book since I used his input."

"Of course."

She was impressed by how much disbelief Whittaker crammed into each word. Rolling her eyes, she gave in to her exasperation. "Okay, fine. Yes, I might have had means to kill him, since I probably had access to whatever type of gun shot him." She pointed to the day planner. "This shows that I had the opportunity to kill him, knowing his address. But again, I have absolutely no motive to do so."

Whittaker shrugged. "Motives are often hidden. You're a writer, as you say, so let's talk hypothetically. What motive could there be?"

"Well, let's see, we can discount a crime of passion since if the murder had taken place in his house—not that you can confirm that," she interjected before the detective could do so. "I would have had time to cool down on the way there. If I can recall, the most common motives for premeditated murder are love, greed, envy, and thrill. I can assure you that I didn't love him. Quite the opposite really, he disgusted me."

"Yet you chose to meet with him," Freeman spoke up.

Cassie looked over in surprise. She had almost forgotten he was there. "Well, he was a resource. But this meeting was going to be the last."

"Why? Did he scare you? Threaten you?" Freeman asked.

"No, I wasn't scared of him, just appalled at his lack of respect for others. He bragged about how much property he destroyed, or what others had done. The man had no remorse that he was destroying peoples' lives. No, I didn't love Mr. Montgomery, far from it. So love wasn't the motive."

"What about…"

"Greed doesn't work either, since he didn't have any money that I'm aware of. A couple of jail sentences probably drained any prior funds. And envy doesn't work either. There was nothing about him to envy."

"So that just leaves thrill," Whittaker said.

She sighed at the obvious note of condemnation in his voice. "Yes, Detective Whittaker, that leaves thrill. So tell me, do I look thrilled right now?"

Was that the ghost of a curve on his lips?

"This isn't supposed to be the thrilling part."

She shook her head. "No, the murder is. But trust me, I might write about murder, and I might think about murder a lot, but a real death? I don't even kill bugs; I catch and release them. Well, not mosquitoes, they deserve to die. But I save crickets from my cat and set them free even though they come back, stupid things. I feel horrible when I see a dead animal on the side of the road. And when my cousin told me he had gone hunting and killed a squirrel, I kicked him."

"Those are animals. Many people are more sympathetic towards animals than their own kind," Freeman said.

"Well, sometimes animals deserve more sympathy than humans. But I don't hurt humans either. Never been in a fight, well, a fist fight that is, with another person. I don't kill real people, gentleman, just fictional ones. And there are times I have trouble doing that."

"What do you mean, you have trouble killing fictional people?" Freeman asked.

"Sometimes I don't want to kill off characters when I'm writing. I actually get depressed when a character I like is killed."

Whittaker and Freeman exchanged glances. She wasn't surprised to see confusion on their faces.

"Don't you, as the author, kind of control that?" Whittaker asked.

She smiled, for the first time since dinner feeling genuine amusement. "Oh no, no. Ask any author; you really don't control the characters after a while. You might think you do, but they truly take on lives of their own. A good writer just follows along." She could tell by their blank expressions they didn't have a clue what the hell she was saying. Oh well. Most non-authors didn't get it. They never would.

Whittaker asked her a few more questions about her relationship with Seth—which she again insisted she didn't have—and some more questions regarding her actions that day. They also repeated questions several times, deliberately she assumed.

After a while, she could tell they were winding down, thank God. She was exhausted answering all the questions and wondered if it was just as tiresome to ask them.

Finally, Whittaker leaned back in his chair. "Ms. Ellis, we appreciate your time and assistance. We ask you not to reveal anything that you've been told here."

She felt an almost orgasmic sense of relief that she wasn't going to continue her research by visiting jail cells. "Don't worry, I'm good at keeping secrets. I didn't even tell anyone that my book was being released until today."

He didn't seem impressed. "Please call us if you think of anything to add to your statements."

"So I'm free to go?"

He nodded. "Do you need us to arrange a ride home?"

She didn't want to spend another minute with the police. "I'll manage, thank you. I can call my father."

Downstairs, in the lobby, she had to stand for a moment and breath the fresher air. Then that air rushed out as she saw her agent, Aaron Kaufman. He ran over, grabbed her hands, and drew her towards the door.

"Oh, Cassie. Are you all right? Michelle called me and told me what happened. Are you okay?"

She smiled, so grateful to see a familiar face that she forgot to be nervous around him. "It's okay, Aaron. They skipped the beatings and thumbscrews part of the interrogation."

He looked down at her, concern in his chocolate brown eyes. "Let's get you home. Come on."

She let him take her arm to guide her out of the police station. Once outside, she took a deep breath. Any hope that the air outside would be fresher than the air in the station vanished immediately. Even after the sun went down, July nights in Baltimore were hot and muggy. The entire summer was hot and muggy. And smoggy. Baltimore never seemed to forget its industrial roots. At least the air didn't.

Aaron squeezed her hand. "Seriously, is everything all right? When Michelle said you were taken in for questioning for the murder of Seth

Montgomery, I couldn't believe it. Isn't that the arsonist you've been talking to?"

"He is…well, he was."

"Why would they think you had anything to do with his murder? I mean, you write about murder, but I have trouble visualizing you actually killing somebody." Stopping at a silver BMW, he opened the door for her.

Cassie mustered up a smile as she slid onto a butter-soft leather seat. "Hell, if I wanted to kill someone for real, I would've killed you months ago for all your millions of suggested changes."

He smiled back as he started the engine and pulled out of the parking space. "True. I suppose I should be worried. You do come up with some unique and graphic ways to kill people. Sometimes I'm scared by what goes on in that brain of yours."

Cassie closed her eyes in bliss as the air conditioner wafted fresh, cool air over her. Aaron's car smelled nice: like leather, money, and the lightest touch of cologne. She inhaled and tried to clear the lingering taint from the interview room. "I keep telling people they should be nicer to me. Especially after I started shooting."

"Seriously, why do they think you did it?"

"Well, I think I was the last person to see him alive…uh…not including the murderer, of course."

His eyes widened at that. "What? You saw him today?"

"Yes, we met after lunch. I'm not sure when he was killed, some time this afternoon, I assume. But the real incriminating evidence is my day planner. They found it at the scene of the crime."

"So? You just said you met him. You must have left it behind." He shrugged.

She began to twirl a curl around her finger. "Well, that would work had I not met him at Starbucks and he was killed at his home. At least, I think he was."

"Oh shit. How did your day planner get there?"

"That's the question for the ages, isn't it? Anyway Aaron, I can't tell you how much I appreciate you coming to check on me. How did Michelle find you?"

"She looked my number up on the Internet. She called your father first, but he was out of the house."

Oh crap. Cassie hoped Michelle didn't leave her father a message. He would be worried coming home and hearing that.

"Yes, he would have been at the school since tonight was parent-teacher conferences. Again, thanks again for coming to my rescue."

"My pleasure. It doesn't look good for my latest and greatest author to be arrested." He looked at her and frowned. "Don't make that face. I was just kidding, of course, trying to lighten the mood. This won't affect anything with DSG. They shouldn't even find out. Besides, the police didn't arrest you, did they? It's only, what is it, circumstantial evidence, right? Seth probably stole your day planner, that's why it was there at his house."

"Yeah, you're right." She hoped. Checking the time, she sucked in a breath. "Oh my God. It's already nine? I was in there for two hours? I remember when I was so gung-ho to get a tour of that place. Now, I think I've seen enough. As a matter of fact, forget the mysteries. I want to write about purple unicorns."

"I'm going to chalk that up to stress and forget you said it. You'll feel better in the morning." Stopping at the light before the expressway, he looked over at her. "So where to, Killer? You live in Federal Hill, right?"

"I do, but, well, do you mind driving me to my dad's instead? He should be home by now."

"No problem. Oh, and make sure to call Michelle and let her know what happened. She was freaking out, but since she doesn't have a car, she called me. I offered to pick her up, but she wanted someone to get there as soon as possible." After that, Aaron fell silent, other than asking for directions. She was grateful the silence gave her plenty of time to get her thoughts in order.

Seth Montgomery was dead, and even though she wasn't close to him, she was saddened. Senseless death always depressed her. If she wanted to psychoanalyze herself, it was probably due to losing her mother at such an early age.

Still, she was curious about the murder. It was the first real murder she'd ever been involved in. She wondered who killed him and why, and whether the police would ever find out. Seth wasn't among the cream of society, so he had probably upset one of his shady friends who then shot him.

But that didn't explain her day planner. Had she left it at the Starbucks? She thought back to the past couple of days, unable to recall when she had last seen it. Maybe Aaron was right and Seth had stolen it. But for what purpose? It wasn't like her day planner had anything valuable other than a bunch of contact info and addresses.

"His house is on the right with the yellow flowers in front."

Anticipating the comfort that only her father could provide, she thanked Aaron and ran up the stairs of the stoop. She didn't even finish knocking before her father yanked open the door. He pulled her inside and enveloped her in his big arms. For the first time since the detective had spoken her name back in Corks, Cassie felt safe and secure.

There was no better cure than a hug from Charles Ellis. That remedy had worked for grief, chicken pox, flu, childhood fears, broken bones, even for a broken heart. She had always been a daddy's girl, and they had gotten even closer after her mother died. Cassie was only ten years old when she lost her mom. Her father had done a wonderful job as a single parent as he supported her throughout her adolescent, teen, and now adult years.

"Are you okay, sweetie?"

"I'm okay, Dad." She realized she did feel fine this time. "It wasn't too bad, honestly. I mean, not that I would volunteer to be interrogated, but I knew I had nothing to do with his death. I feel bad about Seth though."

"Tell me what happened." Her father pulled her inside and across the narrow rowhouse into the kitchen. Cassie drew in more comfort from the space; that kitchen had been such an important part of her life. From meals, to homework, to phone calls, she had spent much of her childhood in the bright yellow room. She had talked for hours and hours on the phone, pacing around the kitchen island. The invention of the cordless phone had been a welcome one for her and her father, who had often gotten tangled up in the cord.

"Actually, let me call Michelle. I'll put her on speaker. That way both of you can hear." She sat down at on a stool and told her father and Michelle all that had happened since the police had shown up at Corks. By the end of her tale, she was up and striding around the island.

Her father sat calmly on the tall green stool. "Well, it doesn't sound like the police think you did it. Wouldn't they have arrested you?"

Cassie shook her head as she paced away. "No, they don't have anything other than circumstantial evidence. The research I discovered while writing my…My book! Oh my God, this murder totally made me forget. Hey Michelle, I'll call you tomorrow, I have to tell Dad the good news." She spun back around to her purse and grabbed another copy of her book. "Look."

A big smile spread across his handsome face, deepening the wrinkles. "Your book is being published?" Then he frowned. "No, your book is published. Let me guess, you didn't want to jinx it by telling anyone." At her nod, he shook his head, but smiled. "That's wonderful news, Cassandra. I'm so proud of you."

He got up and pulled her in for another hug, this one more joyous than comforting. Stepping back, he grinned proudly. "I suppose that explains why you were at Corks. Celebrating, of course."

"Yes, I was. I hope it's okay that I told Michelle first. I should have told you—"

He waved his hand to shush her. "Cassie, she's your best friend, and she edits all your stories. I understand why you told her first. But I wish you hadn't waited to tell us. Bad things don't happen just because you say them out loud."

"I know that, intellectually. But, well..." She sat on a stool as she tried to figure out how to put her feelings into words. "It just feels like every time things are going well, something bad happens. Sometimes little things, like losing something I wanted. Sometimes big things, like Mom dying, which was the worst. Sometimes it's things that seem huge at the time, like that cheating jerk, Derek. And look now. I try to be careful and hold tight to the news about the book. I finally tell someone...and pow, I'm dragged into an interrogation for murder."

"It's coincidence, young lady, and you know that. And I thought you said it was more an interview than an interrogation."

She sighed. "It was. And I know it's probably just coincidence. I wish I could be the optimist you are. But hey, I have too much of Mom and her pessimism."

Her father turned around with a snort before grabbing wine glasses from the cabinet. "You have too much of your grandmother, really."

"Bite your tongue, Dad. I'm not that bad."

Cassie got up to pace again and watched in surprise as her father pulled out a split of champagne from the refrigerator. She stared at the orange label. "You just happen to have chilled champagne on hand? My favorite champagne?"

"Hey, I know my daughter. I can recognize suppressed excitement." He smiled at her over his bifocals. "Well, it's hard sometimes to tell your normal fidgeting from you hiding something. It's been building for a while, so I figured you'd tell me when you were ready. When you said you were meeting Michelle at Corks, I figured tonight was the night."

Cassie shook her head. "You do know your daughter."

He cocked his head to the side as he popped the cork. "Honestly, I'm just glad it's not a guy. I was afraid my girl had finally met 'the one.'"

She hugged him from behind as he poured the champagne. "No, Dad, I'm still your girl. Besides, I don't have time for a man. Especially now. I've got to promote the book, so I'll be going to local bookstores, conferences, and wine festivals." With her father, she toasted her success, hoping she wasn't jinxing it again.

He took a sip of champagne and closed his eyes in appreciation. "I do enjoy Veuve Clicquot, I'm glad you introduced me to it. And you'll be selling your books at wine festivals, huh? That sounds like a hardship. Are there actually book buyers there, or is it just an excuse to drink wine?"

She grinned. "There are some book buyers, and there's not much competition from other authors. Besides, I can do both, can't I?"

"As long as you're not in jail for murder, Cassie." He paused, the glass partway to his lips. "You're really not worried?"

"Now that I'm out of that interview room, no. I swear, after a couple of hours in there, I was ready to confess to anything just to get out of that room. But it was apparent they didn't think I did it, or they would've pressed harder and longer. I hope they catch the real murderer, and not just so it proves I'm innocent. I want the killer brought to justice. Hopefully, Detective Whittaker will come through. He seems like a really good detective."

"I thought there were two detectives."

"Yeah, well, there were. But Detective Whittaker was more…um, I don't know, aggressive? He is probably the primary detective, and he has a very strong presence." She took a sip of champagne, thinking with an inward laugh that was one way to put it. Aloud she said, "But I don't know. This just seems like a random act of violence."

"Baltimore is known for that," her father said. "Look, it's late. Do you want to spend the night here tonight?"

"No, I need to get home to Donner."

"That's a good point," he said, picking up his car keys from the table.

She told her father more about the book release during the short drive from his place to hers. After kissing him goodnight, she raced up the stairs to her stoop and unlocked her door. She turned to wave at her father, who waited, as always, to make sure she safely entered before driving off.

With a sigh of relief for being home at last, she stepped inside.

And was immediately attacked.

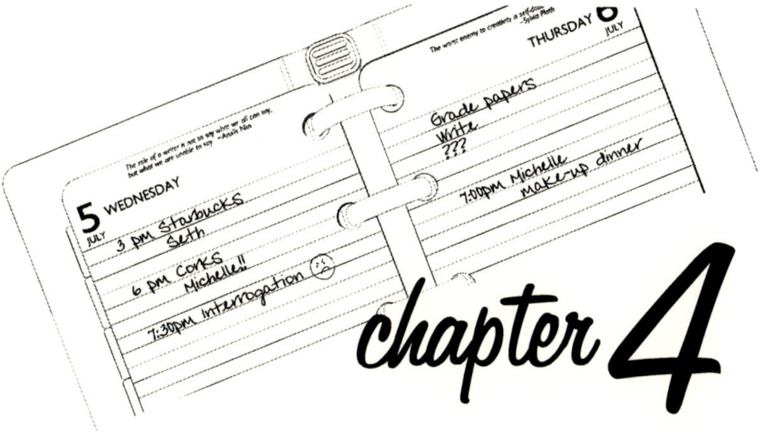

chapter 4

Even buzzed on champagne and exhausted from her interview, Cassie was able to handle the attack. After all, she knew Donner would be starving.

She smiled down at the sleek Russian Blue who was desperately clawing his way up her slacks. "Ow. Not these pants, they're actually nice. I'm sorry, kitty. I realize I've inconvenienced you by coming home late, but it wasn't my fault. I was in jail."

She cuddled the cat against her chest as she hurried the length of her rowhouse to the kitchen. She took comfort from the normalcy of a purring cat after her very odd night. Why did her evening have to end this way? She had looked forward to her announcement for months, when she could finally reveal her success…and revel in it.

Being questioned by the police as a potential suspect in a murder case wasn't how she had envisioned celebrating her first book. Oh well, at least Saturday promised to be an exciting day for the book launch.

She put the cat down on the kitchen floor and opened a cabinet. Donner meowed pitifully the entire time.

"You don't care that I was in jail? Okay, it wasn't quite jail. But it could've been." She dumped kibble into his bowl. Since he just leapt at the food and started chomping, he wasn't concerned about her prison prospects. Was she? Leaving Donner to his food, she went back to the living room and flopped down on the couch.

All in all, it hadn't been a bad experience. Not that she had ever wanted to be interviewed in relation to a murder, but it wasn't like she had anything to do with it. It was just a coincidence. She wondered if the police had found out anything else between the time she left and now.

She played with the tassel on one of the green throw pillows and tried to resist what she wanted to do. She should just forget about the investigation and put it all behind her. That's what she should do.

So why was she reaching for the remote? She picked it up, thought better of it, and set it back down. Then picked it up again. Set it down again. After a whole ten seconds, she picked it up again and even got as far as turning on the television. With a curse, she forced herself to turn it off and got up to pace her house.

Distraction. She needed a distraction. What would keep her from turning on that television, short of chopping the electrical cord with her chef knife? Maybe she should read something. Her living room was full of books, after all. Her gaze landed on the custom-built bookcases she had installed against her staircase. They were the reward to herself once she had finished the renovations she'd made to her home. Looking around at it now, she was filled with pride. Like her book, here was something that had sprung from her imagination and hard work into beautiful reality.

She had purchased the house at the age of twenty-one with trust fund money from her grandmother. The neighborhood was in the process of revitalizing back then. Now, it was a popular location for young professionals. Like many areas of Baltimore, her street and the surrounding areas were safe. However, just a few streets over, the neighborhood was more… questionable. Baltimore was odd. There were imaginary lines that split the good areas from the bad, and neither side breached their boundaries.

She hadn't worried about those invisible boundaries when she saw the house for the first time. She had just fallen in love with it. With her imagination, it didn't take much effort for her to realize that, with a little sweat equity, the rowhouse would turn into a beautiful home. Okay, a lot of sweat equity. But it was worth every minute.

She had more time than money, so she did the work herself, or with friends and family. Her inclination to research and discover things hands-on led her into one do-it-yourself project after another. Paint. Tile. Crown molding. After trial and error—plenty of errors—the house was amazing. She'd come out of her weeks of combat covered in bruises, cuts, splinters, and paint. Now, seven years later, she swore she still found paint underneath her fingernails.

Yes, the results had been worth it, she thought as she appreciated the deep earth tones she had chosen for the walls. They looked very rich with the exposed brick on the east wall.

Walls hadn't been the only surface she changed. She had personally stripped and sanded the original hardwood floors before applying layers of primer and varnish. She had "borrowed" the Oriental rug from her bedroom at her father's house and loved seeing it in her living room as a reminder of her childhood.

And, of course, her house had books.

And the beautiful bookcases. They had been carefully planned and built to follow the increasing height of the staircase wall. Upstairs, there were even more bookcases. And each shelf was full. Still, she didn't seem to have room for all of her beloved books. Each time she would buy a new bookcase, she'd end up buying twice as many books to fill it. She wasn't sure who loved her more, the bookstores or the local wood craftsmen.

She wandered over to one of those beautiful cases now. She let her fingers trail along the polished wood as she scanned the titles. Maybe some J.D. Robb. She selected a well-worn edition of *Portrait in Death* and turned back to the couch. No. She wasn't in the mood for Eve and Roarke. Something a little more familiar, comforting. Panning her gaze along the carefully ordered array, she smiled and chose *Trixie Belden and The Mystery off Glen Road*, a twin of the book that had brought her and Michelle together all those years ago.

No sooner had she sat back on the couch, legs curled beneath her, did she know her attempts at diversion weren't going to work. "I can't freaking stand it any more! I give up." Tossing the book onto the coffee table, she snatched up the remote.

Turning on the eleven o'clock news, she started to bite her nails. She was appalled to realize she didn't know if she was hoping they would announce her name in connection with the murder, or hoping they wouldn't. She scowled. She didn't want to be mentioned. Right?

The newscast had just begun. A huge water main break in downtown was the headline story. She had to watch through five minutes of annoyed commuters complaining about the inconvenience and harassed-looking public employees apologizing for the same.

After coverage of another murder—Baltimore never lacked for murders—they finally mentioned Seth Montgomery. Cassie sucked in a breath and held it as she waited to see if they would name her as a person of interest, but the coverage was very brief. The announcer didn't report anything the detectives hadn't told her. She was surprised to hear them mention Seth by name. They must've informed the next of kin, whoever that was.

Had he been married? Perhaps his wife had killed him. When Cassie first started researching murders for *Mailbox Murders*, in which the husband was the murderer, she had assumed that most murders were committed by spouses or significant others. She had been surprised to find out that only accounted for eleven percent of the murders in the United States.

Perhaps Seth had been cheating on this hypothetical wife. Picturing sleazy Seth meeting some woman at a motel for a quickie was one image she wished she could erase. As the mental image formed in her head, she grimaced and wished for Brain Brillo. Although her very active imagination was useful for her writing, there were times she wished she could turn it off.

Still, she liked the cheating angle. A man who enjoyed burning buildings and had no respect for life and property probably wouldn't worry much about fidelity either. So Seth cheated on his wife, and the wife discovered his adultery. Perhaps this wife…Cassie decided to call her Hillary; that was a good name for a cheated-upon wife. Perhaps this Hillary followed Seth to try and identify his mistress. So Hillary followed him to Starbucks and assumed the worst when she saw her man having a Frappuccino with Cassie.

Then the scorned wife stole the day planner out of her purse—although Cassie didn't know how—as proof of the illicit affair.

Cassie lifted up her laptop, opened up a new word document, and began typing.

> Hillary waited for Seth to come home. She fumed in the car as he walked back into their house, a home they had purchased together. And now the bastard thought he could just cheat on her?
>
> She stomped up the stoop and slammed open the door. The sunlight silhouetted her body, outlining the shape of the gun.
>
> Seth leaped from the ratty couch in the living room. "What's wrong, hon?" His panic increased his already strong Baltimore accent, elongating the "o"s.
>
> "You bastard!" Hillary threw the day planner across the room. When Seth bent down to pick up the book, she shot him.
>
> Hillary stood over the body of her now late husband, her face full of regret that their marriage had come to this. It had been so promising until she discovered his infidelity. Sure, there was also his little problem with arson, but she had stood next to him through his entire jail sentence, and this is how the bastard paid—

Cassie stopped typing and shook her head. Now that she thought of it, Seth had mentioned that while he had been married, the woman divorced him when he went to prison.

"I can't say I blame her," Cassie said to Donner as he strutted back into the room, licking his chops. He leaped into her lap, and she scratched him behind his ears, enjoying the resulting purr.

That scenario was lame. Cheesy. And how would her fictional, cheated-upon wife have stolen the day planner, anyway? If Hillary had snuck into the Starbucks and stolen it from her purse, wouldn't Seth have seen her?

Nope, she just couldn't suspend her disbelief on this imagined scene. If any of her students had turned in something like this for class, they would receive a bad grade for the sheer implausibility. She highlighted the text and hit the Delete key.

Maybe she should start working on *Merlot Murders*. No. She didn't want to write about fictional murder after finding out about a real one.

Closing the laptop, she tucked it beneath her arm and went upstairs to her room. Preparations for bed helped to calm some of her yet-unsettled thoughts, but she knew her imagination wasn't done with her yet. Before trying to go to sleep, she said a short prayer for Seth, and another one for any of his family and friends…including Hillary.

* * *

After sleeping fitfully, she didn't want to get up, but her furry alarm clock was quite insistent. After the third nibble on her toes, she decided that she'd better wake up and feed the cat before she ended being breakfast herself.

"All right, Donner, I'll get up." She glared at the cat, then relented and reached down to smooth his blue-gray fur. "You know, if you were a sexy man, I wouldn't mind the toe nibbling."

She sighed at the empty half of her queen-sized bed. Not that it looked like she had spent the night alone. The deep blue sheets and covers were a tangled mess, the fabric twisted into knots from her tossing and turning.

She could have used a man last night, to hold her and comfort her. Maybe it was her Catholic upbringing, but she was feeling guilt over Seth's death. Cassie knew, logically, that she had nothing to do with his murder, but she still wondered. After all, she spent much of her time daydreaming about murders and imagining people's deaths. It wasn't like she believed just thinking these things could cause them to come true in real life…but still.

Shrugging off the uncomfortable feeling, she grabbed her laptop and, to Donner's great joy, headed downstairs. After pouring some kibble in his bowl, she started making her own breakfast. She threw a bagel in the toaster and turned on the electric kettle for tea. Then she turned on the more important electrical equipment in her life: the police scanner and her laptop.

She wasn't surprised to see several e-mails from Michelle and Aaron. She read Michelle's first, which included a couple of links to articles about Seth's death. She had to immediately follow the links, of course. There still wasn't any mention of her name nor any additional information in those articles.

She shot an e-mail back to Michelle and let her know that she was fine before going on to read the e-mails from Aaron. He had scheduled additional book signings in local bookstores. Great, but that would eat into her free time. The price of fame, she reminded herself as she wrote the dates on her whiteboard calendar.

She went to the living room to get her day planner from her purse and stopped just short of closing her fingers on the shoulder strap.

She no longer had her day planner.

"Note to self, get new day planner," she mumbled, hurrying back to the kitchen. She would need one soon. Although she relied more on the large whiteboard for organizing her day and week, she tried to synch it with a day planner to make sure she could check plans while she was out. Even then, she often double-booked herself and had to make far too many apologies for canceling or rescheduling appointments.

"New day planner," she wrote on the whiteboard. A growl from her stomach reminded her of breakfast. Of course the bagel was cold, her hot water lukewarm. Where had all the time gone?

Deciding to shower and dress first, she abandoned the thought of breakfast for now and ran back upstairs. Clean, in a cool outfit of khaki shorts and green tank top, hair tamed back in a ponytail, she felt ready to get to work.

She flew down the stairs, hoping the inside of her house would hold the cooler air of night a little longer than usual. She was trying to avoid using the air conditioning. The box air units always ate up a lot of expensive electricity and still didn't do such a great job cooling down the brick rowhouse.

Turning the teakettle back on and chewing on her cold bagel, she started to check her work e-mail. She was pleased there weren't too many from her students. She liked the freedom of teaching online courses, but she was amazed at the number of idiots who signed up for them. While she hadn't found one to top the student who asked why he needed a computer to take an online class, this semester's bunch was still mind-boggling.

As always, she had an e-mail from the Excuser, who claimed he was unable to complete his assignment due to a power outage. "A thunderstorm?" Cassie muttered. After checking the weather in the city he had listed on his registration, she wrote him back asking how that could be true when Austin was currently experiencing a drought. She clicked *Send* and rolled her eyes, quite certain that tomorrow's e-mail would explain that he was visiting somewhere else.

Next up on the complaints list was the Whiner. Whiner complained about the difficulty of the assignment and how the course had unfair requirements.

"Dear Whiner," she typed. *"For the third time, let me remind you that my course syllabus, which follows university guidelines, was given out at the beginning of the semester and you signed the acknowledgment form."* Just for the sense of wicked vindication, she hovered her mouse pointer over the *Send* button before going back into the message and deleting the "third time" phrase as well as her personal nickname for the female student. Not that keeping it there wasn't tempting enough.

Moving on, she said a short thanksgiving prayer that Plagiarizing Boy had dropped out of the class after getting caught on two stories, so she didn't have to run any assignments through the detection software. She still had to give him credit for plagiarizing from a Japanese author. If she hadn't been suspicious and run that through the Alta Vista translation program, he might have gotten away with it.

She managed to finish her grading in a couple of hours, despite the cat's attempts to distract her by sitting on the laptop. She moved the cat once more and checked her personal e-mail. She was thrilled to see a message from her book reviewer friend, Christine Schmidt, with the accompanying link to the review that was posted on her blog. She felt the cold bagel flutter in her belly as she clicked the link and closed her eyes for a moment before reading the review.

But she read in growing delight, reaching for her phone and finding Christine's contact info even as she read the last line. "Oh, please be there," she said as the phone rang once, twice, a third time.

Christine answered on the fourth ring. "Christine, *Baltimore Dispatch.*"

"Cassandra Ellis, new and upcoming author of *Mailbox Murders.*"

"Cassie! Does this mean you've seen my blog?"

"I have. I can't believe how effusive you were about the book." She saw her reflection in the computer screen—no wonder her cheeks were starting to hurt. Her grin was enormous. "Complimenting my research, my characters, my plot. And giving it five stars! That's so awesome."

"Well, your book's awesome. It was well done for a first novel. Hell, it was well done for a fiftieth novel. Hopefully, people will read the post today and order the book. Or read *The Baltimore Dispatch* book review on Sunday and buy it then. Of course, they'll have to buy the paper first."

Cassie pictured the woman on the other end: sitting at her desk, running a hand through her short blond hair, sorrow for the state of the journalistic world evident on her face. Christine often bemoaned the dying newspaper business and joked that the name of the paper actually referred to what was happening to the newspaper employees each day.

"Well, that's why you've been smart enough to branch out to the Internet as well," said Cassie.

"Thanks. The advertising on the blog does generate some income. Oh, well, I'm sure I'll strike it rich when my book is published." Christine laughed.

"Of course. Won't we all?" Cassie laughed as well. Published author or not, she knew she'd never make enough to give up her day job. "That reminds me. Did you contact my agent?"

"I did, but unfortunately, he doesn't represent literary fiction."

"Oh." So, Aaron had hated it. Cassie knew him well enough to know that the agent would've made an exception if he had liked the writing. "I'm sorry. Look, it took me years to find an agent, I'm sure you'll find someone soon."

"I hope so. But I don't mean to bring you down this afternoon, just days away from your finest hour."

"No worries," Cassie said. "Besides, your article made me so happy, it's hard to dim it."

Christine laughed again, more enthusiastically this time. "Well, I just hope it helps. And we're still on for Wednesday's show, right?"

"Absolutely. I'll see you next Wednesday."

"Looking forward to it. And congratulations again, Cassie."

She hung up, then rubbed her temple. Why was she getting a caffeine withdrawal headache? The spot her teacup occupied while she was working was empty. Then she remembered: she hadn't managed to actually make a cup of tea yet that morning.

Morning. A glance at the clock confirmed morning was almost over. She had to do something before this headache became bad, so with a sigh she got up to refill the electric kettle again. After she had managed to burn up two teakettles, her father had bought this one with an automatic turn-off feature. When she was in the groove and writing, even the shrill noise of a whistling kettle didn't knock her back into the real world. This time, she waited at the counter for the minute it took for the water to boil and poured it into her patiently waiting teacup.

Taking the cup over to the table, she opened up her iTunes program, selected her "Killing Music" playlist, and prepared to write. Excited to be starting a new mystery novel, inspiration struck and her fingers flew over the keys, throwing in characters, words, and phrases like a chef throws together ingredients for his finest meal.

Two hours later, Cassie was stuck, and her head was killing her. She never did drink the tea. She walked over to the refrigerator for an emergency Coke and considered her story.

After consulting her books and the Internet, she had selected the poison that would work best for her victims. Ricin, a quick acting poison that affected the nervous system, was perfect. But she wasn't certain how to get the poison into the wine. Cork was permeable, so if she had a long, thin needle, she could inject the poison through the cork. But where could one get a needle long enough? And thin enough not to leave an obvious hole, yet still strong enough to penetrate the cork?

Pausing *That's The Night The Lights Went Out In Georgia*, she got her cell phone and speed-dialed Paul Larson, her medical expert. He had been a paramedic for over twenty years and taught first aid courses at a local community college. She'd met him and Liam there when she'd taken a first aid and CPR class.

He didn't answer his work phone. After leaving a message, Cassie tried to go back to writing. But she couldn't, not without knowing how to inject the poison. Paul had a cell phone, didn't he? Yes. He'd called her from it once or twice. She searched through her cell phone call log, but didn't find the number.

"I know I wrote it down somewhere." Rooting through her notebooks, online, and through her purse didn't turn up any results, not even with Donner's help.

She leaned back in her chair and sighed. Of course, she knew where it was, in the damn day planner. But she didn't have it any more. She was just going to have to force herself to keep writing without it, as much as it irked her need for instant research gratification. Something her father and Michelle both teased her about.

Shaking her head, she placed her fingers back on the keyboard, ready to start writing again no matter what. She waited for inspiration to strike. And waited.

It was no use. Even listening to *Janie's Got a Gun* did nothing to get her over the block. Yes, she was addicted to instant research gratification. So what? She had to solve the puzzle of how the murderer would get the poison in the wine before she went ahead with the death scene. After all, what if it couldn't work?

Sighing again, she went back to her purse and pawed through the bag until she found the card. As she dialed the number, she hoped he would understand.

Work on Montgomery case
Check C.E. contacts?

THURSDAY 06 JULY 08:45:04

chapter 5

Deep in concentration, Whittaker didn't even glance up from the file on Montgomery when the phone rang. Reaching over for the receiver, he answered automatically. "Homicide, Whittaker speaking."

He lifted a hand and signaled Freeman when he heard who was on the line. "Hello, Ms. Ellis. Do you have any additional information for us?"

When she said no, he wondered why she was calling. So he asked.

"Well…"

The pause went on for such a long moment that Whittaker thought she had to be working up the guts to confess to the murder.

"I was hoping that you had access to my day planner," she said at last. "I need a phone number from it. For Paul Larson?"

"It's stored in the Evidence Room, so I don't have it."

"I should have known that," she muttered.

He smiled, since she couldn't see him. Then a long, disappointed, and resigned sigh from the other end of the connection made him take pity on her. He reached for the Montgomery file and pulled it closer.

"Hold on, Ms. Ellis. I did take the time to copy the pages, so I should have the info you need." He located the number and read it off to her.

"Thank you so much, Detective Whittaker," the writer said, relief as well as embarrassment apparent in her voice. "I, well, I need to ask Paul something, um, important."

He wondered why she sounded embarrassed. What question did she have for the man she had labeled as a medical expert? Personal or professional? "You're welcome, Ms. Ellis. And thank you again for your time yesterday." He ignored Freeman's raised eyebrow.

"Have you found out anything else?" she asked. "I watched the news and they mentioned Seth Montgomery's name, so I assume that means you've informed next of kin. Do you have any more leads?"

"We're doing everything possible, Ms. Ellis. Thank you for your concern."

He hung up the phone, shaking his head. "She needed a number out of her day planner, can you believe that? I guess it's good that she used the business card I gave her. We'll have to tell Requisitions that those cards do come in handy. Worth the tax dollars." He laughed. "I tell you, if she's guilty, it's pretty arrogant of her to call here."

"Do you think she's guilty?"

"No." Whittaker shook his head again. "Her reactions were totally off when we brought her in. No guilt. And while I think she's clever, I don't think she's clever enough to fake such a readable face. Not that she demonstrated the typical witness reaction either. I've never seen anyone take notes in the interview room before. Well, other than us, of course."

"Do you think she's involved?" persisted Freeman.

Whittaker shrugged, tapping the scanned day planner pages together to align them before placing them back into the file. "Not directly."

"But you think she's connected?"

"Yes, connected. Her day planner got to Montgomery's rowhouse somehow. Whether that's thanks to Montgomery or thanks to the killer, that's still to be determined."

"Do you think she's pretty?"

"Yes, she's…" He frowned at Freeman. "What the hell kind of question is that?"

Freeman snorted. "A fun one. What kind of answer was that?"

Whittaker considered for a moment. "An honest one. She is pretty. Not that that will influence my opinion of her. We've seen beautiful killers before. Remember Renee Sigler? Beautiful, gorgeous, and killed her rich husband without batting an eye."

"We've seen ugly ones too."

Whittaker locked eyes with his partner. "Errol Davidson," they said simultaneously.

Whittaker shuddered. "That was one ugly man. Ugly and stupid. Why he didn't think we'd find the bloody bat in his car trunk, I don't know." He poked at the Montgomery folder on his battered desk. "I don't think this one is going to be as easy to solve though."

"Nothing on Montgomery's family or friends?"

"Doesn't have many of either. His parents died years ago, his father while in prison. One ex-wife who divorced him while he was serving year one of five of his first sentence. She's solidly alibied, lives in North Carolina and was at work until 1700 yesterday."

"I checked the neighbors," Freeman added, indicating his notes. "No one saw anything, heard anything, or knew anything. Not surprising for that neighborhood, no one ever sees anything. Still, it helps confirm Ms. Ellis' innocence. She'd be noticed in that neighborhood. Especially with that hair."

Whittaker nodded. "It is a fiery red, isn't it?" He thought again about Cassie, as he often had since they had interviewed her. Too often. "Did we set up a hotline for anonymous tips?"

His partner nodded as he got up to get coffee. "Set it up yesterday, but seriously doubt we'll get any information out of it. In that neighborhood, it's not so much that people are afraid to talk, it's more they don't even bother to notice. It's amazing enough that a neighbor called in about the gunshots." Freeman sat down and leaned back. "And none of Montgomery's victims checked out either, right?"

Whittaker shook his head. "No, that was the first thing I checked this morning, since Ms. Ellis was a probable wash. Montgomery's fires never killed anyone, so no revenge killing there. And the last time he was prosecuted and jailed was ten years ago. Besides, none of them did a lot of damage. He wasn't very good at arson, just used kerosene."

"Not too original."

"No, Ms. Ellis is probably correct that he wasn't too bright."

"Since nothing about Montgomery raises flags," Freeman said. "We'll need to research more about Ms. Ellis. Well, you can. I had an idea about the Fulbright case I wanted to review."

Whittaker read through the file again, concentrating on the people listed in Cassie's day planner. She had an entire section for experts and listed their information including e-mails, addresses, and what topics they covered. There were dozens of names. Medical experts, gun experts, legal experts, even one she listed as an expert on prenatal violent trauma. Now why in hell would she need to know that?

Turning to his computer, he clicked on an icon and felt guilty. Downloading that application was one of the few things against the rules he had ever done, but he just couldn't stand using the approved browser.

"You just clicked on that fox again, didn't you?" Freeman asked. "I can see the guilt all over your face."

"Keep it down," Whittaker hissed, his eyes darting left and right to see if anyone had overheard.

Freeman rolled his eyes. "Boy, no one cares that you downloaded a stupid browser."

"I care. You know I don't like to break rules."

Freeman's grin vanished. "Listen, Whittaker…oh, never mind. What are you looking up?"

"I'm running all the names in her book to see what pops up."

"I've seen that list, you'll be at it for hours," Freeman snorted.

"Yeah, she must be damned persuasive." Whittaker was impressed despite himself. Many of her resources were well respected experts and some were hard to contact. More than one of the articles on Mark Griffin called him a loner, so she must have managed to charm him. He could understand the appeal. She was intelligent, witty, clever, and damn it, she was pretty.

He shot a glare over the monitor toward Freeman, who was once again bent over his work, before returning his attention to the computer display. It didn't surprise him that Mark Griffin had agreed to spend time with her, especially if she flattered him by asking questions. He could easily envision Ms. Ellis doing that…and not as a manipulative move. She had seemed so inquisitive in the interview room, where most people would have been cowed and scared.

He admired that all-out curiosity…although he hoped that her curiosity didn't affect her the way it affected the proverbial cat.

He sat up straight when a blog post popped up on the search engine. It was not only written by Christine Schmidt, the media expert, but it was also about Cassandra Ellis, newly published author. This merited a closer look.

The book review discussed the upcoming release of Ms. Ellis' mystery novel, *Mailbox Murders.*

He wasn't surprised to see the reviewer complimented Ms. Ellis on her excellent research skills in addition to praising her writing and plotting abilities.

"Well, I found something interesting about Ms. Ellis."

"Oh?"

Whittaker swiveled the computer monitor around to show his partner. "A blog entry, by Christine Schmidt, posted today, about the release of Ms. Ellis' book. You know what a blog is, don't you?"

"Of course," said Freeman.

Whittaker stared at him and waited.

"Okay," said Freeman, giving in. "I mostly know what that's about. Blogging is sort of doing a diary online, right? You just write about whatever you did that day."

"Or, about topics upon which you are an expert. In fact, many of the people that Ms. Ellis used for experts were probably found online, thanks to their blogs. Except for Mark Griffin. He's pretty much a recluse, real world or virtual."

"I don't get why you would want everyone to know every single thing you did that day. What you ate for breakfast, how many times you took a shit."

Whittaker snorted. "Okay, most blogs aren't that bad. Now, Twitter… that can be pathetic. Way too much information."

From the expression on his partner's face, he could tell Freeman was dying to ask what Twitter was, and whether it had anything to do with birds. He laughed when instead Freeman turned to his own computer and pecked at the keys, obviously looking up Twitter.

Whittaker did his best to keep up on technology. First of all, because he enjoyed it. And the Internet, including social media, had proven to be a valuable tool in solving some murder cases. One person had even tweeted "rest in peace" wishes to a friend—before the friend's body even had been discovered.

Freeman pushed his keyboard aside in disgust. "Okay, Twitter does seem stupider. Anyway, what did this blog say?"

Whittaker summed it up for his partner. "It says a more complete review will be posted this Sunday in *The Baltimore Dispatch*."

He held back a smile at Freeman's relief. Newspapers he understood. Freeman was one of the few people who still read Baltimore's newspaper in the actual print edition.

Freeman tapped the latest edition of the *Dispatch*, as usual atop all the paperwork in his inbox tray. "So, do you think the timing of this blog thing and the timing of Montgomery's death are related?"

"It's possible. Ms. Ellis doesn't mention his name, although she does mention a few others. I wonder if she cleared that with them. We should probably interview all of her contacts."

Freeman sighed. "Are you sure we're not following a wild goose, Whittaker? We don't know Ms. Ellis is involved in this; the day planner could be just a coincidence."

"I don't believe in coincidence. Besides, it's not like we have any other leads from Montgomery. Family? Nothing. Friends? Montgomery didn't have any. Victims? All alibied and accounted for, and again, he wasn't very good as an arsonist. Workplace? Considering he couldn't hold a job for more than three months, nada there as well. Neighborhood? Zip. So we're left to pursue this angle. There's something about Ms. Ellis, I'm just not sure what it is."

"But you'd love to find out, right?" Freeman waggled his eyebrows.

Whittaker rolled his eyes. "I'm making another copy of this list so we can leave one in the file and take the other one with us." He got up, ignoring Freeman's groan of agony. Heading for the copier, he passed the other detectives busy at their desks. After fighting with the ancient copier for a few minutes, he got it to spit out another copy of the day planner pages. He threw the copy down on Freeman's desk and returned the original copy back to the file.

"Anyone really interesting on the list?" Freeman asked. "Hey, why are they mostly guys?"

"At first guess, I'd say it's because there aren't that many women involved in the fields Ms. Ellis is interested in. Like arson, murder, guns, and so on. At second guess, I'd say she probably has an easier time charming information out of men than women."

"This Solange Gavreau might be a woman," Freeman stated. "Sounds French…and sexy. Let's start with her."

Whittaker shook his head. "Keep it up and I'll tell your wife about this."

"You wouldn't dare," Freeman rebutted. "You like having a partner too much."

"But it would be a damn easy murder to solve, at least. I'd get to mark that one closed pretty quickly."

"You think? I've always suspected Jordan asks me all the questions about the murders we're investigating in order to learn from them. She watches those Discovery shows too. Calls them 'How to get away with murder' shows. She figures she'll see how everyone else got caught and not make the same mistakes."

Whittaker shook his head again. "Your wife scares me, man."

Freeman looked around and whispered. "Me, too."

Laughing, Whittaker kicked Freeman's chair. "Come on, get your butt out of that seat, we need to get going."

After five hours, they had nothing to show for it except for a number of discussions, including one with Solange Gavreau, who did turn out to be French and as sexy as Freeman had imagined. Whittaker found her cold, but not cold enough to be a murderer. Somehow, she seemed inappropriately delighted that Ms. Ellis was in trouble.

They also gained some new knowledge about the effects of gunshot on a fetus, and some glowing accounts about the smart and friendly Cassandra Ellis. And, from the author's best friend Michelle Edwards, a bit of guilt about how they had disrupted what had been a celebration by pulling Ms. Ellis into interview. But no real leads.

That was a typical day, Whittaker thought as he crossed off their most recent visit. Most days were all research, little real outcome. Probably a lot like Ms. Ellis' job, now that he thought about it.

They did find one interesting connection, although it didn't pan out. Paul Larson's paramedic station handled Montgomery's area, but Larson hadn't been on the response team at that time. He had been at his office, along with Liam Brody, preparing for their evening first aid class. Since Brody was another of Ms. Ellis' contacts, Whittaker and Freeman managed to establish two alibis at once.

While they ate lunch in the car, air conditioning cranked full blast, Freeman checked the next contact on the list. Whittaker laughed when a big blot of mayo spurted from Freeman's sandwich and onto the list. Taking the papers, he carefully wiped the mayonnaise from the list with some of his napkins. "Hmm, the next name is Christine Schmidt, media expert."

"The one who wrote the blog?"

"One and the same," said Whittaker, taking a new napkin to make sure his hands were thoroughly clean before reaching in his pocket for his smartphone. "She's listed as a book expert. But still, she's media. It feels wrong to voluntarily talk to media."

"It does seem to go against some police code." Freeman raised an eyebrow. "I don't mean that literally of course, since you would know if there was truly a rule against it in the General Orders. You have those memorized, right?"

From long practice, Whittaker ignored his partner's jibe as he googled up Christine Schmidt on his smartphone. "Then again, she does book reviews for *The Baltimore Dispatch*."

"I thought she did them for her blog."

"She does reviews for both. Surprised that *The Baltimore Dispatch* lets her do that though."

"Wait, you mean we have to actually go to the den of the lion to meet with this woman? That does feel wrong."

Whittaker started the car and slid into traffic. "We'll have to be careful not to let her know why we're asking her questions about Ms. Ellis. I'd hate for her to put two and two together and realize we have her murder mystery author as a murder suspect."

* * *

Christine Schmidt seemed happy to see them. Whittaker was nearly overwhelmed by the rampant curiosity burning in her green eyes. "Hello, fellows, you just increased my level of respect here. Two handsome homicide cops visiting me at work. People might actually start treating me as a real journalist now instead of a bookworm. What can I do for you in return?"

Trying for casual, Whittaker said that her name had come up in the course of an investigation—just routine, of course. He worked the conversation to confirm her whereabouts at the time of the murder. Not surprisingly, she had been on the phone with a couple of authors during the time period.

He thanked her for her cooperation and turned to leave. Then, making it appear as an afterthought, he turned back.

"By the way, what book will you be reviewing this weekend?"

"A very good debut author in the mystery genre," answered Christine. "Cassandra Ellis, author of *Mailbox Murders*. She's going to be awesome. Lives here in Baltimore."

"No kidding." Whittaker asked a few more questions, taking the opening Christine had given him to get her opinion of the author without cluing her in to his real reason for asking. He hoped. He never felt comfortable talking to the media.

"Good job, boy," Freeman said after they were on the street again. "You were damn subtle on asking about Ms. Ellis."

Whittaker glanced over his shoulder at the brick building housing the *Dispatch*. "I hope so. Hard to get information out of a subject without letting her know what we're doing. But she appears to be in the clear. Let's head out and confirm those author calls she claimed to make before we head home. Hopefully, we'll solve this case before Sunday. If not, can you bring your copy of Sunday's *Baltimore Dispatch* in on Monday so we'll have the book review on file?"

Freeman grinned. "Sure thing. You can have it for your scrapbook album on pretty Ms. Ellis."

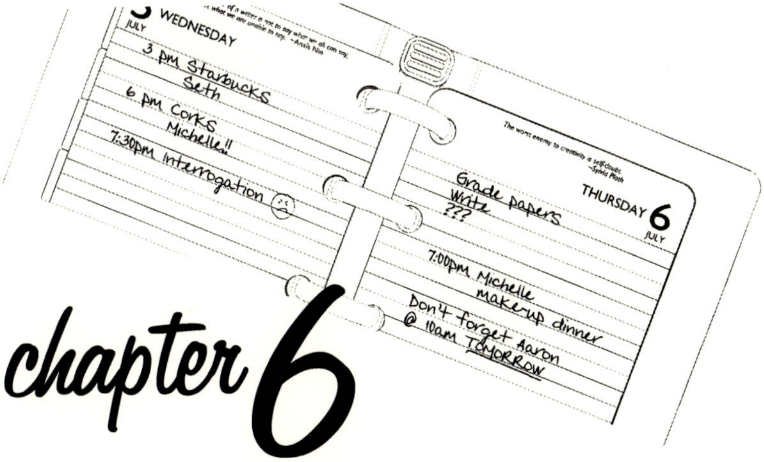

chapter 6

"There, the first few pages of your scrapbook are done." Michelle patted the page and smiled at her work. "You sure you don't mind me cutting up the dustjacket from your book?"

"I don't mind at all. I've got thirty more copies," Cassie said, pointing at a stack of books in her living room. "I can sacrifice one."

"Cool. And I printed out Christine's wonderful blog post. You scored big there with that connection. I printed out your listing on Amazon and the bio. We'll have to make sure to get all the reviews too. Can you grab me some copies of your postcard and bookmarks?"

Cassie took her wine glass with her as she got the marketing materials. Coming back, she shook her head at her best friend's pure concentration as she worked. "Thanks. I've never had the patience to do this kind of stuff—not sure how you manage it. You were never that great in the patience department either."

"I can be patient sometimes. I just have to work on it. Or have an important enough reason. You're an important enough reason."

"Thanks, Chelle." Cassie headed over to stir the bouillabaisse she had simmering on the stove top.

"Besides, you feed me. No, not you," Michelle said to Donner, who had jumped up on the table to inspect her work. "Speaking of patience and lack of it, by the way, you seem to have patience enough to cook fancy food."

"Well, as you said, it's important. Good food and good wine are incredibly important."

"Amen to that." Keeping her eyes and one hand on her work, Michelle raised her glass in a toast. "Aren't you going to have a book release party?"

"Aaron and I argued about that, actually. I didn't want to jinx anything by announcing the book ahead of time, so I refused to do one on the release date. So we're having a one-month anniversary party in August. I'll send out invites this week. So…" Cassie set down the wooden spoon and leaned against the counter. "Should we include the reports of Seth's death in this scrapbook?"

Michelle looked up with a scowl. "Don't be stupid, Cassie. First of all, his murder has nothing to do with you. Second of all, no, this is a happy scrapbook. We're not including any of your rejection letters, either."

"Well, it is related to my writing career. He was one of my contacts, after all. And hell, being accused of his murder gave me the opportunity to see the Baltimore police interview rooms. I can use that."

"Cassandra Lynn Ellis. You were not accused of murder. Stop being so damned pessimistic."

"Hey, if I was pessimistic, I'd be worried that the police were about to come knocking on my door. And honestly, I'm not worried." As soon as the words were out of her mouth, Cassie couldn't help but to take a breath, watch the front door, and wait for the bell to ring. Or for the door to come bursting from the frame with a SWAT squad pouring in with the splintered remains. Any second now.

When nothing happened, she knocked three times on the counter. "Or, even worse, I'd be worried someone else I know is going to be killed." She knocked again.

"Okay, chickie, I think you've been thinking about murder too much. We live in Baltimore, one of the top murder capitals in the United States. It's not surprising we know someone who has been killed. One of my employees was killed last year."

"And were you brought it for questioning?"

"Well, no."

"Did your employee have your day planner in his house?"

Michelle took a sip of wine. "Her house. And no, can't say she did. Fine, you have a right to worry and wonder. But this isn't one of your stories, Cassie." She tilted her head and grinned. "Although it does have a sexy hero."

"Detective Whittaker is hardly a hero," Cassie said, scowling.

Michelle's eyebrows rose. "Actually, I was talking about your agent. Who rode to your rescue, I might add. But your answer is more interesting." She drawled the last word. "Cassie's got the hots for a cop."

"Do not. It just makes sense that I've been thinking about him." All the time, actually. "It's good research, that's all."

"What, Marty's going to hook up with a sexy cop?"

"My main character already has a guy. But she might get dragged into interview. I have firsthand experience now, remember."

"Which is exactly how you need to treat this, Cass," Michelle said firmly.

Cassie stirred the saffron into the soup and said a silent prayer of thanks for her best friend. Michelle was the perfect remedy for bouts of worry or self-pity.

Michelle cleared her throat. "Now, I'm going to do something shocking in this house. In ten minutes, I am banning any thought or mention of murder."

Cassie smiled. "I'm not sure I can do that, actually...why in ten minutes?"

"Well, that should give me enough time to tell you about my visit today."

"A murdering visit?" Cassie thought it would be a good idea to sit down for this one. She checked the heat under the soup and took her wine back to the living room.

"A visit about murder. I received a visit from your detectives."

Cassie was glad she had chosen to sit. Had she still been standing, her knees would have buckled. "They interviewed you? Why? Oh God, they do think I did it."

"I don't think so, Cassie. Detective Whittaker said it was routine."

"They *always* say that. Routine, my ass. They aren't about to ask you if you think I went and killed someone."

"I didn't get the impression they thought that. I mean, Detective Whittaker did ask me—and he is sexy, isn't he? Even when he's so serious. Anyway, he asked me when you had invited me to Corks, the purpose of the dinner. I tried to guilt them on that one, told them they had interrupted our celebration and all. Things like that. Oh, they asked whether you were on time or not."

Cassie snorted. "Like you'd know. You were late."

"Yeah, that's what I told him. Then the other detective..."

"Freeman."

"Right. He asked me if that was a typical pattern."

"So they could establish whether I could expect you to be late. I wonder when the murder actually took place, the timing of it."

"Well, they asked me what I was doing between three and six, so that's a pretty big window. I was at work for most of the period, and provided some names to confirm it. Don't you have an alibi or something? Someone who saw you?"

"Probably not." Cassie shrugged. "I met with Seth for about a half hour at Starbucks. Unlike you, he was on time."

"I'd rather be late than a stupid arsonist. Or a smart arsonist for that matter."

"I'd rather that for you as well. Anyway, we met for about a half hour, then it was such a pretty day that I biked over to Federal Hill and wrote outside for a while. I didn't see anyone I knew. It was mostly just tourists around. But I stayed there until about five, then headed home to get ready for dinner. Left the house forty-five minutes later to walk to Corks."

"Did you see anyone then?"

"Not that I knew. Not until I got to Corks at five minutes before six. So I wonder when the murder was. It would have to be earlier. Much earlier, actually, since there'd have to be time for the uniforms to arrive, then call in Homicide." Cassie swirled the wine in her glass around as she stared into space and visualized the scene: the body spread out on the floor, the blood, and the soiled day planner.

"Then enough time for the detectives to be called in and travel to the scene, find my day planner, see that I was the last to see Seth alive. And see I had a dinner reservation that same night, and head to Corks. How did the police even know about the murder?"

"Well," said Michelle, after a sip from her glass, "you said he was killed by gunfire. Perhaps someone heard the gunshot and called it in."

Cassie blinked and sharpened her attention on her friend. "That makes sense. So that would be a quick response, then. Still, they'd need enough time to do some investigating."

"And the 'knock on doors'," Michelle agreed. "See, I watch cop shows."

Cassie waved a hand. "They probably had uniforms do that, at least initially." She rested her chin on her hand and calculated backwards. "So I'm thinking the murder was probably around four fifteen or so. Enough time for him to get home—I met him in his area—and for the killer to determine Seth was alone and wait for a time when the streets were empty. Then he could get into Seth's home, drop the planner, and shoot him."

"He? Do you think it's a man?"

"Perhaps. Guns, like poison, are less hands-on, so women do prefer to use guns more often than something more direct like knives or strangling. But it's rather violent. I'm just using 'he' as an example. Anyway, what else did they ask you?"

"Not much really. Whether I knew Seth. I told him only through you talking about him. I did volunteer information, though. When I told him about how we were celebrating the book, I mentioned how you're a good writer since you're so good at imagining things that you've never personally experienced. I thought that was a subtle way to let him know you'd never actually kill anyone."

Cassie had to smile. "That was subtle, for you."

Michelle's return smile was pure wickedness. "I thought about saying that if you were a killer, you would have killed Solange while we were in college before you'd kill someone you barely knew."

"Damn straight. I thought about calling her though, when I was on the way to the police station. I wasn't sure if I needed a lawyer or not. I still don't know." Cassie bit her bottom lip. "If they're calling you, I must be under suspicion. Or my friends are. They're probably using my damned day planner to contact some of you."

"Or it's routine, Cassie, since they don't have any other leads. Stop worrying. Please? For me?"

Cassie reached over and squeezed her hand. "Thanks. I'll try to stop. For you."

"Anyway, enough about murder. From now on, no talk of murder, no thinking murder. Unless, of course, it's how I'm going to kill you in Scrabble after dinner."

* * *

Thanks to the magic of Michelle, who kept up a constant chatter on non-murder subjects, Cassie managed to make it through dinner and most of one game of Scrabble without talking or thinking of the banned topic. It wasn't her fault that her tiles spelled out anthrax. In fact, it was her best scoring wordplay ever.

Cassie gloated as she tallied up the scores. "Okay, so adding the 'n' to your 'ratio', that makes it 'ration', only worth seven points there. But hey, the 'x' is on the double letter score, so that's sixteen points. Plus nine for a total of twenty-five points. On the triple word score, that's seventy-five. Plus fifty points for a Bingo. So that's one hundred thirty-two for that play!"

"Okay, this game's over. No way I can catch up now. But I cry foul. I said no thinking of murder." Michelle turned and spoke to Donner, who was pouting in the corner since he didn't get any bouillabaisse. "Didn't I tell her no murder?"

"Hey, anthrax is used more for biological warfare than murder. Did you know that the anthrax used by the United States is believed to have been developed not too far from here, at Fort Detrick? Sadly, it was created when a scientist there accidentally infected himself with the Vollum strain. They call it Vollum-1B."

"That's horrible. They should've at least named it after the scientist."

"Well, they might have. His last name started with a B. Umm…what's that singer who did so well on that British television show?" Noting their first bottle of wine was finished, she went to fetch a new one.

Despite the shift in topic, Michelle's answer was instant. "*Britain's Got Talent.* Susan Boyle."

"Right. The scientist's last name was Boyle." Cassie frowned as she opened the wine refrigerator. "No, Boyles. William Boyles."

"Your memory frightens me."

"Hey, I like trivia." She chose another Riesling out of the fridge.

"Yeah, especially if it's about death. They should put out a new *Trivial Pursuit* for you."

"The Morbid Edition?" Cassie giggled as she got her waiter's corkscrew from the drawer. Unfolding the knife, she prepared to cut the foil. And stopped.

"What's wrong?"

"What? Oh, nothing's wrong. It's just…" Cassie stared at the foil capsule as she realized her plotting problem might not be that hard."There are holes in this foil."

Michelle came into the kitchen. "Yes. They're decorative. Why do you care?"

"Well, see, I'm trying to figure out how to put poison in a bottle of wine, unnoticed, of course."

"Cassie, I said 'no murder'!" Michelle poked her in the arm. "I meant it."

"Don't ruin my epiphany. This is important for the book I'm working on."

Michelle sighed and leaned against the counter. "All right, let's hear it."

"I figured cork is permeable enough that a small needle mark wouldn't show. Anyway, according to my medical expert…" She paused, remembering who she had to call to get Paul's phone number. "Anyway, he thought dental needles, like those used to give Novocaine, would be long and sturdy enough. But we were concerned that a big needle like that would leave too noticeable a hole. Especially in the foil. But these have holes already."

Michelle took the bottle from her. "I don't know. Cork is permeable, but it's pretty strong and tough. Most needles, and thank you very much for making me think of the dentist, are designed to go through soft things, like skin or gums. Flesh."

"Do you have a better idea, Einstein?" Cassie snatched the bottle back.

Michelle grabbed it again. "Actually, I do. You're a purist—you use a waiter's corkscrew. But the CO_2 openers have a slender needle that is designed to pierce the cork."

Cassie reclaimed her bottle. "I don't want to inject carbon dioxide into the bottle."

"I know that, Cassandra. But you wanted to brainstorm, so hear me out. What if you remove the cartridge…"

Cassie considered the possibilities. "I could put in whatever I wanted. Stay here, I'll be right back." Abandoning the wine and her astonished friend, Cassie headed for the front door. She jammed on her helmet, released her bike from the rack, and was halfway out the door before Michelle reacted.

"Hey! Where are you going? What about me?"

Cassie didn't pause. "I cooked, you can wash the dishes. I won't be gone long. Hopefully they'll have what I want at Ray's."

She jumped on her bike and pedaled the ten blocks to Ray's Liquors, a more upscale store than the one in her neighborhood. It also stayed open longer. She rushed into the accessories aisle, not even bothering to remove her helmet. She scanned along the array of ice buckets, coasters, and paper cocktail umbrellas until she spied what she wanted. Score! The last one, too, so it must be meant to be. She didn't even bother with the price, this was research. Examining the CO_2 opener through its packaging while she waited at the checkout, she considered the needle size. It just might work.

Excited and eager for some hands-on research, she raced back home, her new opener rattling in the saddlebag.

"I got it," she panted, shouldering open the front door and dragging her bike through.

"Cassie?" Michelle stepped out of the kitchen, drying her hands on a dishtowel. "You're crazy to go racing out on a muggy night like this."

Cassie stowed her bike and helmet, trying to get her breath. Now that the air, however humid, wasn't whooshing past her body, she was miserable. She grabbed the bag and stepped next to the box air conditioner.

"Hey, thanks for doing the dishes. You know I didn't really expect you to."

Michelle tossed the towel aside and reached for opener. "Yeah, yeah. Give me that; I want to see if it works."

"Mine!" Cassie yanked back the bag.

Michelle folded her arms and tapped her foot. "And which of us knows how it's supposed to work?"

Reluctantly, Cassie handed her over the corkscrew. Without fanfare, Michelle tore into the packaging and threw the plastic on the counter. "By the way, guys love these things. The more gadgety something is, the better."

Cassie leaned on the counter and watched as her friend unscrewed the top of the device and removed the CO_2 cartridge. Cassie passed her over the bottle of Riesling, now beaded with condensation from being left out of the fridge.

"Here goes." Michelle set the opener on top of the bottle and pushed down. The opener's needle slid down easily and pierced the cork. "See? It could work."

"It will work," Cassie said.

Michelle's nose wrinkled. "Yeah, but how will you get the poison into the bottle? I didn't think that far ahead."

"Like this." Cassie rummaged through a kitchen drawer. "Aha! Here." Removing the bulb from a turkey baster, she fitted it into the opener. "So, just fill this up with poison, then use the bulb to apply pressure."

"Well, don't do it now," Michelle said. "I want to drink this wine before it gets any warmer. If you're up for another game. So let me show you how this is really supposed to work…skipping the adding poison part."

Cassie snorted, but she nodded and watched as Michelle put the CO_2 cartridge back in and pressed the button. In seconds, the cork popped out, impaled on the needle.

"Wow…I can get used to that. Sure, I'm up for another game. And let me guess, no murder words, right?"

"No murder words. But an extra ten points for each sexual word."

Cassie shook her head and laughed. "Only you, Michelle."

* * *

Cassie hunched over her laptop and hoped the burn she felt on her telltale fair complexion could be excused to the high heat index for the day. She hadn't understood the meaning of half the words Michelle had played in that last game of Scrabble the night before, so she had been looking up the terms on Urban Dictionary as she waited for her appointment with her agent, Aaron Kaufman.

Her overactive imagination had gone wild from information overload. Definitely not something to have done in a public setting.

She switched screens to something far safer and hoped Aaron's current appointment ran overtime so she'd have time to cool down. She glanced up as the door opened, keeping her grimace inside. Talk about bad timing.

"It was wonderful talking to you, my dear. You can pick up that form from my secretary, she has it ready."

With curiosity, Cassie eyed the woman who followed Aaron. She was older and…sturdy. Cassie always struggled while writing to describe that size frame. Sturdy would have to do. She didn't like *chubby* or *pleasantly plump.* Although the woman did seem very pleasant.

The woman had long, pure white hair and wore a flowing, lime-green skirt with a bright yellow tunic. Next to Aaron's conservative dark pinstriped suit, the cheery bright colors popped even more.

"I'll be sure to do so. Take care, Aaron."

She even sounded pleasant. Cassie watched as the white-haired woman shook hands with the agent and went to the receptionist's desk.

It was only then that Aaron turned to greet Cassie, his handsome face breaking into a warm smile. Not having a murder to distract her, butterflies flew around her stomach, as they did whenever the attractive agent focused his full attention on her. His wavy, dark hair and warm brown eyes always left her feeling flustered.

"Cassie, it's good to see you again, especially looking so much better than you did the last time I saw you. You were so pale. Now you have some nice healthy color in your cheeks."

If only he knew what had been responsible for that.

"So, I just got a note from DSG that advance book sales are doing well, even better than expected," he went on. "*Mailbox Murders* is going to break the records of any of my first-time authors."

"*Mailbox Murders*?" At this, the older woman at the receptionist desk turned to face them. "Then you must be Cassandra Ellis. I loved your book; Aaron sent me an advance copy. I can't believe it was your first story."

Cassie blushed; she still wasn't sure how to receive praise. "Well, it was my first published novel, but not my first story. I've been writing since I was eight."

The older woman laughed. "And I thought I was precocious at ten years old. We'll have to compare our original stories one day then. I'm Linda Kowalski, by the way, since Aaron here is neglecting his duties."

Aaron gave Linda a chagrined smile. "Oh, my apologies, ladies. Linda, this is Cassandra Ellis. Cassie, Linda Kowalksi, although she writes under the name LeAnn Kowles." He waved a hand at Linda. "Linda produced a number of psychic mystery novels for DSG." He moved his hand and rested it lightly on Cassie's shoulder. "Cassie is our up-and-coming murder mystery novelist. I expect her to be the next James Patterson."

Cassie blushed again, in part due to Aaron's praise and in part because she recognized Linda's pen name. Aaron had sent her some of Linda's books, but she hadn't bothered to read them. "Oh, I doubt I'll ever be that good or well known."

"Oh, if your first book is any indication, I think I can predict great success," Linda said.

"And Linda ought to know, she's the psychic," Aaron said with a devilish grin.

"Really?" Cassie did her best to hide any trace of skepticism.

"I do try…but Dorian is better." If Linda had picked up on any of Cassie's reaction, she didn't show it. "Anyway, I should let you get to your appointment. It was great meeting you, Cassie."

Cassie waited until Linda was in the elevator before she turned to Aaron. "Dorian? Is that her main character?"

He frowned at her. "I don't know who Dorian is but her main character's name is Penelope. You should know that, I sent you her books. I always send my authors each other's books. That way we can get some good reviews from each other."

"Well, as a new author, I'm hardly going to be an influential reviewer. And, well…I don't believe in psychics."

Aaron shrugged as he stepped back, ushering her into his office ahead of him. "You think I do? But it makes for good fiction, and it's a popular genre. Linda's a good writer, even if she is a little ditzy."

Cassie admired the view of the harbor as she took a seat in one of the lush chairs opposite the large desk. The office suited the man, she thought. Slick, gorgeous, confident, and functional.

"Would you like coffee, water, soda?"

"No, thank you. Caitlin already asked. I'm fine."

"Good. Hold my calls." Aaron said to Caitlin, then closed the door and took his place in the sumptuous leather executive chair. He sat back and Cassie almost laughed when he steepled his fingers together. She had never seen someone do that in real life. "So, Cassie, now it's time to market this story."

That sobered her up. "I know. It's not my favorite thing, since writing is my passion. But I know it's a necessary evil."

"Marketing isn't evil, Cassie. You have a good book, a good product. Therefore, the purpose of marketing is to bring an entertaining, well-researched book to the readers."

"Yes, I suppose you're right."

"Besides, if we were evil, we'd find a way to use your contact's murder as a marketing opportunity. A headline like, *'Up and coming murder mystery author under suspicion for real Baltimore* City *murder'* would bring in the sales."

"Aaron!" Cassie couldn't believe it.

He waved away her shock. "I'm not saying we do that, Cassie. Although it would be a great press release. I'm just saying if we were evil, we could try and benefit from the murder. You know, invite the police to your one-month release party." He shook his head. "I still can't believe you were worried about jinxing something."

"Well, it seems like something has been jinxed, don't you think?" She played with a thread on her khakis and wished that he'd switch topics. She'd even be happy talking about additional book signings.

"Coincidence, Cassie. Just coincidence."

"I'm not so sure the police think so." She glanced up as something occurred to her. "Did you get a visit from the police?"

Aaron furrowed his brow. "They called, but I haven't had a chance to call them back yet and set up an appointment."

Cassie slouched in her seat and looked out the window in disgust, ignoring the view. "God, they're talking to everyone."

"About what? Do they want me to verify your whereabouts or something?"

"Actually, they'll probably ask you if you knew Seth and can account for your whereabouts between three and six on Wednesday."

"*My* whereabouts?" he squeaked, turning so pale Cassie thought he might pass out. "Why would they ask me about that?"

"Routine calls, evidently. It's not a big deal, Aaron. Unless you want to confess to killing Seth," she added in a teasing voice.

The color rushed back into his face. "Of course not. I hate the sight of blood. I would never kill anyone."

"Neither would I...well, on paper, maybe, but not in real life. Anyway, talking about wanting to murder, why don't we go over the marketing schedule?"

Aaron opened his calendar, then stared at her. "How is the marketing schedule about murder?"

Cassie kept her voice and expression light. "Well, if you've booked up more of my weekends on book signings, it'll make me want to kill you... or myself. One of those." She pulled out her new day planner.

Of course he had booked her on more signings.

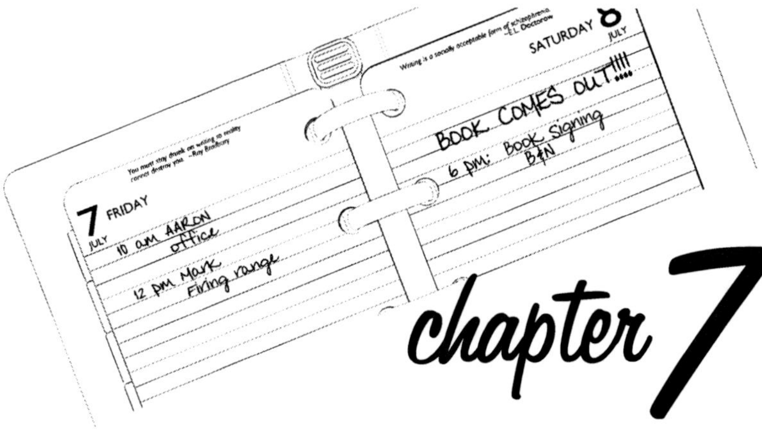

chapter 7

"Ooh, shiny." Cassie glanced sidelong toward her companion and hoped that his ear protectors prevented him from hearing her words. She couldn't help herself; the gun *was* shiny.

"I'm going to ignore that, Cassie," Mark Griffin said as he finished unpacking his equipment.

She ducked her head. Of course he heard it. Their high-tech electronic ear muffs only muffled loud noises, so voices were clear.

"Guns are not 'shiny'."

"This one is."

"Okay, fine, it's shiny. But it's not 'ooh, shiny'," he lisped.

She had to laugh. It wasn't often that Mark made jokes. A former Marine, he took everything seriously, especially where weapons were concerned. After all, he had been an instructor for years with the USMC Weapons Training Battalion.

Even now that he was retired, he practiced his marksmanship often using his extensive firearms collection. He even had a shooting range on his property in Carroll County, but he came to an indoor range during bad weather such as they were having this evening. Cassie hoped the thunderstorms currently happening would cool down the temperature, but she doubted they would.

Mark had also kept his Marine tough body, even though he was as old as her father. Of course, her father never had a Marine-tough body to keep.

But Mark didn't look as old as her father did, other than the fact that his hair—what little he had in his buzzed military cut—was a silvery gray.

Cassie had been shooting with him ever since her introductory class at On Target. After the class, she had asked so many questions of the staff that he wandered over and started contributing to the conversation. Since then, he'd taken her out a number of times on the firing range, both his personal one and the one at On Target. He was a careful and patient teacher who tolerated her questions, regardless of the frequency…or the oddity.

Not to mention he had a lot of cool guns, like this one. "It's made of stainless steel, right?"

He nodded. "Yes, this is the Colt SSP Semi-Automatic, chambered in 9mm Luger. SSP stands for Stainless Steel Pistol. It's extremely rare, there are probably only ten to twenty in existence."

"Why?" she asked, again with internal thanks for his patience and indulgence when it came to her need to know.

"It was one of the losing models of the U.S. Army trials for a new service sidearm in the early '80s. Colt only made fifty or so for the competition, and many of them were destroyed afterward. I'm very fortunate to have one, and two original magazines to go with it. It just arrived, so you should feel honored I'm letting you shoot it. After I do, of course."

She examined the pistol and magazines closely. As Mark always did, he was careful to show her the gun components. When he discussed the double stack magazine, double/single action trigger, safety lever, and magazine release, she was proud that she easily understood the use of the components.

It had taken quite a while for her to feel comfortable handling guns, especially since she knew she had a habit of allowing her mind and imagination to wander. But on the firing range, she did her best to concentrate since she was handling something that, used improperly, could kill someone. It was the one place where she did not allow herself to daydream.

Okay, she didn't allow herself to daydream *much*. However, she remembered Mark telling her to practice shooting while imagining a life or death situation. With that stern expression on his face, he had lectured her. "That way you'll train yourself how to react if the worst happened and you did face an armed enemy. If you had never practiced with the surge of adrenalin flowing through your body, you wouldn't be able to maintain proper shooting posture in a real gunfight."

Not that she wanted to be in a real gunfight. She'd leave that to her fictional characters to fight the bad guys. She preferred to never look at the wrong end of a gun barrel.

As Seth had, she thought. She shivered as she remembered that Seth Montgomery's last moments had involved a view of a gun barrel. She didn't see him as being a particular brave man, so he probably screamed like a girl when the shooter charged in and broke down the door. The shooter, lust for revenge evident on his face, would lift the pistol—one-handed, she thought. Most people wouldn't use the proper two-handed techniques she had been taught. He'd point it directly at Seth and announce, "This is for burning down my house." Seth would stutter out an apology—

"Cassandra Ellis. Are you paying attention?" Mark demanded, a frown deepening the wrinkles around his tanned face.

"Sorry, Mark. Mind wandered." She forced her attention back to the moment.

"Not here, Cassie. Pay attention here."

She nodded and watched as Mark loaded the magazines. She never could load the magazines at that speed. The last time she tried, she'd ended up knocking the entire box of ammunition onto the ground.

She'd never be able to shoot as well as he did, either. Well, he was her gun expert for a reason. But there were a few things she could do just as well.

"Want me to attach the target?" At his nod, she reached up, opened the binder clip, and attached the large paper sheet of a man-shaped target to the holder. There. See? Perfect. There was something she could do just as well as Mark. "How far back do you want it?"

"Seventy-five feet," he said.

"Of course," Cassie said as she sent the target all the way to the far wall. Backing up to the clear glass window, she examined his posture as he got ready to fire.

She took in his stance, noticing the weapon gripped in his right hand, his right arm nearly straight; the elbow of his left supporting arm noticeably bent straight down. It was a classic example of the Weaver stance.

She remembered when he had first mentioned the name of that stance, she wondered what it had to do with weaving. And whether the weaving meant moving back and forth or something to do with sewing. She had almost asked that question when he went on to explain it was named after Jack Weaver, a California Deputy Sheriff who had developed it for pistol competitions.

Mark had taught her, however, to use the Isosceles stance, which she preferred since she didn't have the upper body strength that the Weaver stance required. Not that she always maintained the right positioning either. It was probably why she wasn't as a good as Mark.

He fired off fifteen shots in quick succession. She didn't even have to look at the paper to know all of them were dead on. The target would also be dead, were it a non-paper target. She snorted. "Non-paper target" always amused her. What an understatement.

When the slide locked back, he dropped out the first magazine and laid the gun on the ledge for her to take a turn. She worried for a moment that he'd make her shoot at the same distance he had, but thankfully, he brought the target back to twenty-five feet. She'd have been lucky to have gotten any shots on the target if he had left it at seventy-five.

"Let's see what you can do with it," Mark said as he loaded up the second magazine.

Making sure to focus on what she was doing, she got into her position, slapped the magazine into the gun, racked the slide to chamber a round, and lifted the gun. When she felt she had the correct aim, she pulled the trigger. Surveying the results, she decided her first shot was pretty good, so she aimed again.

Click.

She bit her lip when nothing happened; she hated misfires. She waited, gun aimed downrange in case this was just a hangfire. She had been taught about hangfires in class and still made sure to wait a few seconds to see if the powder would ignite, even though Mark teased her about it. According to him, thanks to modern gunpowder, no one had had a hangfire since the Vietnam War. Still, she waited, then looked at the gun. The slide hadn't closed fully, and she could see a bright copper round jammed against the breech.

"You've got a malfunction, Cassie. You may have limp-wristed again."

She frowned at that. She hadn't limp-wristed for months now. Mark had told her that this was caused when she hadn't held the pistol firmly enough, so the recoil interfered with the regular slide cycle. This caused the casing of a round to get stuck in the ejection port. But this didn't look to her like a slide malfunction, it looked different. She didn't know what to call it, but she hadn't limp-wristed that shot.

She tapped the magazine and racked the slide again, discharging the unfired round. Taking aim again, she fired off the next thirteen rounds with no problem. She even managed to do a half-decent job on the target as well.

After setting down the gun, she turned back to Mark. "I did not limp-wrist it."

He smiled at her indulgently. "If you say so. I'm glad you were able to clear it yourself instead of giving it to me like you usually do."

"Well, I'm learning. But I hate it when the gun doesn't fire right."

He nodded. "The worst noises in the world are a click when you expect a bang, and a bang when you expect a click. Nice grouping, by the way."

She smiled happily. That almost made up for the limp-wrist comment.

He sent the target back to seventy-five feet.

"You're not changing targets?" Cassie asked, since there were a number of shots now in the center of the target.

"Going for the head this time," Mark said and took his stance.

She winced as he got them all dead center. Perhaps she should have said she wouldn't want to be on the other end of the gun barrel if Mark was handling the gun.

Most of the shooters at the range weren't as good as he was, nor did they even try to be. Many people seemed to think the solution to taking down a target was to have a lot of ammunition, instead of a lot of skill.

She looked around the firing range, checking out the other shooters. It was the middle of the day, so there weren't too many. Hmmm, if someone was so inclined, it would be a good time to commit a murder at the gun range. It wasn't the first time she played with the idea, and she again wondered if such a thing could be set up to look like an accident. Regardless, a blatant murder attempt would be a really bad idea in a place like this, with so many people armed with all kinds of firearms. Every time she started imagining this scene, it ended up very badly for the killer as dozens of weapons unloaded into his sorry—

The sight of a stern, wrinkled face only inches from her eyes stopped her imagination cold. She gave him a chagrined grin, then walked forward to take her turn. To make certain Mark couldn't claim she limp-wristed this time, she took aim, carefully and firmly gripped the gun, and started firing. And cursed when her second shot resulted once again in a malfunction. She cleared it and went on to shoot well, but she was frustrated.

"I did not limp-wrist it," she said in self-defense when he came to switch places with him.

"I think you might be right," he said as he took her magazine and loaded it instead of using the other he had ready and waiting.

When his second shot also ended up with a malfunction, she felt relieved and vindicated. It wasn't her fault. Whew. She blew an errant curl away from her eyes.

He shook his head, corrected the problem, and kept shooting until the slide locked back. He ejected the magazine and motioned to her to come closer. "There, you were right. You weren't limp-wristing. I think the spring is not quite right in that magazine, so it's interfering with the cycle. We'll just use the one magazine."

That seemed to work for the rest of their practice session. While she waited for her turn, she wondered if she could use a gun like this, one that had a consistent stoppage—Mark hated when she used the word *jam*—in one of her books. She wouldn't want Marty's gun to do that, of course, but if the bad guy's gun did that, it might make for a good and dramatic scene. But how would Marty know to expect it?

She took out her notepad and wrote down that idea before going back to watch the others on the range. Often, she played a game of deciding who she would want to rescue her if she was ever taken hostage. Besides Mark, of course.

There was a tall black man two lanes over who had a very smooth pull on his trigger and was also consistently hitting the bulls-eye at seventy-five feet. She'd probably choose him.

She would not choose either of the pair of twenty-something males at the end of the range. Instead, she wanted to go behind them and yank up their baggy pants. At least she knew if there ever was a shooting at the range, she'd be able to escape before they would. They'd be tripping all over their clothes.

She put any thoughts of pants, or murders on the range, or other stories out of her mind when it was her turn to shoot. Now that it wasn't jamming—now that there wasn't a stoppage—the gun was nice to handle. They took turns shooting it until they ran out of ammunition.

After walking out both doors of the shooting area, she removed her earphones and earplugs. "So, are you up for lunch?"

He nodded as he checked out and made sure he had everything in his bag. "I am. Go wash your hands."

She shook her head in amusement as she headed to the restroom. Mark always sounded like a dad admonishing his daughter to wash up before dinner when he reminded her to wash her hands after shooting. But he wanted to make sure she got rid of the gunpowder and lead residue.

She looked at herself in the mirror as she cleaned her hands. The ear muffs always smooshed her hair, pressing down on the curls. The yellow goggles she wore for eye protection turned her eyes an interesting shade of green. She had originally purchased the goggles when she tried playing racquetball. The one and only time she tried, that was. After hitting herself twice with the racquet and hitting her opponent with the racquet and the ball—at the same time—she decided racquetball was not for her.

She returned and answered Mark's inquiring glance with an impudent grin. "I washed behind my ears too, Daddy." She laughed at the slight flush that darkened his tanned cheeks. There were people at the shooting range who already speculated on her relationship with Mark. This should give those gossips some fodder for interesting discussions.

She amused herself by humming *Secret Lovers* as she waited for Mark to return. He frowned at her when he recognized the song, then hefted his bag strap over his shoulder. "Do you have to encourage them?"

At her impertinent nod, he sighed. "Fine. What do you say to heading to Panera's?"

She beamed at him. She adored the sandwich and soup shop, and he knew it. "I'd say yes."

Ten minutes later, she parked next to his gray pickup and stepped out of the coolness of her car and into the sauna of the outside air. She had been right, the thunderstorms hadn't brought any relief at all. "So, are you ready to be a published author?" she asked.

With her encouragement—much encouragement—Mark had put together a book of his gun collections with pictures and explanatory paragraphs. They both were amused to have release dates within a week of each other.

"Shouldn't I be asking you that?" He opened the door for her.

Eyeing the menu high on the wall behind the order counter, she frowned when she realized it wasn't the day for her favorite soup. Darn it, she never managed to come on the right days. She'd just have a sandwich then. "Well, you have to admit, the publishing process has been much easier for you. I'd been trying to get published for six years now before I got lucky. You come up with one proposal—"

"Actually, you came up with it. And wrote the book, too."

She waited to respond until after their turn to order. "Well, it was my idea. But my point is, it was much easier for you to get your non-fiction book accepted and contracted than it was for me. It was even easier during the writing and editing process."

"Since it's mostly just pictures of my guns, and a short description of each, it was rather easy. The bio was the hardest part to write. I don't like writing about myself."

"No one does." She tried to grab her tray from the counter, but Mark beat her to it. Used to his behavior, she went and collected utensils and napkins before following him to a booth. "Still, maybe I should switch to nonfiction."

He carefully unfolded his napkin onto his lap before picking up his spoon. "I suggest you switch topics, then, and don't write nonfiction about murders. I don't want you doing any hands-on research."

She shuddered. "No thanks. This situation with Seth Montgomery is the closest I want to get to real-life murder. I still can't believe he was killed."

"I can believe it. People in his…shall we say 'line of work' tend to hang out with bad characters, Cassie. It doesn't surprise me that he came to a bad end."

"I suppose. Still, I had just seen him a few hours before he was killed."

"Which explains why the police visited me."

She cursed under her breath. "They got to you as well? They *are* going to everyone in my day planner."

"Don't worry about it. Detective Freeman stated it was just a routine follow-up."

"Yeah, they keep saying that. It's not routine to me." She tried to remember who all was in the day planner. Just about everyone she knew.

"Not to me either, honestly. Never is. Especially since I don't have an alibi, since I was home alone. Course, unless they're idiots, they'd realize I would have made sure to actually have an alibi if I had done it. They didn't look like idiots, unlike many cops and MPs I've known. So they should be able to find the real killer. Though many cases in Baltimore remain unsolved, right?"

"Depends on the case. And the detective." She suspected Detective Whittaker had a higher case resolution rate than most. "And the motive. Some are easy to solve, since the motive is obvious. The random ones are the hardest to solve."

"This one sounds random."

Chewing a bite of her sandwich, she wanted to agree. She really did. She just wished she knew how her day planner ended up there.

"Cassie? Cassandra Ellis?"

Cassie glanced around for the source of the voice. It was vaguely familiar. A distinctive head of bright white hair was enough of an identification. She swallowed hastily as Linda Kowalski hurried over to their table.

"Hello, Linda," Cassie said.

The psychic mystery author looked slightly more subdued this time, dressed in a white skirt with a bright yellow top. Cassie introduced her to Mark, or tried to, but Linda gave him the barest of glances before focusing all her attention on Cassie.

"I'm so glad I ran into you here. We need to talk. I was just about to call Aaron to get your number."

"You were? Why?"

"Dorian has been talking about you. At least, I think he was talking about you. He kept saying 'Red.' I figured he meant you, with your copper curls." She gestured towards Cassie's hair.

"Is this Dorian making predictions about me or something?"

Linda slid into the booth, forcing Cassie to move over. "He said that Red needs help."

Cassie glanced at Mark and tried to wordlessly apologize for the odd interruption. Then she regarded Linda, wondering if the other author had forgotten to take some kind of medication that morning. "Well, that's… interesting, Linda, but I think I'm okay."

"Are you sure? Dorian is seldom wrong."

"Perhaps Dorian is speaking of someone else. I'm fine."

Linda finally acknowledged Mark's presence. "Is she, really?"

He nodded seriously. "I believe so. Thank you for your concern, though."

Linda frowned. "Dorian is seldom wrong. The mistake must have been mine, then." She rooted around in her yellow purse, one that perfectly matched her blouse.

Out of the corner of her eye, Cassie saw Mark tense, and just as quickly relax again when all Linda produced was a couple of business cards.

"Here. This is my card. If you do need help, of any kind, please call me." She handed a second one to Mark. "And one to you as well, Mark Griffin. Nice to meet you." She smiled charmingly at both of them and went to the counter to order a coffee.

They both looked at their cards. It was done in pastels, with a picture of an exotic bird on one side. "Psychic Consortium" was written in a flowing script at the top. Below that was printed a phone number and address in a more conservative font. *Consortium? Who else is in it? This Dorian person, maybe?* Cassie shrugged and put the card in her purse.

"Mark?"

He was still staring at the card. "What…interesting friends you have, Cassandra." He covered something that sounded like a cough with one hand and reached for his wallet with the other.

"Well, she's not quite my friend. She's a fellow author, actually. Aaron represents her as well."

"You could use some help, you know. Perhaps she knows something about the murder. Info from the great beyond."

She cocked her head to the side. "Seriously?"

He gave her a look that, for Mark, passed as amused. "No, not really."

Cassie poked her straw around the ice in her cup. "Hopefully, I won't need a psychic. I'll put my faith in the police and wish them good luck in solving the case."

\+ ×

Stupid media!
Get book.

SATURDAY 08 JULY 10:08:47

chapter 8

"Damn it!" Slamming down the phone, Whittaker cursed his luck and tried to calm down from the call.

"So, based on your one word, pissed-off answers," Freeman said, "I'm going to guess that was the media. What are they calling about? None of our cases are headliners."

"The Montgomery case will be, since someone managed to leak Ms. Ellis' involvement and her upcoming murder mystery. The newscasters are going to cream themselves over this story."

Freeman released a long, drawn-out whistle. "Oh, shit."

"Yeah, understatement of the year. I have to admit, it's probably our fault for visiting Christine Schmidt. I bet she, or some other reporter, used their contacts here to find out why we were interested in Ms. Ellis. Now this reporter—a crime beat one, not a book reviewer—calls and wants to know if there was any overlap between Mr. Montgomery's murder and Ms. Ellis' book."

"Well, is there?"

"How the hell should I know? I haven't read it. It doesn't come out until Saturday." Whittaker flung a hand toward the screen. "Unless…"

"Unless?" prompted Freeman.

"I assume the author gets copies before the rest of the public. I could get one from her. And, I should warn her that she's probably going to be getting some phone calls." He dialed the author's number, but didn't get an answer.

Frustrated, he stood up. "Think I'll head over there, see what's going on. Besides, you know I always say you can tell a lot about people from their surroundings." He looked up her pertinent information, including her address and license plate number.

* * *

Fifteen minutes later, he pulled up next to her rowhouse. The neighborhood was a nice one, he noted, based on the newness and quality of the parked cars and the cleanliness of the street.

He took the three steps up her stoop and rang the doorbell. If it wasn't for the fact that he parked behind her car, he would have wondered if she was home or if she'd left for on a long vacation. Her flowers outside were wilted and crying for water, and the mailbox was overflowing with mail, most of which was junk mail.

When she opened the door, he saw surprise, then concern, then resignation.

"Detective Whittaker, um, come in. I wasn't expecting you." She sighed and looked at the cell phone in her hand, scowling as it started to ring. "I wasn't expecting a lot of things."

He raised an eyebrow at her reaction, especially when she lowered the phone. "Are you going to answer?"

"No. It's just another damned reporter, calling now that they've got the connection between me and Seth Montgomery." She whirled on him. "How the hell did they find the connection between me and Seth?"

Whittaker hid his wince. "Why don't we talk about that?"

She sighed and headed towards the living room. "Fine. Have a seat." She flopped down, and just as quickly bounced back up. "Can I offer you some coffee?"

"I never say no to coffee, but only if it's no trouble."

"No, I definitely could use a cup or two…or a whole pot…myself." She headed to the back of the narrow house toward the kitchen.

He chose a cranberry-colored armchair that was wedged diagonally against the brick wall. There was no way he was sitting on that green sofa. That would put his back to the door and an open window.

Relaxing as much as he could, he turned to look around her house. An individual's surroundings could reveal so much about the person. He never was able resisted his impulse to analyze, whether or not he was on the job.

The first floor of the rowhouse had an open floor plan, allowing him to see all the way back to the kitchen. She had used her television to separate the living room from the dining area. At least, he assumed it was her dining room. There was a small table crammed up against the east wall. The room narrowed at that point, thanks to the stairs on the west wall, and the stairway wall was filled with bookcases, lined up in increasing height.

He went to get a closer look at her books. Books also told him about a person. There were hundreds of murder mysteries, dozens of true crime novels, and an entire bookcase filled with reference books on murder, weapons, and death. And one bookshelf that included over twenty copies of her own book.

Interesting woman, he thought, sniffing the air appreciatively when he smelled the coffee brewing. Without a doubt, this was going to be much better than the mud served at the station house.

The rest of the house—the minimal part that wasn't books—also gave a clear picture of its inhabitant. A little cluttered, but not messy. The nice architecture and narrow width that Baltimore rowhouses were known for. A bold use of color and actual curtains hanging from the windows. He hadn't quite gotten around to that in his place.

Whittaker was interrupted from his inspection of her house by a nudge against his leg. He jumped and glanced down to see a dark gray cat staring up at him with unblinking yellow eyes. He hadn't even heard it come into the room.

"Oh, sorry about that," Cassie said from the kitchen. "That's Donner. He's very friendly. I hope you're not allergic."

"No, just didn't realize you have a cat."

"Of course I have a cat. Aren't all writers supposed to have cats?" She laughed and pulled two mugs out of the cupboard. Whittaker watched as she poured him a cup.

"How do you take your coffee?" she asked.

"Oh, black is fine. I'm not picky, and I'm sure it's better than what we have at the station."

"Here you go."

"Thanks." He took the cup and wandered back to the books.

"What's Trixie Belden?" he asked, scanning down the colorful spines that filled one bookcase. The titles started with Trixie Belden and ended with either *The Mystery Of Something* or *The Something Mystery.*

"Trixie Belden is a teen detective. Like Nancy Drew, but better," she explained with a light laugh. "When I was a kid, I used to read all the series mysteries, especially Trixie Belden. But I also read Nancy Drew, Hardy Boys, Rick Brant, even the Bobbsey Twins. Did you ever read those, Detective Whittaker?"

"I read a few Hardy Boys," he admitted, sipping some coffee and turning back to face her. He had been right, it was better than what he normally got.

"I loved how they collected the clues," she said. "How they solved the crimes and caught the bad guys. I loved good succeeding over evil. And as I got older, my taste in books aged as well. And I started reading murder mysteries, true crime stories, police procedurals…just about anything I could get my hands on, as you can see." She waved her hands again in the direction of her book shelves. "And that's just the first floor. I have more books upstairs."

"*More* books?" He shook his head in disbelief. He thought his friend Ian owned a lot of books, mostly of the sci-fi variety, but Cassie had him beat with just the books on her first floor. She could start her own library.

She cursed again when the phone in her pocket rang. Her scowl turned to relief when she saw the readout on the phone. "One minute, Detective Whittaker. Hello Christine, thanks for calling me back."

The reporter. Whittaker turned so she wouldn't see the face he made and headed to the armchair. He preferred to be sitting for her response.

"So, was my message correct?" She listened for a few minutes. "Yeah, that's what I thought." Then she turned and nailed him with a glare so hard it would have knocked him off his feet if he hadn't been sitting down. "No, that's okay, Christine, you were just doing your job. I understand. Talk to you later."

She closed the phone with a snap and stalked over to sit on the couch. "Okay, I understand that you were also just doing your job. But you do realize that your visit to Christine Schmidt is how this whole thing got leaked, right?"

"As you said, it's my job. I have to follow leads," he said, keeping his face and voice calm and businesslike.

"So, now I'm a lead?" She huffed out a breath. "You think I had something to do with murder?"

He glanced over at the hundreds of books on mysteries and murders. Sensing she was about to explode, he held up a hand. "Yes, Ms. Ellis, you are a lead. Whether or not you had something to do with the murder remains to be seen. The facts stand. As far as we've been able to deduce, you were the last person to see him alive. Your day planner was at the scene of the crime. These are leads, and as such, we have to follow them."

The phone rang again. This time, they both ignored it.

She brought her legs up and wrapped her arms around her knees. "So you interviewed everyone I know?"

"We contacted everyone in your day planner, although there are some we're waiting to hear back from. It was just a routine follow-up, as we informed them."

"So you asked them for their whereabouts at the time of murder, whether anyone could confirm that, whether they knew Seth, and how they knew me."

"Good guess," he allowed with a nod.

"It wasn't a guess," she said, a glint of anger sparking in her icy blue eyes. "My firearms expert, Mark Griffin, told me. As did my best friend Michelle Edwards. But I didn't realize you'd contacted everyone in the damned thing. Nor did I realize what would happen if you talked to Christine. But when all these reporters started calling me, I figured what had happened." She leaned back on the plush cushions and closed her eyes.

"Which was?"

She opened one eye. "Can't you guess?"

"I don't guess, I deduce," he said gravely. When she snorted, he continued. "And I deduced that when we visited Ms. Schmidt, and mentioned both your name and Mr. Montgomery's, she alerted one of their crime reporters. That reporter then used contacts at the station to find out you had been brought in for questioning."

"Nice deducing, Detective. That would be precisely what happened."

The phone rang again. She checked the display but ignored the call. He took a sip of coffee and savored it. When someone was preparing to eat crow for admitting he was at fault, it was better to start out with a pleasant taste.. "I'll apologize that my actions, and those of my department, led to this inconvenience."

She let out a long sigh. "Well, I suppose if it leads you to the murderer, I won't complain. Not that I think any of my friends or contacts are murderers."

"Just arsonists?"

"Former arsonist. And really, most of my contacts aren't actually the criminal element; they just came in contact with said element. I just hope you find the killer. Seth wasn't a friend, precisely, but I'm sorry he's dead. In fact, I was going to send a sympathy card to his family, if he has any left." She raised her eyebrows, obviously hoping he'd answer the indirect question.

He made sure to keep his face extra bland.

"Wow," she said. "You're really good at this not revealing anything business. I'll stop trying to get info out of you." She smiled at him, lowering her lashes coyly. "Mostly."

He couldn't help it, he had to smile at that.

"Hey, you have dimples!"

He dropped the smile. What the hell was he doing anyway? He was usually much better at controlling his reactions. "Yes, I'm aware of that."

"Well, I wasn't."

He arched an eyebrow. "I seldom smile or show off the dimples in interview, oddly enough."

"I suppose not." She cocked her head. "You've never had anything amusing happen in interview?"

He shrugged. There were plenty of times he'd had to hold back a smile or a laugh. People were idiots. "Plenty. It's amazing what people will blurt out. However, we do our best not to react."

"But afterward?"

"We maintain our professionalism at all times, Ms. Ellis. In fact, as much as I am enjoying your coffee, I need to return to the station. I came over to personally apologize for any inconvenience our investigation has caused you...and also to ask if I could borrow a copy of your book."

"My book?" She glanced over at the bookshelf that contained the multiple copies. "I'm going to guess that it's not because you're a big fan. Do you think the book's involved? It's not a copycat murder, I can tell you that."

"How do you know that?"

"Well, the murderer in *Mailbox Murders* used a shotgun. And while I'm sure you won't tell me the weapon used on Montgomery, the spatter pattern didn't indicate a shotgun."

"No, it wasn't a shotgun." He shook his head at her raised eyebrows. "And no, I won't tell you the weapon used."

He had to hold back another smile when she rolled her eyes at him.

"Fine. Anyway, I'm guessing again here and not expecting you to tell me anything about the location of the murder, but the book is called *Mailbox Murders* for a reason. The victims were gunned down while getting their mail." She stood up and got a book from the shelf.

"Someone going postal?"

She grinned at him. "That, I think, was actually a joke."

Shit, it was a joke. What was he doing telling jokes?

She laughed. "But no, it wasn't a mailman on a murder spree. It was just an easy place to ambush the victims, since most people have an established pattern of when they get the mail. And you're out in the open when you head towards your mailbox. At least in the suburbs. Not so much here, where your mailbox is on your stoop."

"Oh, yes, talking about that, you have mail. A lot of it."

"I always do. I forget to get it." She shrugged and handed him the book. "Do you want me to sign it for you?"

With effort, he held back the smile. "No. I'll return it after we get the copy I ordered." He took the book and placed it in his briefcase, then stood up to take his leave.

"Of course you will. If not, it might be construed as accepting a bribe."

He frowned at her. He hoped people wouldn't think that.

She shook her head as she saw him to the door. "Detective Whittaker, I'm not serious."

"Of course." He smiled again, but it was polite and professional. "Thank you for your time. I'll be in touch."

* * *

He muttered to himself the entire way back to the station. "I'll be in touch. What a stupid thing to say. Especially if she takes it as a double entendre. Not that it was. At least, not much." He let himself visualize being in touch with her, then shook his head. "She's involved in this case. I smiled at her. And made a joke. I never smile or make jokes with witnesses."

He shook his head as he waited at a red light. Thank God Freeman hadn't been there to see his behavior. It was simply unacceptable. Not that he—or Freeman—thought Ms. Ellis had committed the murder. But, it was an active case, and she wasn't completely cleared. His gut told him she was innocent. But he couldn't pull out his gut feeling if anyone questioned his relationship with her. Not that he had a relationship with her. Not that he wanted...

Okay, if things were different, he might pursue a relationship...well, a date or two with her. She was pretty, he had admitted as much to Freeman, but he was more attracted to her curiosity and intelligence.

In general, he didn't do relationships. Previous girlfriends didn't understand anything about his being a homicide detective. They complained about the hours he put in, were appalled by what he told them about his investigations, and hated that he was a police officer. Somehow, he didn't think she would have problems with any of that. Definitely not with hearing the details. In fact, she'd pester him to tell her things. They'd probably fight about it and—

And wasn't he getting ahead of himself here? First things first, he needed to solve this murder. Not just because he owed it to the victim and was dedicated to his job, but because he wanted to prove her innocent.

He shook his head at that notion. It sure didn't sound like the impartiality he prided himself on.

The ringing phone interrupted his personal self doubt. He used his hands-free device to answer. "Whittaker here. Oh, Mr. Kaufman, thank you for calling me back."

chapter 9

"This guy is a jerk. A total, full of himself jerk." Whittaker stopped himself short of kicking his desk.

Freeman looked up from his paperwork. "So you keep saying… although sometimes the words are worse than jerk. You're speaking of Ms. Ellis' agent, right?"

"Correct. Aaron Kaufman." He made a rude sound. "I went to his office last night. I tried reaching you but you didn't answer. Anyway, I went up to meet him. Slick building, slick office, even slicker of a suit."

Freeman rolled his eyes. "This from the man who doesn't think a suit is any good unless it's from a foreign country."

Whittaker shrugged and continued pacing. "Mine are British, that's quality. His look is from the pages of GQ, that's slick."

"You're jealous."

"Of what, his look? I don't even read GQ."

"It ain't the look you're jealous of. Anyway, for God's sake, sit down; you're annoying me with your pacing."

Whittaker froze into place. "I never pace." He headed towards his chair.

"Like I said, you're jealous. Love makes you crazy."

"I'm not jealous. Or in love." Whittaker sent his partner a disgusted glare, then took a deep breath. "Anyway, I asked the guy what he was doing on July 5th between 1500 and 1800 hours, and he started hemming and hawing."

"Hemming and hawing?" Freeman asked dubiously.

"Shut up, that's what he was doing. Anyway, I kept pressing. And as much as I'd like it to be this jerk to be the killer, his alibi is unassailable. And, of course, the reason for his hemming and hawing."

"Something embarrassing?"

Whittaker smirked. "Oh yeah. Definitely embarrassing. You see, I meant it when I said his look was from GQ. And that day, he decided to take the magazine's advice…and it went really, really wrong." He paused, relishing the moment even while he felt a twinge of sympathy for the agent's mistake.

Freeman was practically lying across the scattered files and papers on his desk. "Well, don't kill me with suspense, tell me!"

So he did.

"Oh, man." Freeman winced, but then laughed. "No wonder he hemmed and hawed. And yes, the emergency room is a solid alibi. We should e-mail that around the bullpen."

"Probably shouldn't. Not appropriate." Whittaker frowned, uncomfortable as he remembered his own rather inappropriate thoughts regarding Ms. Ellis. "I never smile," he muttered to himself as he watched Freeman turn gleefully towards his computer

"I won't put in any names, and I'll use 'allegedly' a lot. You know, like 'allegedly, we heard a witness used this as an alleged alibi' and…" Freeman stopped his slow typing. "Are you okay?"

"Yeah. Yes, I'm okay." Whittaker straightened some papers on his desk. "Look, you don't think Ms. Ellis is guilty, do you?"

Freeman stopped the hunting and pecking on his keyboard. "I don't. You don't. There's no actual evidence, just circumstantial. Her alibi is weak, but if we tried really hard, we might be able to find someone who saw her writing at that time. Do we need to?"

"No. It would be a waste of resources. We should focus only on finding the killer. Do our job."

"Sounds like a plan. After I send out this e-mail."

Whittaker laughed, then followed his own advice to focus and do his job.

* * *

Cassie tried to do her job, but phone calls kept interrupting her. Since her connection had been leaked to the media, it was all over the local news stations.

Which was a shame.

It was Saturday, July 8th. The day her book was released. It was a day she should have been accepting congratulatory calls, not calls from people asking about the murder.

She was tired of telling people she was innocent, tired of explaining that she didn't know anything, tired of saying that the investigation was ongoing.

But Aaron's call almost did her in. He was so cheerful.

"Good morning, Cassie," he trilled. "How is my most famous author today?"

She actually lowered the cellphone and stared at it in disbelief before putting it back up to her ear. "Tell me you're not happy about this situation."

"All publicity is good publicity, Cassie. How many times did you hear 'Cassandra Ellis, author of *Mailbox Murders'* yesterday? People are *so* going to buy the book today! Tonight's book signing at Barnes and Noble is going to be a huge hit, I'm sure. Too bad people's attention spans are so short. I wonder if they'll still be talking about this Wednesday when you're on the cable show."

She smacked her hand on the kitchen counter. "Aaron. Someone has died. This is not a sales opportunity."

He sighed. "Cassie. You barely knew the guy. This is so totally a sales opportunity."

"What, you want to have a death sale or something? Ten percent off the book if you mention Seth Montgomery by name? Twenty off if you know something about the murder?"

"Well, it does sound like the police need some help, actually. Can you believe that the detective who interviewed you came to my office? *My* office. To ask me what I was doing on Wednesday."

She sat down on the bench in her kitchen and leaned her head on her free hand. "I'm sorry, Aaron, I really am. I hope you were able to provide a better alibi than I was. I was out writing so no one could confirm my whereabouts."

She waited, could almost swear that Aaron hemmed and hawed before answering. "No, I was fine. But I don't understand why they even talked to me. I didn't even know Seth Montgomery."

"They're contacting everyone in my day planner."

"That damn planner," he said. "Did you ever remember where you saw it last?"

"Why does everyone ask that? No. No, I don't remember where I last saw it."

"Well, you had it on Monday morning, when you came to my office," he reminded.

She got up to pour herself some water from the refrigerator. "True. I had to have it then, since we went over all the promo opportunities then. But after that, I couldn't tell you. And I was swamped Monday, Tuesday, and Wednesday meeting with people to prepare for the book release. I could've lost it anywhere."

"I still say that arsonist guy stole it. That's how it got to his house."

She shrugged. "I suppose."

"So, let's talk about how to capitalize on this," he said.

Cassie sucked in a breath. "You have to be kidding."

"It's an opportunity, Cassie. Besides, think of it this way, at least something good will come out of this…this sad death."

She closed her eyes. "Aaron, why don't we talk about this later? I have a headache…and another incoming phone call. See you tonight."

"If it's a reporter, plug the book," he said before she switched over.

"Hello, this is Cassie," she said through gritted teeth. "Oh, hello, Solange." Great, she thought, this conversation wasn't going to be any better.

At least she didn't have to do it over the phone. Solange invited her to meet at Donna's, a Baltimore area coffee bar with a location halfway between them. Cassie decided it was at least an opportunity to give Solange her free signed copy of *Mailbox Murders* and save on postage. She was sending one to each of her subject matter experts.

Cassie paused as she parked in a garage near the coffee shop. Not only was she dreading the conversation with Solange, but she didn't want to leave the blessed cool of her car either. Sucking it up, she sprinted through the heat to Donna's. That was a mistake. She arrived flushed, sweating, and feeling even worse-looking than usual compared to her college classmate, who always managed to look perfect.

At the University of Maryland, where they had lived in the same dorm for four years, the men had drooled over Solange. Tall and statuesque—and far more comfortable with her height and figure than Cassie was—Solange always turned heads. She exuded femininity and confidence, from her platinum blond hair to her perfected French pout.

Cassie looked down at herself and cursed herself for not changing before heading over to Donna's. Not only was she sweaty and miserable from her sprint, she was also dressed in Keds, denim shorts, and an Orioles shirt. At least the O's shirt was a new one. Solange, on the other hand, wore high heeled sandals, a short black skirt, and a sleeveless blouse of white silk. Cassie had to admire the woman; she'd never be brave enough to wear white to drink coffee. Sure way to ensure she would spill some on herself.

"So, *ma chérie*, I think you might need a lawyer," Solange began after they got their coffees.

Yes, it was going to be a bad conversation, thought Cassie with an inward grimace. Solange had spent four years in college trying to prove her superiority. Aaron wasn't the only one selfish enough to use Seth's murder for his own benefit.

"I don't think I need a lawyer, Solange," Cassie said firmly. "I didn't do anything."

"Oh, Cassandra, your *naiveté* is so charming. One doesn't need to have done something to need a lawyer. One just needs to be suspected of doing something."

"The police don't suspect me. They interviewed me, yes, but only due to some…um, unusual circumstances."

"You mean because your day planner was found at the scene of the murder," Solange said, smiling like a killer who had just found her next victim.

"How do you know that?" Cassie demanded. "That information wasn't leaked."

"Well, it wasn't leaked to the media…yet. But I have contacts in the police department and I used them. You're my friend, after all."

You just wanted to gloat, Cassie thought as she sipped her coffee. "Well, I'd appreciate it if that information could remain between us. Client-lawyer privilege, right?"

"*Certainement.* And shall I send the invoice to your home? My going rate is two hundred an hour."

Cassie cursed herself for walking into that trap. "That's fine, Solange. After all, our friendship has to end somewhere, right?" She saw the anger flash in the other woman's eyes, but only for a moment. *Touché.*

"Oh, Cassandra, you just don't have a sense of humor. I was joking about the fee. After all, I know the writing profession doesn't pay all that much, even now that your little book is being published."

Cassie had forgotten just how good the woman was at verbal battles. In the past, she had just surrendered; it wasn't worth the fight. But she was having a bad day—hell, a bad week—and Solange was a perfect target.

"If payment secures confidentiality, I am more than willing. After all, money seems to be the only way that you keep information to yourself. In fact, money seems to be the best way to get you to do a lot of things."

Cassie must have struck a nerve. She watched in fascination as the woman's nostrils actually flared in a struggle for control.

"I suppose I was wrong, you do have a sense of humor. Not a good one, but a sense of humor. But this isn't a laughing matter. I would recommend you get a lawyer. It looks suspicious, what with your day planner being at his residence and you being the last person to see this man alive." Solange smoothed back her already perfect hair. "Why you would even associate with someone like that is beyond me."

Why I associate with you is beyond me, Cassie thought. But perhaps something could be gained. Aloud, she asked, "Did your…contacts at the station give you any information about the weapon? The time and location of the murder? The positioning of the body?"

Solange wrinkled her nose. "We didn't get into graphic detail, but yes, my source told me the weapon was a Davis P-380."

"Not surprising it's a cheap handgun," Cassie said. "Probably black market. Easy to buy, hard to trace."

"See, and that's another thing that makes you look guilty." Solange traced designs in the foam of her latte with a wooden stirrer. "You know so much about guns, murder, and violence."

"Knowing and doing are two different things." Cassie indulged herself in a quick mental image of using that knowledge on Solange. The woman wouldn't look quite so perfect after sipping a non-fat, no-foam, double espresso, two pumps of ricin latte. Maybe she should change her work in progress and have the killer poison coffee instead of wine. Hmm…but what about the title? *The Macchiato Murders*?

Shaking those thoughts out of her head, she reminded herself that Solange was a potential resource…and a friend, sort of. "Did you get the time of death?"

Solange picked up her smartphone. "16:14. Or 4:14 P.M. for you Americans."

Cassie hid a smile that she had guessed so close to the correct time. "Anything else interesting that was passed on?"

Solange tapped some keys. "I know he was found in his home after a neighbor called in some gunshots." She looked up, a perfect eyebrow arched. "What, are you going to try and solve the murder now?"

"I'm just curious."

"Well, you should beware that curiosity doesn't kill the Cassandra." Solange set the phone down. "Talking about curiosity, I was wondering what else is going on in your life? Have you managed to find a boyfriend yet?"

Cassie gritted her teeth. Here was another sore spot that Solange always probed. "No, been rather busy with writing."

Solange shook her head. "You've always had your priorities wrong. I think in college you spent more time surrounded by books than boys."

Cassie sipped her coffee in order to stifle the urge to react. "I feel my priorities were fine. Unlike you, I don't need a man to feel personally validated. Anyway, I think I've had enough coffee, thank you." She stood up, tried to make a three-point toss with her coffee cup, and missed. She gritted her teeth and headed over to pick it up.

"Does that mean you don't want to see the crime scene photos?"

Cassie froze in place for a second, then turned back to the table and made a grab. "You have them?"

Solange jerked her phone back. "I do."

Cassie didn't care if she was giving Solange the satisfaction of being in a superior position. She sat down again and held out her hand. "Please, may I see them?"

She wasn't surprised to see the Frenchwoman give a smile of triumph before passing her the phone. She was so going to owe Solange for this.

She thought she was prepared as she started thumbing through the images. After all, she had seen plenty of such photos before. But never of someone she knew. Before, they had just been of "the body" or "the victim." Now, they were of Seth Montgomery, someone she knew. And, she thought, noting the neon bright timestamps on the photos, someone she had met with not even four hours before this photo was taken.

More than coffee left a bitter taste in her mouth. Her stomach churned as she made herself look more closely at the details.

Seth was splayed, his body half on the ratty couch, half on the filthy carpet below. Several bullet wounds were apparent in his torso with dark, red-black blood staining his clothes and the floor beneath. His eyes were open and staring.

And damn it, right next to him, within a hand's reach, was her stupid day planner. How the hell did it get there?

She analyzed the pictures as much as she could on the small screen. Nothing jumped out at her as a sign of who would have done this, who would have taken her day planner to implicate her.

"Can you e-mail these to me?" she asked, unable to take her eyes off the screen.

"Well, I don't know, Cassie. After all, I technically shouldn't have these pictures. It would be worse if you had them. After all, the police might come again and find them on your computer. It will make you look guilty. Well, guiltier."

"Please." Cassie swallowed down the bile in her throat as well as her pride. "I'd really appreciate it."

The self-satisfied gleam in Solange's eyes increased. "*Bien sur,* since you said please." Solange pushed some buttons on the device, then stood up and gracefully tossed her cup in the trash can.

"Thank you," Cassie said. She picked up her cup off the floor and walked across the street with Solange to the parking garage.

It was too hot to take the stairs, so they used the elevator. Not that it was much better. The humidity in the elevator car was worse than outside and carried the lovely smell of stale urine. Cassie tried to hold her breath.

When the elevator stopped on the second floor, Solange stepped out, then paused, keeping her hand on the doors so they stayed open. "Good luck with this, Cassie. I still think you're going to need a lawyer. I'd be happy to help, of course."

"Of course she had to get in the last word," snarled Cassie to herself after the doors wheezed closed and the elevator jerked to continue its ascent to the fourth floor. "Happy to help, she says. I'd rather be dead. Or rather she'd be dead." Okay, so maybe she wasn't ready to change the title of *The Merlot Murders,* but she was seriously considering adding a character like Solange to the story. She smiled, feeling better just thinking about it.

It was the most cathartic aspect of her writing. When someone irritated her, all she had to do was make them into a character, a villain or a victim.

Solange...Cassie sighed, being honest with herself. Solange was an irritant. Like a mosquito. A French mosquito, she thought, picturing the insect with a beret and a striped shirt. And ricin, honestly, was nasty business. So maybe she would write it that Solange's fictional doppelganger would get sick and recover, not actually die.

She was halfway into her car when she noticed the book on the back seat. "Crap!" Grabbing it with one hand, she pulled out her cell phone with the other. "Maybe she hasn't left yet...she's probably fixing her face in the mirror." She hit the speed dial number for Solange and rushed for the stairs.

She was on the third floor landing when she heard the scream, followed by several horribly loud cracks.

Gunshots.

chapter 10

Echoes reverberated in the garage and in Cassie's head as she stood paralyzed for a moment. Swallowing the shock, the panic, and the fear, she ran down the next flight of stairs, missing the last step and slamming down on her right knee. The pain helped clear out the last of the shock as she scrambled back up and lurched towards the body she could see lying on the cement floor.

Solange.

She was face down, her blond hair spread around her head and saturated with fresh blood and brain matter. Two other vicious wounds pierced her back. The blood had turned the white silk shirt a deep, deep red with pink at the edges.

Cassie sucked in a deep breath and dialed 9-1-1.

"What's your emergency?" came the voice.

She struggled to give a concise answer. "This is Cassie Ellis. I have a gunshot victim at the Penn Street Garage, um, the corner of Pratt and Penn. Second floor, back of the building. Please send an ambulance and police." Although as she stared at Solange, she didn't think they'd need an ambulance.

"The appropriate authorities have been contacted. Did you witness the shooting?"

"No. I, uh, I heard it. I was on another floor of the parking garage and ran down."

"Are you in a safe location? Is the shooter still there?"

Cassie looked around. She hadn't even thought of the shooter. "I'm safe. The shooter wasn't around when I got down here."

"How about the victim? Is he breathing? Conscious?"

"She. I mean, she, not he." Cassie tried to stop her shuddering so she could tell if Solange was breathing. But there was no way that anyone could live through the head shot. "No. I think—I think she's dead. She's been shot in the head, there's lots of blood and…stuff, and two other shots in her back. I, I've been trained in first aid, I'll see if I can help. I'm setting the phone on speaker." She dropped the phone twice before she managed to activate the speaker. Crawling over, she tried to find a pulse on Solange.

"Ms. Ellis, can you give me more information about the victim?"

"Um, female. Late twenties. She's dead, I can't believe this, she's dead." She had to sit and put her head between her knees before she passed out. She thought she had felt sick looking at pictures of Seth. That didn't compare at all to this. The smell alone had her gagging. And there was blood everywhere; she had blood on her hands and knees.

"Ma'am, can you begin CPR on the victim?"

Cassie looked up again at Solange. "I think, I think it's too late. Her brain is all over the ground…and well, I'm not supposed to disturb a crime scene."

"Okay, ma'am, then why don't we just wait until the ambulance arrives?"

The sound of sirens had her raising her head and thinking again. Oh, God, here was another shooting victim that was connected to her.

She grabbed the phone again, smearing blood on it. "Look, I hear the sirens but I really need to make another phone call, is that okay?"

"We'd prefer you to stay on the line until the authorities arrive."

She nodded, then realized the woman couldn't see her. "Okay," she whispered. She waited until the ambulance screeched to a stop and the paramedics rushed out. Hoping for a familiar face, she looked for Paul, but his station was near Patterson Park. They wouldn't come down this close to the harbor.

She got herself out of the way and watched as the paramedics worked and the police secured the area. She grabbed her purse from the floor where she had dropped it and pulled out Whittaker's card. Perhaps she needed to add him to her speed dial.

Although she had wondered if he'd answer his work line on a Saturday, she wasn't surprised when he picked up.

"Whittaker."

"Hello, Detective Whittaker? This is Cassandra Ellis. Um, I think you probably need to get down here."

"Where is here? What happened?"

"Penn Street parking garage. And, um, someone shot Solange."

"Gavreau? Did you call 9-1-1?"

She closed her eyes. Great, he had all of her contacts memorized. "Yes. And yes, but it's too late. She's dead." Her stomach rebelled and she had to fight to quell the nausea.

"Stay right there. Don't call or talk to anyone else."

Cassie closed the phone and stared blindly at the activity going on in the corner. She explained herself and her presence to the police officer who trotted over to ask who she had called and what she was doing. She figured he was an exception to the "don't talk to anyone" rule from Whittaker. Then she just stood there and thought.

It was funny what death did for the memory. Now, she could remember more enjoyable times with Solange. Playing board games with everyone on their dorm floor. The parties on the weekends. Sometimes, Solange was even friendly and fun at those events, as long as her blood alcohol content was high enough to make her forget her superior airs.

When her mind veered to the less pleasant memories, Cassie cut off those thoughts. It seemed disrespectful to think bad things about the woman lying dead only fifty feet away.

She looked over again. The paramedics were no longer rushing, so obviously they had decided it was a lost cause.

Staring down at the floor, she finally let herself think what she'd been avoiding since she heard the gunshots…

It was no longer a coincidence.

She might have been able to chalk it up to Baltimore's high murder rate that she had known one person who was shot and killed. Even with her day planner present at the scene. But not two. And not when they were not only people she had known, but both had been resources she had used for her murder mysteries.

Was it her fault? Where they dead because of her?

Were all her friends and contacts in danger?

* * *

Stepping out of the car, Whittaker noticed Ms. Ellis first. Not the body, not the responders, but the woman, standing alone next to a concrete wall, looking miserable and lost.

He deliberately kept his face and mind blank when she made eye contact. For a moment he saw hope flash through the misery dragging her features.

He took a deep breath. Right now, Solange Gavreau needed him a lot more than Ms. Ellis did. Then he cursed inwardly. Since when did he have to remind himself of his responsibilities? They were supposed to be ingrained. Was this how his father had been corrupted? A seemingly innocent start?

He gritted his teeth and focused on the present situation. This was not the time to think of the past.

While Freeman talked to the uniforms, he went to check the body. From the position the body lay in, it looked as if Gavreau had turned away from the shooter and tried to escape. Her purse was near the car with its contents scattered everywhere. Had she dropped it while turning to flee, or when her body had fallen?

He made a mental note to request a rush on the ballistics to see if the gun matched the one used in the Montgomery murder. Not that they would rush anything, they never did, but he would at least request it.

The screech of bad brakes alerted him to the arrival of another car. Not only did he know instantly that the new arrivals were official, since the crime scene was closed off, but he recognized the squeal. He had been yelling at Wertz and Garcia to take their car into Maintenance for weeks now.

He strode over to the homicide detectives. "Get off my crime scene."

"Your crime scene?" Wertz asked, raising one eyebrow. "We were next on roll."

"Yeah, but we got this one."

Garcia joined his partner. "Why? That your girlfriend or something?" he asked, nodding towards Ms. Ellis.

"Don't be stupid," Whittaker said. "This case is connected to one of ours, the Montgomery case."

"Yeah? The murder mystery author one? That her?" Both men took a long stare at the woman.

"Yes, that's her."

"She's hot."

Whittaker scowled at Garcia. "She's a witness."

"A hot witness," Garcia said with a leer.

Wertz had other concerns. "Not a suspect?"

Whittaker shrugged. "We didn't think so for the first murder. We haven't had a chance to talk to her for this one. Anyway, can you let dispatch know we've got it? I've got to talk to the witness."

They grumbled, but left.

He turned and headed back. Noticing something on the bottom step of the stairway, he went to investigate. It was a book. Red and black and…a mailbox. He cursed.

"It's not part of the crime scene," Ms. Ellis said quietly behind him.

He turned around to face her. "No?"

"I dropped it when I fell. I was already heading down with the book when I heard the gunshots. I had originally gotten it from the car to give to Solange since I had forgotten to take it with me when we met at Donna's."

Whittaker signaled to Freeman for him to come over. His partner needed to hear this too. "You had just met with her at Donna's? I assume you mean the coffee shop?"

"Yes. Solange called me and invited me out for coffee."

"Do you often meet for coffee?" Freeman asked as he joined them in time to hear.

"Not really. She's a friend, well, sort of. But we're not close. Our relationship is…was rather antagonistic, really. She actually invited me over to gloat over my misfortune of being involved in the murder." She bit her lip. "Now I'm involved in another one."

"Who suggested this location?" Whittaker asked.

She took so long to answer he was worried at first that she was trying to figure out a lie. Shaking his head, he realized she wouldn't be taking so long if she was trying to create a fake story. Most likely, she was such a stickler for detail she was trying to recall the entire conversation verbatim. While he appreciated that, he wished she'd just answer already.

"She did. Well, she suggested a Donna's, and I chose this one since it's in between her home and mine. She lives in Roland Park, although you probably already know that."

Damn it. He had hoped that the location had been the lawyer's choice, not the author's. Not that it mattered. If Ms. Ellis had committed the murder or had even been involved, she could have planned it out regardless. "When did she call you?"

She dug out her cell phone and punched a few buttons. "Looks like 10:18 A.M."

"And—"

She answered his next question before he could ask. "And we met twenty minutes or so later. Probably stayed there for thirty minutes or so. We left at, actually I can tell you that exactly." Again she played with her phone.

Whittaker was close enough that he could see that she accessed the Internet, then a mail client of some sort.

"Um, 11:23 A.M., exactly."

"You know this how?"

She hesitated, a guilty expression crossing her face. "Solange e-mailed me something right before we left the coffee shop."

"Something?"

She looked even guiltier. "Why don't we save that for interview?" she asked. "We are doing that again, right?"

He traded glances with Freeman. "That would probably be best, Ms. Ellis."

She sighed before nodding.

"One last question. Didn't meeting Ms. Gavreau interfere with your plans today? After all, this is the release date for your book, right?" That had to suck for her, he thought, that this happened on her big day.

She grimaced. "I didn't have plans until six tonight, when I was supposed to have a book signing at Barnes and Noble." She glanced at the display of her cell phone. "I'm not sure I'll make that. Do you mind if I call Aaron to warn him? He won't be happy."

He nodded and watched as she moved aside to place the call. She couldn't be too happy about any of this, either. From the position of her shoulders, high and tense, and the low, tight sound of her voice, he guessed she was battling back tears as she spoke to her agent.

He checked his watch. There was almost six hours remaining between now and her book signing. Unless something odd came up during interview, there was no reason they shouldn't be able to finish in time for her to make it. Not that he'd let her time concerns affect the interview.

"Crime Scene finding anything?" he asked Freeman, who wandered back over, making notes.

"Got some cartridges; they'll check them for prints. Won't find them most likely, but they'll check. It's better than the Montgomery scene, the killer must've taken any cartridges that time. That book onsite?"

Whittaker lifted the book, which he still gripped in his left hand.

"Yes and no. Ms. Ellis said she dropped the book herself when she fell down here after hearing the shots. I'll still give it to Crime Scene, have them check for prints."

Freeman nodded. "Sounds good. Uniforms checked the garage but didn't find anyone except for a couple of tourists who seem terrified to talk to cops. Foreign, so perhaps it's not safe to talk to the police where they're from. They're waiting downstairs. The uniforms also canvassed the area, found a few people who heard shots. So far, no one saw anyone running from the garage, but maybe they don't know what they saw."

"Maybe," Whittaker said, "but if Ms. Ellis didn't even manage to see the killer, he must be pretty damn fast and careful. I'd assume he went out the back stairs, past the body."

"Looks like it, since the door was still wedged open a little," agreed Freeman, checking his notes. "They're dusting for prints there too. Why don't I call a marked car for Ms. Ellis, then we'll go talk to the witnesses? We'll meet her as soon as possible back at the station."

"Sounds good," Whittaker said, "but I bet we won't find anything useful."

* * *

He'd been right. No one had seen or heard anything other than gunshots. Hopefully Ms. Ellis would know something that could help.

He sighed once as he and Freeman made their way to the interview rooms.

Freeman punched him lightly in the arm. "What's up?"

"Nothing. It's just hot."

"It's more than that, Whittaker, and you know it. What's your—" Freeman stopped, then called out to a colleague. "Hey Morris! You don't look like you got any rest on that vacation of yours. What were you doing all that time, huh?"

Whittaker had been concentrating on how to lie to his partner, but looked over at Freeman's teasing. He hadn't seen Morris since his fellow detective left for his honeymoon. He managed a wave at the other detective before Freeman yanked him into an empty interview room.

Forget about lying. That wouldn't work on Freeman.

"This have to do with Ms. Ellis?"

"I…I don't know. I guess I'm just questioning now whether she's innocent, of this murder or the previous one. It's a lot of coincidences."

"Well, it's not a coincidence if she's involved. She doesn't necessarily have to have pulled the trigger to be involved. She might just be the center of it."

"True. Do you think she could be bullshitting us?"

Freeman took a moment before answering. "I'm not discounting the fact that she could be. We wondered if she could have been clever enough to deliberately throw suspicion on herself. She is clever all right, but as such, I think she's smart enough to know that you and I are clever as well. I don't think she'd risk another session in interview."

"I feel bad for her," Whittaker blurted out. He couldn't believe he said that aloud. Good thing it was Freeman, he'd understand and not judge him. Too bad he couldn't stop judging himself.

"I do too. I like her. You like her."

Whittaker started to protest his innocence, but Freeman waved it aside. "Now who's bullshitting? Look, I'm not saying you're going to ask her to marry you, or that you want to sleep with her. I'm just saying you like her. She's a likeable person."

Whittaker couldn't disagree. "But I'm not supposed to go into interview with prior conceptions."

"Ah, so you're second guessing your impartiality."

Whittaker didn't reply, but he didn't have to.

"And knowing you," Freeman went on, "you're thinking that makes you a bad cop."

He didn't say "like your father," but Whittaker thought it anyway. "I'm not supposed to go into interview with prior conceptions," he repeated.

"You're human, Whittaker. You have prior conceptions, we all do. You have instincts. It's what makes you a good cop, right?"

Whittaker nodded.

"You like her. You trust her," Freeman said and opened the door to the interview room. "Trust yourself."

Taking his partner's advice, Whittaker strode into the room and started the interview. "Detectives Whittaker and Freeman in interview with Cassandra Ellis, Saturday, July 8th at approximately 1430 hours, regarding the murder of Solange Gavreau." Whittaker said as he sat down and pulled out his notebook. He nodded to Officer Pamela Rivera in the corner. "Ms. Ellis, can you confirm you came in on your own volition."

"I did," she said quietly.

"Ms. Ellis, how would you characterize your relationship with Ms. Gavreau?" he began.

She winced. "Well, I've known her for over ten years. We met in college, at the University of Maryland in College Park. We lived in the same dorm, had many of the same friends. Still have some friends in common."

"That's not characterizing the relationship, Ms. Ellis, and we all know it."

She sighed. "No, I suppose it wasn't. Let's see. I wouldn't quite call it adversarial, but it wasn't actually friendly either. Solange was competitive."

"Can you give some examples of this competition?" Freeman asked.

"Well, we were in similar courses. Even though I was an English major, I was still taking Criminal Justice classes due to my interest in mysteries. She was taking those courses for pre-law. And, we both did very well.

But, Solange wanted to get better grades. On the classwork, on the tests, or just in general."

"But that was college. Why was your relationship still adversarial after so many years?" Freeman asked.

Whittaker saw the effect his partner's calm, "confide in me" voice had on Ms. Ellis. He had seen that technique work on dozens of victims, witnesses, and suspects since he had partnered with Freeman. That voice was his partner's best tool; whether it was to inspire actual comfort to a distraught victim or encourage a suspect to confess his or her guilt, it never failed.

"Solange isn't…wasn't that good at letting things go. She still felt we were in competition. She would deliberately set things up to compete. If she thought I was attracted to a man, she'd go after him."

"Why didn't you just avoid her if you weren't really friends?" Whittaker asked.

"Girl dynamics."

He blinked at her. "Girl dynamics?"

She nodded. "Yeah, girl dynamics. In any group of girls, there are always those in the group who don't get along with others in the group. But you still pretend to be friends. Especially if you have friends in common or if you met them through friends. I have a lot of friends of friends that aren't really my friends but I still pretend to be friends with them so it doesn't upset my real friends."

Whittaker tried to parse that sentence as she continued.

"Solange and I have friends in common, Jody Berber and Kathryn Campbell, who would often throw parties or coordinate gatherings. They'd invite us both. I might not invite Solange to my own things, but I didn't avoid her either. Besides, Baltimore's a small town. We'd bump into each other here and there."

Which gave Whittaker a good lead-in to start asking the hard questions. "And you bumped into each other today?"

"Not exactly. She called me, invited me out for coffee."

"You didn't find this suspicious, since you were so adversarial?" Freeman asked.

"No, I knew exactly what she wanted. She wanted to gloat over my bad fortune."

"So you consider it bad fortune to be involved in a real-life mystery?" Whittaker asked, not surprised when her eyes flashed with anger. "I would think an author would enjoy the publicity."

"It's not publicity; it's people's lives," she replied heatedly.

"Research then." Whittaker kicked back in his chair. "So Ms. Gavreau called you today. You've already stated that she invited you, but the location was your idea. Who arrived first?"

"She was there when I arrived. We got coffee, sat down, and talked about Seth's murder. She advised me to get a lawyer, even offered her help. I told her I didn't need one, since I was innocent. You'll notice I still haven't gotten a lawyer."

"It probably doesn't help that your legal expert is the one killed."

She flinched and wrapped her arms tight around her torso.

"And there goes your competition too." Whittaker saw her jaw clench and tried to ignore the bite of guilt. This was his job, damn it.

"I told you, I did not compete with her, she competed with me."

"Still, it was probably irritating," Freeman put in.

"Many people are irritating, but I don't kill them. At least not in real life," she said, and winced.

Whittaker caught her implication. "You kill them in fiction then." He watched her waffle about telling the truth. God, she was so easy to read.

"I do. It's good therapy, really. I'll name a victim after someone, not literally, that would be too obvious. I'll change the name a little, like make a Smith into a Jones, or something. But, again, I do it in fiction, on paper. Not in real life, not for real."

He believed her, but shrugged anyway. "Why not?"

She gaped. "Um, I don't know. Because killing real people is illegal? Because it's immoral? Because it's rather harsh to eliminate a life just because they annoy you?"

"So when, exactly, would it be appropriate to eliminate a life?" Freeman asked.

"Self defense," she said. "Or to protect another. War. That's about it. I don't even believe in the death penalty."

Whittaker couldn't believe it. Didn't believe in the death penalty? Now that might be a bone of contention if they started dating. Dating? What the hell was he thinking? He forced his mind back on business. "Okay, so the only way you would have killed Ms. Gavreau is if she had threatened you. So how did she threaten you?"

She lifted an eyebrow. "She didn't. And when I said self-defense, I meant a life-or-death scenario. Not a confrontation of words in a coffee bar."

Freeman sat up straight in his chair. "You had a confrontation?"

"We had a battle of wits. Solange is good, very good, at the veiled barb. She enjoyed taking pokes at me about everything. The situation with Seth," she hesitated, then kept going. "How little money I had, my lack of a love life."

Whittaker felt Freeman nudge his shoe at Ms. Ellis' last comment. He didn't dare glance at his partner, certain he'd see a knowing smirk behind that calm, neutral face.

"What did she say about Mr. Montgomery?" Whittaker asked, while vowing to get revenge on his partner later.

She took a deep breath. "Well, evidently, Solange had a source in the police department, as she knew about my damned day planner being on scene."

Damn. Whittaker hated leaks to the public. "Did she tell you her source?"

"Of course not," Ms. Ellis said. "She'd never give me that advantage. She did tell me though, the time of death. The weapon."

"Did she now? Care to share what she said?" Whittaker asked.

He kept his face as still as stone as she told them information that damn it, should have remained confidential. She was watching him for some sign to confirm the facts, but he wasn't going to give her one. He sat, silent, waiting.

But he did flinch when she admitted Ms. Gavreau even had access to crime scene photos. "You saw the photos?"

"I did. She had them on her phone. She also, well, she forwarded them to me too. I haven't opened the e-mail yet, didn't have a chance."

"Ms. Ellis. I'd appreciate if you could please forward me those e-mails and delete them. As you know, you are not authorized to have such information. They're evidence." *And they'd make you look guilty as hell for having them on your computer,* he thought. "It's also best if you keep the information she shared to yourself."

She nodded. "All right. I can do that. I didn't want to get anyone in trouble. Not her source…nor Solange." She stared at the table. "It's funny how death changes your opinion of a person. She wasn't so bad. But I wish I could look at the pictures again. I couldn't get a good look on her phone. I wanted to review them more thoroughly at home."

"For your research?" He deliberately laced his words with dripping sarcasm. "Going to put this into a book?"

"No! I want…I want to help."

He sneered. "You think you can do a better job than experienced police officers? Those trained to do this?"

"I just want to help. I want to know. And now, I want to protect my friends. Do you think they're in danger?"

He wished he could respond to the worried appeal in her bright blue eyes. But that wasn't his job—finding the murderer was. He didn't allow his face to change.

"We aren't able to draw any conclusions regarding that yet. We haven't even established if these murders are connected."

"Other than by me, of course. I'm now the last person to see two people alive." She leaned her head back and stared at the ceiling. "Shit, no one is ever going to want to go have coffee with me again. You end up dead afterward."

"Again, you shouldn't draw conclusions."

She sputtered. "You can honestly say you don't think they're connected? You think it's just coincidence?"

He opened his mouth to answer, but she just waved a hand in his direction.

"I know, I know. You can't answer at this time. You have to keep an open mind. It's an open investigation and all leads are being pursued. You'll ask the questions here."

He heard Officer Rivera in the corner fight back a laugh.

"These things are all true, Ms. Ellis," Freeman said. "Other than that last one, we wouldn't say anything that trite. And questions are good. Do you have any for us?"

"Sure, who's next? What other friend or contact of mine is going to die?" She looked up at the ceiling again.

As he saw her swallow hard and blink back tears, Whittaker felt a pull of sympathy. He smothered it. "We will do our best to make certain that this murderer, or murderers if the crimes aren't related, is caught before anyone else is hurt. And perhaps, it would be best if you would let us conduct a search of your computer and your house."

At this she straightened in her seat, a look of shock crossing her face. "You still think I did this?"

It took everything he had to keep his face frozen and voice impassive. "If you didn't do it, a search could help eliminate you by giving us free access to everything. We could get a warrant, of course, but it would look better if you volunteered."

She put her face in her hands. "Of course. Go ahead, search my computer, my home. Hell, you can do that while I go to the book signing. Won't that be fun?"

chapter 11

It was supposed to be fun. Exciting. Triumphant even.

Her first book release. Her first book signing. All her life she had dreamed about this day, seeing her name in print on a glossy book cover. Having people come and actually buy her book, ask for her autograph. This was supposed to be the most enjoyable part of being an author, the reward for all the hard work, revising, editing, and more revising. It was supposed to be her best day ever.

Instead, it was her worst.

Aaron had already suggested, as kindly as he could, that she might try to smile since no one was going to approach a depressed, sad-faced author. She had changed into a turquoise and black patterned wraparound dress, but not even the cheerful geometric design could brighten her mood.

After all, each time she reached for a copy of her book to sign—and there was a steady stream of people buying it—she'd see the word *murder*. And immediately think of Solange and her last few moments of life.

She could imagine the scene: Solange sashaying through the parking garage and pulling out her keys as she approached the car. The beautiful Frenchwoman's normally composed face scrunching up in terror as she looked straight down a gun barrel as it raised into position.

She pictured Solange turning around and fleeing, the rush of adrenalin pulsing through her body to give her the speed to run for her life, the fierce sound of blood thumping in her ears. The next scene played in slow motion: the muzzle flash and the dispersing smoke cloud as the gun released its killing missiles into Solange's helpless body.

But this wasn't one of her stories. She couldn't flip her point of view to look at the killer. That figure remained dark and fuzzy.

Who would do this? And why?

"Stop thinking about it, Cassie," her father said for the fifteenth time that evening from his position near her chair. He hadn't been more than five feet away from her since he had picked her up at the police station. "Let's get through this first. Enjoy it."

Aaron stopped his patrol looking for potential customers and walked over. He laid his hand on her shoulder and squeezed once. "Please try, Cassie. Your first book signing should be something exciting, something you'll always remember."

"Oh, I'll remember this," she said sarcastically. "Won't ever forget this day, I can promise you that."

Michelle patted her knee in sympathy. Cassie reached over to grab her hand and what little comfort she could draw from her friend.

She tried to smile as she looked around the bookstore. They had originally placed her in a small space on the second floor by the escalator. But when people had crowded in, blocking the entrance to the second floor, the staff moved her to a more open area on the first floor. They had even gotten a second chair for Michelle, who was helping to handle the signings when the line was long.

Thankfully, it started to slow down later that evening. Of course, the late-night customers were even more interesting.

Cassie noticed a new arrival. She couldn't help but notice. She stared in fascination as the middle-aged woman, a total Baltimore "hon" with a large hairdo and too-tight Spandex, headed straight up to the large display poster Aaron had put up and stopped only inches away from it, as if she couldn't read it any other way.

"Oh, look, Butch," she said in a carrying voice to the man next to her. He was attractively attired in a wife-beater T-shirt, tattered denim shorts, and sandals with socks. "It's that author. You know, the one who killed that man."

Cassie lowered her head to the table. She turned to Aaron, silently begging him for advice on how to handle this. He shrugged, the action wrinkling his blue linen shirt before he straightened it again.

She tried to smile as the couple approached the table.

"Are you that author?"

Cassie pointed at the sign holder that included her picture. "I am the author of *Mailbox Murders*, yes."

The man grunted and squinted at her. "You don't look like no killer."

She forced another smile. "I'm not a killer. I didn't kill Seth Montgomery. I'm an author. I write books." She pointed helpfully at the stack next to her. "With words."

Aaron stopped fussing with his shirt and hissed.

Luckily, the couple seemed oblivious to her patronizing tone. The woman picked up a book. "WBAL said you killed a man."

"First of all, WBAL is a television station, it doesn't say anything. Second of all, I was only brought in for questioning." Cassie took a deep breath. "And that's not why I'm here. I'm here to sign books. If you'd be interested in purchasing one of them, I'd be happy to sign it. Do you like mysteries?" *Do you even know how to read*? she thought, then chastised herself for being harsh. These people might be very intelligent, and just making a choice to dress and act like morons.

"I don't do much reading. Cal does, though," the woman said, pride evident in her voice as she pointed at a young boy wearing an Orioles jersey with the number eight on the back. "Cal, come here. I gots someone I want you to meet."

The boy came over obediently, carrying an armload of books. "Can I get these please? And hello, ma'am," he said pleasantly to Cassie.

The woman looked over at her husband, then back at the boy. "Oh, I ain't sure we can afford all of dem, hon. Anyway, I wanted you to meet this woman." She looked over at the board. "Miss Ellis. She's a writer. Like you wanna be."

The boy smiled enthusiastically as he balanced the books in one hand and shook Cassie's with the other. "It's great to meet you, Ms. Ellis. I hope to be an author one day."

"Yeah?" Cassie asked, flashing her first true smile of the afternoon. "That's great, what do you like to write?" *Please don't say books about vampires. Please don't say books about vampires.*

"Science fiction, actually. I love Heinlein, Asimov, Roy, Bradbury."

She was simultaneously impressed and chagrined. Impressed by the choices. Even though she loved to write mystery novels, she read across the spectrum of genres. She was one of the few in her class who didn't mind reading different authors for her Masters in Fine Arts degree. She liked all books.

But chagrined because she had been prepared to judge this kid based on his parents. Time to make up for it. "Those are good writers, Cal. Good role models to follow as well."

"He definitely likes science," his mother said, draping an arm around him. "He's even taking some courses for CTY at John Hopkins."

"*Johns* Hopkins, Mom," Cal said, ducking his head to escape.

"Sorry, you're right. *Johns* Hopkins," the woman repeated, accenting the "s" on the first name. "He's a bright boy. Cal, that is, not Johns Hopkins. Though I supposed he was too."

The boy was bright, Cassie thought. CTY—Center for Talented Youth—was a summer program for gifted youth, or whatever they were called these days. She had taken courses there when she was in high school.

"Yep, Cal is smart," Butch said, poking a finger at the books in his son's hands. "But those courses are expensive. I'm not sure we can afford the books, too."

As the boy's face fell, Cassie grabbed her purse. "Look, I got a gift card from the store for doing this promotion."

Oh, she was lying through her teeth, but something about this earnest young man had touched her. So she didn't get anything from the store. But she received gift cards every birthday and holiday, and had quite a collection. "Why don't I buy Cal's books today in order to help an aspiring author? And I'll throw in one of my books, too. See if I can bring you over to the dark side and get you interested in mysteries."

The whole family protested, but Cassie was adamant. "Look, I insist. This might be the only positive part of my day. And you can help me by recommending my book to others, okay?"

She wore them down until they accepted. As they left the store, she heard the father mutter, "She's pretty nice for a killer."

This time, she found the humor in the situation and had to chuckle. She shook her head as she left the register and returned to the table.

"That was nice of you, sweetheart," her father said, meeting her halfway.

Shrugging, she took the tea he passed to her. "I like supporting young authors. And I felt bad for judging the parents so harshly at first. They seem to be good parents, making sure that their son has a chance to succeed."

"That's what all parents want for their kids. What I want for you. What your mother wanted for you. She'd be so proud of what you've done," he said, pointing to her books. "Your success. You've worked hard, and you're achieving your dream."

She closed her eyes. "Then why is it turning into a nightmare?"

Her father pulled her in for a hug. "I don't know, Cassie. I don't know why this is happening, I don't know who would do this. But it's not your fault. I promise you."

"No, it's the killer's fault, I know that." Carefully balancing her tea, she turned her head and rested it on her father's shoulder. "You know, I even had a character going through this in *Mailbox Murders.* You know, thinking it was his fault and all. Marty had to talk some sense into him."

Her father laughed. "That's right, I remember that scene. Marty had some good advice. You should listen to her. She's very clever."

She leaned back and grinned at him. "Yes, she is." She let him go and stepped back as they walked back to the table together. "Thanks, Dad. Now go on home, it's getting late and Michelle's here to keep me company."

A few more people came up to purchase books. Some seemed to be interested in mysteries, others had heard her name on the news, and of course, her friends came as well. She winced as her college friend, Jody Berber, someone who had been very close to Solange, approached the table. The tears in the brunette's eyes made it clear she knew the bad news.

"Oh Cassie, have you heard about Solange?"

Cassie started to answer, then was grateful when Michelle interceded. "Yes, we've both heard about it. It's so hard to believe."

"I *know.*" Jody wailed the last word. "I just saw her last week, we made plans to go down to D.C. next weekend. I can't believe I'll never see her again." She sniffled, but still smiled at Aaron when he handed her a handkerchief. "He's cute, who's that?" she whispered, leaning closer to Cassie and Michelle.

"Aaron Kaufman, Cassie's agent," Michelle answered.

"Oh, wow, I didn't realize you got such a nice benefit from writing. It's so cool that you're a published author now. I had to come, even after hearing the news, so I can get a signed copy. Although I don't think I'll read it yet. I don't think I can read about murder after finding out that someone killed Solange."

"I'm not sure I can write about murder anymore," Cassie told Michelle after Jody had left.

"Yes, you can, Cassie. You're too good to stop. Please don't let this prevent you from doing what you should be doing."

"Maybe I should go back to writing about Kerfluffel," Cassie muttered.

Michelle laughed and hugged her. "Well, there is a lack of purple unicorns in the literary world right now, but I don't think you should nix writing mysteries because of what happened. Maybe you should take a break from it. We can go to the beach or something. I have vacation time."

Cassie shot a glance in Aaron's direction to make sure he hadn't overheard. He was talking to one of the store managers, giving one of those smooth sales pitches he was so good at. "Aaron would kill me. Do you know how many venues he's got scheduled in the next few weeks? And he keeps asking me if I've started the third book for the contract."

"Look, if you need a break, you need a break. You've had a very stressful week. At least you haven't been stressing about the book release."

"Way to find the silver lining, Michelle. I guess I haven't stressed so much over that. I thought I'd be worried whether anyone would show up at this signing. Instead I'm worried about who might be killed next. You called all the people on my contact list, right?"

"Everyone that you could remember having in the day planner, yes. I let them know what happened to Solange, let them know that the police have not officially connected the murders, but told them to be careful."

"Good. Thanks for doing that." Cassie felt some relief that they had done what they could to protect her friends. "Detective Whittaker will probably be pissed we did that, but I don't care. I want them to be warned. Besides, you didn't specify exactly what happened to Solange, right?"

Michelle shook her head. "Just that she'd been killed. No details. You didn't share any with me either."

"No, and I'm not going to. You don't need those images in your mind."

"You don't either, Cassie. What do you say after the signing, you'll come to my house for the night? I'll grab Donner and his stuff and take him to my apartment. That way you don't have to go home tonight and see what the investigators did to your house."

Cassie sighed, both in relief and at the thought of what was happening to her home. "It'll probably be a mess. That sounds like a good idea."

"Do you need a change of clothes from your place?"

"No, I've left a few things at your house the last time I was there. It's not like I can borrow your clothes, Shorty."

"Oh, that was on purpose? I thought you had just forgotten to take them, like you forget to take your wallet whenever we go out to eat."

"Look, the last time wasn't my fault," Cassie protested, her temporary good mood disappearing as she remembered that night at Corks.

"Stop thinking about it, Cassie. Think about tonight. We'll have fun. I'll grab the cat and some alcohol, and we'll have a party."

"Alcohol sounds good. Oh, here comes another person."

Cassie smiled at the newcomer. He looked twenty-something. The hair beneath the Boston Red Sox cap was fashionably unkempt and his clothes had that distressed look that came off the rack instead of from natural wear.

"Can I help you?"

"Yeah, can I get you to sign this book?"

She pulled out a pen. She would have preferred to use her favorite mechanical pencil, but Aaron, her father, and Michelle had collectively put their feet down that she had to use an ink pen.

"Of course. What name should I write?" She opened the book to the title page and waited, pen poised lightly on the paper, for his instructions.

"To Seth Montgomery," the man said.

Cassie choked in shock. She stared at the young man. "Your name is Seth Montgomery?"

He blushed. "Well, no, my name is Gene Harris. But I figured, you know, if you signed the book to that Seth Montgomery guy, I could probably sell it on eBay and say that it was left at the murder scene. Maybe put some fake blood on it or something. Uhm..." He pointed at the table, breaking her stare. "Can I get another one, one that's not messed up?"

Cassie followed his pointing finger to the book in front of her and saw why he wanted a new one. Her pen had slipped in her surprise, making a mark so hard and deep several pages beneath were ruined.

She pushed the copy aside and reached for another, leaning close to Michelle, who was regarding the man with complete disbelief. "Alcohol sounds really good."

chapter 12

Worry and guilt were killing her.

Cassie had barely slept the previous night, despite Michelle's best attempts at diversion. Michelle hadn't let her watch or look up any of the media coverage of Solange's case. Instead, they played Scrabble and consumed a couple of bottles of wine between them.

So she had a hangover on top of everything else.

Not the way she had envisioned spending the night after her book launch.

And today was even worse.

It felt weird to know that strangers had been in her place, searching out her secrets, going through every drawer and closet. She stood in the middle of her living room, unsure what to do, where to go. Donner prowled uneasily, his fur standing up as he sniffed at the unfamiliar human and chemical scents on furniture and carpeting.

Cassie wasn't worried about the police finding anything to implicate her, but having her home searched was still embarrassing. Now the entire Baltimore police force would know about her battery-operated boyfriend.

But she wanted this investigation over, this mystery solved. She would do anything to speed up the process of finding Seth and Solange's killer. She didn't want this…this…person to kill any more of her friends.

She thought about calling those she'd listed in her day planner again just to make sure they were all okay this morning.

No. There was something more important to do first. Steeling herself, she called Jody, figuring someone closer to Solange would have the phone number she needed. She took a few more moments to compose herself before placing the second call, this time international.

But as much as she'd tried to prepare, she hadn't been ready to talk to Solange's parents. Being an author didn't make finding words any easier. She struggled, tongue-tied, to tell them she was sorry, that she was shocked, and that she would always remember Solange.

The language barrier didn't help, either. She labored to use her high school French. Although Solange's parents had spoken perfect English when they came to this country on a previous visit, it was obvious they weren't currently capable of speaking any language but their own. In fact, her mother seemed incapable of speech and cried the entire time Cassie offered her inept condolences.

She had to wipe her eyes as she hung up the phone. For a moment she hunched over and hugged herself, wondering if they knew she had been there when their daughter was killed.

And that she was to blame.

Damn it, but she wasn't to blame. The killer was to blame, the killer was to blame, the killer was to blame. She said it over and over in her mind, but it still wouldn't sink in. There was no denying she was involved. Connected.

She unknotted herself and stared at her shelves with their rows of books about murder, feeling distant, dazed, and sick to her stomach.

God, it all seemed so easy, back when she first started writing. Although she had worried about whether someone would take the books and copycat the unique murder methods she created. Her father patiently reminded her that what people chose to do after reading a book—or anything else, like watching a movie, playing a violent video game, or listening to a song played backward—was still their choice. At the time, she had accepted his advice, back when it was all hypothetical and imaginary.

Now, it was real. And she was struggling to not blame herself.

She nearly fell off the couch at the knock on her door. Getting to her feet instead, she went for the peephole, praying it wasn't the media. Catching a glimpse of perfectly styled blond hair, she breathed a sigh of relief. It was the media, but not of the bad sort.

She gladly opened the door for Christine.

"Hello, girl. How are you holding up?" Christine gave her a one-armed hug. Her left arm was full of Sunday newspapers.

"I'm holding. Talk about holding, let me take those." Cassie offered to take the newspapers. "Thanks for bringing these over, I hadn't even thought of it."

Trying to focus on something other than her guilt, she watched Christine glide towards the couch. Christine had what Cassie had always thought of as a "Goldilocks body"—not too short, not too tall, not too fat, not too thin. Christine kept that body just right with long-distance running and covered it in designer clothes. Even today, on a Sunday, she was clad in Calvin Klein jeans and a lavender silk shirt.

And perfectly made up, unlike Cassie, who hadn't bothered with makeup that morning and was still wearing the casual jeans and T-shirt she had stored at Michelle's house.

"You make the rest of us look bad, Christine," Cassie complained. She sat down to read the review and realized Solange's picture was on the front page.

She stared at it instead.

Christine took the paper from her and opened it to the book section. "Skip that, Cassie."

"Does it mention me? Of course it does, that's why you're telling me to avoid it."

Christine sat down on Cassie's coffee table. "Yes, it says that you were first on scene and talks about your connection to the victim. And of course, it mentions your book. But, sweetie, don't let this ruin your first book release. You only get one of those."

"It already has. Yesterday sucked at the book signing. I mean, I got plenty of people there, but some of them referred to me as 'that author who killed that guy.' And that was before the news about Solange came out."

"Well, at least you'll have a story to tell your grandchildren about your launch day then." She grabbed Cassie's hand, sympathy shining in her green eyes. "I'm so sorry about that, Cassie, sorry about your friend."

She tried to shake it off. "Thanks, Christine. And thanks again for the copies of the paper."

"Well, I wanted to make certain that you got some copies. They're selling fast today."

"Oh? Well, thanks even more then. I would've forgotten to get any."

"I'm not surprised. It sounds like you've had a stressful week. Again, I'm sorry for my part in it, telling Mike at the News Desk about the detectives' visit."

Cassie shrugged. "It's your job. You smelled a story."

"I did, although Detective Whittaker tried to play it off. Still, I wish I hadn't said anything to anyone. Although Mike would've made the connection this time, probably. You being pulled in twice for questioning would've gotten his attention." Christine reached over to scratch Donner when he pounced up on the couch. "Can I do anything for you? Want to go out for coffee or anything?"

"I'm bad luck where coffee is concerned," Cassie said bitterly. "The last two people were shot after having coffee with me."

"Really? I hadn't heard about that."

Noticing the gleam of interest in the woman's eyes, Cassie realized she should be careful about what she said. While Christine had helped her with the reviews on her blog and *The Baltimore Dispatch,* and while she had offered to interview her for the cable show on Wednesday, she was still, technically, a reporter. Whatever she said would be most likely reported by Christine to her friend at the news desk.

"Probably a coincidence, but just in case, let me make coffee for you here instead. Actually, what do you say to wine? I could use some." Cassie glanced at her watch. It was after twelve; she could have more wine. Even though she had a headache from the night before.

Christine nodded. "That would be nice. And you're probably right, it's just a coincidence. As are the two murders, right?"

Cassie shrugged as she headed to the refrigerator. "I hope so."

"What do the police think?"

With a snort, Cassie opened the wine. "The police are keeping their thoughts to themselves."

"They tend to do that, unfortunately. In fact, it was one of the reasons I gave your book such good marks for research. The police in your story were just as close-mouthed as they tend to be in real life. Unless you develop a relationship with one."

"I'd like to do that," Cassie muttered.

"Do what?"

She ducked her head in embarrassment. "Um, develop a relationship with a police officer. You know, to get the inside story and all," she hedged. "Actually, Solange had one. She was able to tell me things about Seth's murder that hadn't been released."

"Really, like what?"

Cassie smiled and walked in with the wine and two glasses. "Oh no. I'm not telling you. It'll end up on the front page."

"Oh, I'm not all that bad, Cassie. If I promise it's off the record this time, will you tell me?"

She shook her head as she poured. "Honestly, I promised Detective Whittaker not to share what I learned. You know how it works; they prefer to keep all the information close to the vest. That way, if someone reveals too much, it might be a sign of guilt."

"Good point. Okay, I'll stop badgering you." Christine raised up her glass. "To the success of your book."

Cassie tried to smile, but figured it didn't make it all the way up to her eyes. "To the success of the book. And to all my friends who helped make it happen."

Christine clinked glasses with hers. "I can drink to that."

* * *

After Christine left, Cassie took the time to read both the article about the murder and her review. She felt helpless. She didn't think any of the information she had given helped the detectives. Searching her house wouldn't have given them any more clues either.

Plopping down on the sofa and closing her eyes, she stroked Donner's soft fur when he leaped up to join her. She tried to take comfort from his soft purring when he curled up in her lap. "You just know when I need some loving, huh, fellow? Are you psychic?"

Psychic? Her eyes flew open when she remembered the card Linda had given her.

Deciding that she was more bothered doing nothing than making a fool of herself, she stood up and dislodged Donner. He landed gracefully and ran up the stairs, miffed by her actions. She grabbed her purse off the foyer table and after a hunt, found Linda's card. She barely managed to suppress the urge to roll her eyes when she read *"Psychic Consortium—Find the answers you're looking for."* She wasn't sure which bothered her more, the idea of a self-proclaimed psychic, or the fact that they ended the sentence with a preposition.

That made her smile; she was her mother's daughter. It was her affinity for the English language that had interested her in writing.

Removing the cell phone from the charger, she mustered up the courage to dial. With both trepidation and self disgust, she placed the call.

She was surprised it took over four rings for someone to pick up; shouldn't they have been expecting her call? She chastised herself for her cynicism. She was calling them, after all. She should show some respect.

Maybe.

"Good morning, and thank you for calling the Psychic Consortium. How may I help you?"

Cassie suppressed the urge to suggest they should know, but she had already recognized Linda's voice. *I guess the Psychic Consortium doesn't rate a secretary then.* "Hello, Linda? This is Cassandra Ellis."

"Cassie! I'm so glad you called. Even George was talking about you today. Which is odd. She's normally the quietest of the four of us."

So, there were three others, Cassie thought. "Ah, well, it looks like Dorian was correct. I could use your help."

"So I heard on the news. They've mentioned your name a number of times. Two murders, my word. I'm sorry about your friends."

She almost corrected Linda. Solange was more a friend of friends, and Seth was definitely not a friend, but she opted for a noncommittal grunt instead. "Thank you."

"So, are you calling for help?" Linda asked. "Or do you think I should know what you need already?"

Cassie opted for the noncommittal grunt again.

Linda laughed. "Well then, why don't I use a combination of psychic ability and logic, like Penelope Ramos does? That's my main character, by the way, since you probably haven't read my books."

Cassie was grateful she was on the phone so that Linda couldn't see her blush. "Okay, go ahead."

"Well, this morning, Dorian again said that you are in trouble, so that's the psychic connection. Which sounds like it should be a song that Kermit sings."

This time, it was Cassie's turn to laugh. It sounded like Linda had a sense of humor about all this psychic…stuff.

"Anyway, logically, I've seen for myself that you are in trouble, what with being involved with two real-life murders. And since you're calling me, using the card I gave you, I assume that means you're desperate enough to venture towards the paranormal for help."

Never content to sit still, Cassie stood. Going to the kitchen, she got a glass out of the cabinet. She tucked the phone on her shoulder as she filled the glass with water. "Nice deduction, Linda. And yes, whether you used logic or psychic powers to deduce it, you're right. I need help. The police are doing what they can, but these are my…friends who are dying now and I want it to stop. So I'll do anything. Can you meet anytime soon?"

She checked her schedule on the whiteboard. "I'm free all day today and most of tomorrow, other than a class tomorrow night at seven."

"Well, we have clients coming here most of today, but we're available this afternoon after four."

"Sure, four would be fine. Will I meet with one of you?"

"All of us, actually. Whoops, someone is at the door, Cassie. I'll see you at four."

"Thank you," Cassie said as she realized Linda had already hung up.

She spent the intervening time second-guessing herself and writing. Well, trying to write.

She had tried. She had diligently opened up her file and started typing.

> Marty couldn't believe it as she stood in her friend's newly renovated kitchen.
>
> On the granite countertop, there was a bottle of wine: Elaine's preferred Merlot. A corkscrew with the cork still on it lying next to it.
>
> And lying on the tile floor...was a body.
>
> Elaine.
>
> Her friend was face down, her blond hair spread around her head and saturated with fresh blood—

Cassie stopped and pushed away her laptop in frustration.

Elaine had auburn hair. And most poison victims didn't have head wounds. But Cassie couldn't get the image of the her slain friend out of her mind. It came to her again and again with graphic clarity.

Writing was probably a really, *really* bad idea right now.

Grading would be a better option. Especially since this was for her technical writing course, so none of her students would have written any scenes that included murder victims.

Oh good. She had one e-mail from Misplaced Modifier Man. His e-mails and papers never failed to amuse her and she could use a good laugh right now. After reading that *"I found my missing file folder cleaning my office"* and that *"while typing my report, my computer broke,"* she had to admire the talents of the tidy folder and the typing computer.

But the time and effort required to correct his attached file meant that she didn't think about Solange. It also meant she had to rush to get ready. She ran upstairs to figure out what one wears to a gathering of psychics.

It took her so long to decide on a freeflowing purple skirt and matching top that she ended up running late. Luckily, she was able to find a parking space just outside the address of the Psychic Consortium and executed a quick parallel parking job behind a large truck. She couldn't stop herself from glancing around as she ran into the building. She hoped no one she knew saw her.

Once inside, she was surprised by the professional decor of the office.

Linda was the only one currently in the office. This time, she was wearing a light gray suit that was kept from looking conservative by the orange-red top she wore with it.

Cassie followed Linda down a hallway into a brightly lit room in the back where the older woman gestured her into a chair next to a round office table.

Seating herself on the opposite side, Linda said, "The media says the police haven't made any more headway in the murders. Is that the case? Oh, and that's what I've been able to garner by watching the news, not by any ethereal method. The police have been rather tight-lipped about the entire thing."

Cassie thought about Detective Whittaker's lips. She quickly tried to erase that image before Linda could read her thoughts. She frowned at herself; she didn't believe in that sort of thing anyway.

"No, they don't seem to have much information, at least not that they're sharing. They're following leads, including interviewing many of my friends and acquaintances, but that's just a routine follow-up."

Then she had to swallow a laugh as she realized how much she sounded like Detective Whittaker.

"They haven't interviewed me," Linda said with a disappointed look.

"Well, you weren't in the original day planner that was stolen from me." *Or I lost it, or it mysteriously evaporated and reappeared in Seth's living room.*

"Can I get you anything to drink? Coffee? Water? Soda?"

Cassie nodded. "Coffee would be nice. Cream and sugar, if it's no bother."

When Linda left the room, she took the opportunity to be nosy. She was disappointed. This wasn't what she had expected, at all. No spooky noises, no dark and mysterious objects. She couldn't resist sneaking a peek under the table, just in case Linda had some contraption set up to fake thumping noises.

But no, the place seemed like a normal office space, other than the crystals hanging around. Still, considering their placement near the windows, the ornaments were probably more for a decorative effect than a paranormal one.

Continuing her perusal, she noted the desk in the corner. The desk was cluttered, but Cassie wasn't in any position to judge, since the one in her office at home was just as bad. That was one reason she usually chose to work downstairs at her kitchen table. More room for her clutter—and the quick access to tea and soda.

It appeared that Linda did her writing in this room. Her laptop was open, and Cassie had to suppress the urge to take a peek at the screen. The bookshelves in the room were overflowing with a variety of books. She craned her neck to read a few titles along the spines and was surprised to see that she and Linda had dozens of book in common. There were also a few true crime books that she didn't own. Perhaps Linda would loan her a few.

The room had three doors, all open. One was from the hallway and one had to lead to the kitchen, since that was where Linda had disappeared.

The other door seemed to lead to another room. Perhaps that was the office space for the other members of the Consortium, whoever they were. Cassie was wondering what was back there when she heard what sounded like a quiet plea for help.

She sat still and listened closely, but all she could hear was Linda moving around in the kitchen, the sound of the coffee maker percolating, and the sound of a truck outside. No voices.

Wait. There it was again. A desperate sounding cry for help. A breathy voice called out, "Please, please. Can anyone save us?"

chapter 13

Cassie glanced towards the kitchen again. The coffee maker sputtered out its final gasp, so she had a little time. She stood and tiptoed towards the door. She had only gotten about halfway across the room when the voice stopped her.

"No, no. You're in serious danger," the high-pitched voice called out.

She scrambled back to her seat and tried to look nonchalant just as Linda came back with the coffee. She'd quickly consult with Linda, then leave the office and call Detective Whit—call the police.

"Here you go," Linda said, a pleasant smile on her face as she sat down a tray with their coffee and a plate of cookies.

Cassie wasn't fooled by it. After all, she wrote murder mysteries. She knew the nicest-seeming person could be the worst villain ever. Even a motherly woman who served coffee in china with cute bird patterns could kill viciously.

She wouldn't have expected Linda to be a murderer, though. Honestly, the woman didn't seem bright enough for it. But perhaps she was really clever and only pretended to be an eccentric, ditzy psychic.

Cassie raised the cup to her lips. Then it occurred to her what such a clever woman might add to coffee. That voice she'd heard before…was it someone Linda had kidnapped and stashed away in one of those mysterious back rooms? Perhaps the older woman had heard her victim begging Cassie for help—what better way to get rid of a witness?

She blew on the coffee for cover before setting it back down. Even though she tried to be careful, she still rattled the saucer a bit. The clink of china against china echoed in the quiet room.

Then the voice called out again. "Please, please, can anyone save us?"

Dreading Linda's reaction, Cassie whipped her head towards the room and back.

"Oh, silly me, let me bring in my fids." Linda stood up and disappeared into the room from which the calls for help had come.

Okay, Cassie hadn't expected that reaction.

After a few moments of rustling, Linda returned with a very large white bird on one shoulder and a smaller silvery-gray one on the other. Perched on her finger was a tiny neon-green and yellow creature.

"Fids?" Cassie asked in some confusion. They looked like birds to her.

"Yes. Feathered kids. These are the other members of the Psychic Consortium," Linda said proudly, beaming at her birds.

Cassie gaped at Linda, but this time in disbelief rather than worry. "You've—" She swallowed the *got to be kidding me* that had almost slipped out, replacing it instead with a mumbled repetition of "Psychic Consortium."

The silvery-gray bird on Linda's shoulder was watching her, a calm, keen sense of intelligence in eyes the same color as her favorite champagne. Its face was pure white and the black beak looked sharp.

It cocked its head at her as they made eye contact. "You're in serious danger," it said clearly, in a voice that sounded exactly like the one she'd heard earlier, calling for help.

Shaking her head in amusement now, Cassie's attention went to the white bird. She'd seen something like it before, on a 70s cop show, she thought. A cockatoo, maybe? Bright yellow feathers erupted from the top of its head, and once again, she was struck by the intelligence that glowed from the animal's round dark eyes. She had no doubt the bird was examining her with as much curiosity as she examined it.

A blur of motion attracted her attention to the smallest bird. She was sure it was a parakeet. An elementary school friend of hers had owned one. Lively and full of energy, it bit Linda's ring, bobbed, flicked its tail, turned around in circles, attacked the ring again. Although she was often accused of such restless energy herself, just watching the little creature's constant motion was making her tired. If only energy like that could be bottled, she thought.

"You aren't afraid of them, are you? I can bring the cages out here, but it's such a bother."

Although the final scene from Hitchcock's *The Birds* came unbidden to her mind, Cassie shook her head. "I'm fine."

Linda lifted her hand to the bigger of the two birds on her shoulders. "Step up," she said. The bird stepped obediently onto her finger.

"Houdini, this is Cassandra Ellis. Cassie," Linda repeated carefully. "We are going to help her today. Cassie, this is Houdini. He's quite the escape artist, hence the name. I have yet to find a cage that he can't get out of. Thank goodness I keep his wings clipped."

"It's a cockatoo, right? Wasn't there one of those on that *Baretta* TV show?"

"I thought *Baretta* was before your time, dear, but yes, he did have one. Houdini, introduce yourself to Cassie."

The bird walked across the table to her. It was a big bird, about twelve and a half inches tall. At least it looked big to a city girl used to sparrows and pigeons.

"Hello, pretty lady. Whatcha doin'?" Unlike the gray bird, the voice sounded more…bird-like and his—her?—words were not as clearly enunciated.

Cassie watched cautiously as the cockatoo came up to her. She tried not to wince when it boldly stepped onto her arm and scrambled up to her shoulder, gripping her shirt to pull himself up with beak and claws. It was a weird feeling to have such a big, warm creature so close, to feel the strong grip of its feet and nails. She caught a glimpse of the scimitar-shaped black beak and looked away, trying to act as if it didn't matter she had an animal capable of pecking her eyes out on her shoulder.

"Houdini is a flirt, don't mind him," Linda said.

A flirt? Cassie thought. *And he's a him. I wonder how you can tell he's a boy?*

Linda lifted her hand towards Cassie to bring the little neon green and yellow bird closer.

"This is George. She's a budgerigar. George, this is Cassie."

This bird was quiet, just cocked its head at Cassie as it hopped off of Linda's hand and onto the table.

"Not a parakeet?" Cassie asked, curious now. She loved to learn new things.

Linda frowned. "Generically, yes," she said with a roll of her eyes. "It's what the pet stores call them, so it became popular. Parakeet is, more specifically, a common name for some parrot species with long tails. For example, Indian Ringnecks and Bourkes…"

Whatever those were, thought Cassie, but had to smile at the glow of enthusiasm in Linda's face as she waxed eloquent on a favorite topic. Michelle often told her she started to glow when talking about her research. Now Cassie understood what she meant.

"...so a budgie is a parakeet, but a parakeet is not necessarily a budgie. George is an American Budgie." Linda concluded.

"And is George a boy or a girl? The name's unisex."

Linda nodded smartly. "That was the point, really. You can't tell on budgies whether they are male or female when they are babies, which is when I got George. She's a girl; you can now tell by the color of the cere," Linda pointed at a brownish area above the bird's beak. "On a boy, it would be blue."

"Well, George can be a female name, too."

Linda nodded. "Yes, I know. In fact, I also named her after Nancy Drew's sidekick."

"Nancy Drew." Cassie wrinkled her nose.

"Wait, you're a mystery author, and you don't like Nancy Drew?"

"She was okay. Just a little too perfect. I prefer Trixie Belden," Cassie said as she watched George bop around the tablecloth.

"And this..." Linda announced, slowly sweeping her hand up to her shoulder. "This is Dorian."

"He's beautiful," Cassie said as the bird stepped onto Linda's hand. "And amazing, I can't believe how human he sounded when he talks."

"It is amazing, actually. He's very smart. He's an African Grey. Like Alex?" Linda asked with an inquiring glance at Cassie.

Cassie shook her head. "Who's Alex?"

"He was a famous research bird that did amazing things with language. But I won't bore you with all that."

Cassie made a mental note to google Alex when she got home.

"Dorian isn't as gifted as Alex, not yet, but he does have the best vocabulary of all the birds. Don't you, Dorian?"

"Yes. Yes I do," said the gray parrot with an actual nod.

"Say hello to Cassie, Dorian."

"Hello." It bowed this time.

Cassie couldn't help it, she was charmed. The bird really was beautiful with its gray feathers and bright red tail. She was amused when she realized that Linda's outfit matched Dorian's plumage. She was certain that was deliberate. Amusement reigned again when she realized the bird's name had to be another deliberate choice.

"Is he named Dorian because of Dorian Gray and the fact that he's an African Grey?"

"Yes, his previous owner said that's why he chose that name. The other option was Earl, after the tea."

"And Dorian is the one who said that Red is in danger?" Cassie asked, remembering Linda's words from Friday. And laughed when she remembered Linda had been wearing white and yellow on Friday, matching Houdini.

"Red's in danger," Dorian said.

"Red! Danger!" Houdini screeched in her ear, nearly knocking Cassie off her chair. Even though it was too late, she clamped a hand over her ringing ear.

"Houdini! Inside voice!"

Cassie only heard that from the ear that hadn't been screeched in.

"I'm sorry, my dear, this situation has them a bit anxious."

Cassie swallowed and tried to pop her ears. "So, um, Dorian's the one that said that phrase that I'm not going to repeat again?"

Linda broke off a piece of cookie for Dorian. "Yes. He was the one who predicted you'd be in danger. And I suppose he was right, since your friend died yesterday."

"Well, he should have said 'Red's friend is in danger' then, shouldn't he? That would have been more helpful." Cassie watched the budgie as it half walked, half skated over to her. Gripping her shirt with its claws and beak, it walked up her chest and stood there, staring at her. It came closer, so close she felt a surprising heat against her chin although the little bird wasn't actually touching.

Cassie blinked at it and tried to focus as it got so close to her face. She couldn't stop thinking of the eye-pecking scenes from *The Birds*. The beak and claws did look pretty sharp.

"Unfortunately, predictions like that are often vague. It may be difficult to interpret any prediction until it is too late." Linda sipped her coffee and offered another bit of cookie to the Grey perched back on her shoulder.

Cassie tried to conceal a sneer. It seemed to her if a prediction came post-event, any interpretation could be all too easily twisted into whatever applied.

"I know, I know," Linda said in an amused, tolerant voice. "You don't believe me."

Cassie realized her skepticism must be showing, so she did her best to remove the disbelief off her face before she answered. "Well, no, I don't really believe in psychics. But I'm here, aren't I? And I'm trying to keep an open mind."

"That's better than most people try for," Linda said. "Generally, they want to know if we're psychic, why don't we just figure out the winning lottery numbers and retire? Or they won't bother telling us why they want to talk to us since we should already know."

Cassie felt heat flare in her cheeks, and it had nothing to do with the very warm avian bodies still close to her skin.

Linda started laughing. "So you thought that, too. That's okay, Cassie. I appreciate you trying to keep an open mind."

"I am trying, Linda."

"You don't believe at all in extrasensory powers? Precognition? Telepathy?"

That made her smile. As did the profound relief when Houdini climbed back down her shirt and walked back to his owner.

"What's so funny about telepathy?" Linda wanted to know.

"Well, when Michelle and I were eleven, we tried to work on mental telepathy. See, our parents complained about how much time we both spent on the phone, so we tried to find another way to communicate."

Linda took a delicate sip of her coffee. "And?"

"It was a miserable failure. Neither of us could ever figure out what the other was thinking, at least not word for word. As the years past, we were able to communicate without words, but mainly because we knew each other so well. And because we learned American Sign Language."

"You did?"

"That way we could talk in class, well, without talking. And no one knew what we were saying. It would drive the teachers crazy though. One of them threatened to tie our hands to our desks. But I asked him how we could do our work then."

"Well, I suppose sign language is one way to get around the lack of telepathy. I understand your skepticism with psychics. There are a lot of people out there, intelligent people, who think psychic power is completely bogus. And there are a lot of people, just as intelligent, who believe and have seen proof, at least to their eyes."

"I'm not sure what I believe. More importantly, I'm desperate for help. I know the police are out there, searching for the killer." And interrogating all my friends, again, she thought. "But I need to do something now. So I thought of you. And the, um…" she looked around at the birds. "The Psychic Consortium?"

"Yes, even the most open-minded people have trouble believing that the birds have any powers. But personally, I think most animals have powers we don't understand. We call it instinct, how they are able to react to dangerous situations, usually as a group. But I think it's more. I believe most flocks have the ability to communicate amongst the group, to communicate instantly with each other, and to think as one entity."

Cassie took a sip of her coffee and grimaced. She had let it get way too cold. "What, like the Borg collective?"

The Grey perked up at that. "You will be assimilated," it said, in a mechanical-sounding voice.

Cassie choked on her coffee. Picking up a napkin, she looked at Dorian. "He is smart."

"He's the smartest of the birds. And he has had the best success rate for predictions. He said to me, 'You have to move all these people out of here right now' and 'It's a fire, mister, and all fires are bad' a week before the 2007 wildfires in Southern California. In August of 2005, just days before Hurricane Katrina, he said something about how you could be a meteorologist all your life and never see something like this. Then he said it would be a disaster of epic proportions. It definitely was, wasn't it?"

Cassie nodded. A friend of hers had lived in New Orleans during that time, but hadn't lost too much. She had been smart enough to vacate the area when warned.

"And a few days before 9/11, he said, 'We have a national security matter.' I did try to alert the FBI and CIA, but they didn't take me seriously. They never do." Linda gazed into her coffee and shook her head.

Cassie had to admit, while the last one had been rather vague, the other predictions did seem rather intriguing. Was it possible for a bird to predict the future?

Dorian had finished his cookie and was preening himself. Houdini was nuzzling up to Linda's hand. George continued to just sit on Cassie's chest and stare at her, almost preternaturally still. It freaked Cassie out a little. What was going on in that little bird brain? And just how high were their body temperatures, normally? She was glad it was air conditioned in Linda's office, she didn't think she could take the added heat on her face otherwise.

"Does George even talk?" she wanted to know.

"She does, just not as often. She's a lot shyer than the two boys and often won't talk in front of strangers. It's hard to understand, she has a very small voice. But she's young. I've only had her for two years. Dorian and Houdini are older. They both talk a lot and often won't shut up, especially when it's time to sleep."

Considering how Donner managed to annoy her when she wanted to sleep and he didn't, Cassie winced at the thought of garrulous birds keeping someone awake. "Did you get Dorian and Houdini as babies too?"

"No, they were already adult birds when I got them, about ten years ago. I saw an ad from someone who was moving out of the country and couldn't take any animals along. I thought birds would be nice for companionship, especially since both of them were such talkers. It was the 9/11 prediction that made me realize what these birds can do. At first, I thought it was just Dorian, but then Houdini asked one night, right before I covered his cage 'None of you has ever seen an F-5?' I had no idea what he meant, but three days after that, an F-5 tornado hit Greensburg, Kansas."

"Wow," Cassie said, impressed despite herself.

"Anyway, hopefully that convinces you a little, Cassie. Why don't we get to the reason you are here?"

"Um, well, I suppose that I'm just wondering if you…" She glanced at the birds. Was she supposed to talk to them too? "If any of you have any idea about what is happening with these murders."

"Let us look," Linda said and put her hands together before staring deeply into Cassie's eyes.

After a couple of minutes, Cassie noticed some things. First of all, Linda had lovely eyes. They were hazel, almost a dark army green. And, like the birds, they held a keen intelligence that had been hidden behind the flighty appearance. Second of all, Cassie really hated having someone stare at her this long. Especially since the birds were also watching her. Eight eyes staring at her almost did her in.

She was about to say something to break the silence when Linda closed her eyes and sat up straight. "You know the killer."

"I do?"

"Yes, but you don't know that this person is the killer."

"Do you know who it is?"

Linda shook her head. "No, I can't get a clear picture. Just a vague image from you."

"How vague? Male? Female?"

Linda got up, headed towards the kitchen, and came back with two bottled waters. "It's really vague, Cassie. I can't even see that."

Cassie slouched down in her chair. "Well, what use is that, then?"

Linda laughed before she winced. She put a hand on her forehead. "Headache. Always get them when I do this. And I suppose it's not terribly useful to you. I'm sorry. Sometimes I see more. Perhaps it's because you don't realize it's the killer...or you refuse to believe this person would do something like this. I don't know. What about you, Dorian? Do you know who is doing the killing?"

Swiveling his head first at Linda, then at Cassie, he puffed up his feathers and shook himself before speaking in a low voice. "Can't take no pleasure from killing. There's just some things you gotta do."

"What the hell does that mean?" Cassie asked, staring at the bird. And why had his English just gotten so bad?

Linda shook her head. "I don't know, I'm sorry. Dorian must have his reasons for saying it. Houdini, George? Any ideas?"

Houdini shifted from foot to foot and then answered Dorian. "Doesn't mean you have to like it."

Cassie frowned at the bird. "Like what?"

"The killing, I suppose," Linda guessed. "I think his statement relates to Dorian. They often seem to work together like that. With my previous client, Dorian asked 'What do we say to them?' and Houdini answered, 'Welcome to California.' The client had been talking about her ailing parents and whether she should move back home. Since her parents live in California, it provided her with a good answer." She shook her head. "But I'm not sure what they are trying to say here, unless they think the killer doesn't actually enjoy the killing."

Cassie bit her bottom lip. "So I know the killer, and the killer doesn't actually enjoy the killing?"

Linda nodded. "Yes. I know that might not help much, but perhaps you could let the police know this. It might help in their search."

Cassie snatched up her napkin to hide her expression as much as to muffle a laugh. She tried to imagine talking to Whittaker about her session with the Psychic Consortium. She might not fully believe in psychics—or psychic birds—but she felt she could safely predict his reaction. Raised eyebrows, utter disbelief in his smoky eyes, and a frown on his full lips. Maybe she should just call him and say "a little birdie told me..."

No. No way. She wouldn't be sharing this with the police.

"Well, if you'd like, I could do a tarot card reading," Linda offered. "Perhaps that will help shed some light."

chapter 14

An hour later, the tarot cards only revealed that Cassie was going to have success in her life, following turmoil. Sadly, it didn't reveal the name and address of the murderer. It would be so nice if it did.

"Let me pay you for your time." Cassie dug her arm into the depths of her purse, fishing for her wallet.

Linda shook her head. "No, first time is free. Besides, we didn't really help you. I hope this is all resolved soon. I'm sure it's spoiling what should be a joyful time of your life, having your first book published. I can remember my first time. I was giddy as a chickadee. But I didn't have anyone to celebrate with. It's one reason I went and got the birds. They've celebrated every book release with me since."

Cassie slowly walked down the hallway. While she still wasn't convinced about the abilities of either Linda or her birds, she had enjoyed the time with them. All of them. She'd probably enjoy hanging out with Linda. And Linda seemed a bit lonely.

They had spent the last ten minutes talking about writing after the tarot card reading. Evidently Linda used the cards to help get over writer's block. That was an interesting concept.

She jumped when her cell phone rang. She was so distracted she didn't even bother looking at the display, just flipped open the phone and held it to her ear as she walked out the door.

"Hello."

"Ms. Ellis?"

She knew he couldn't see her location, but she flushed as she recognized Detective Whittaker's voice. "Um, hello Detective Whittaker, how are you? How's the case?" She tried desperately to sound normal.

"That's what I was calling about, actually. I'd like to return your book, our copy came in. And I'd also like to ask you a few more questions. Are you available to come down to the station or could I meet you somewhere?"

"Meet me?" Her voice cracked. She stepped out of the building, blinking as the bright sun blinded her. "Oh, that won't be necessary." Eyes slitted shut, she hurried toward her car, cringing as she realized how guilty that last statement sounded

Not a good idea with a cop. Especially one as observant as Whittaker. Cassie's gut clenched as the silence lengthened on his side of the connection. *Oh God, he's suspicious.* Even though he couldn't see her, she rushed to make it back to her car and away from the Psychic Consortium.

"Actually, I think it's best if I meet you. Where are you located right now?"

"Oh, I'm in...um...Hampden. But I can easily drive down to Headquarters, I'm only about ten minutes from—damn it!" She stared at where her Saturn should have been. Instead, there was an empty space. She looked up at a nearby sign. "Great! I parked in a truck loading zone and my car got towed away. That's never happened before."

Whittaker laughed in her ear, startling her. It was the first time she'd heard him laugh, and she had to lower the phone to stare at it a moment before putting it back to her ear as he spoke again.

"And you've lived in Baltimore for how long? I've been towed twice, and I'm a cop. Once, they even towed my police car. Granted, it's unmarked, but still."

She stood entranced as he laughed again. She'd be willing to bet her advance that he looked incredibly sexy laughing, those dimples winking and the clever gray eyes sparkling. Infected with his humor and her mental image, she started to laugh along with him.

Which seemed to be a mistake, since he stopped laughing and cleared his throat. "Since you're stranded now, I have to come to you. What's your location?

"That's really not necessary, Detective Whittaker. I can call for a cab."

"Oh, it absolutely is. I must rescue a damsel in distress; it's one of those police codes."

"I don't recall reading that one in the General Orders." She wiped her brow and considered. What she had learned of Whittaker in the past couple of days had already taught her it would be useless to continue arguing. Besides, she didn't really want to argue. It was too hot.

But so was he. Maybe being alone with him was a bad idea.

"Ms. Ellis, just tell me your location."

She sighed and gave in. "Fine, if you insist. I'm on the corner of Elm Street and..." She looked up at the 36th Street sign and lied. "34th Street."

"Sure, I'll be there in a minute. And after we talk, I'll be happy to drive you down to the impound lot."

She started to thank him when she realized that he had already hung up. She hitched her bag over her shoulder and sprinted down to the next block. She didn't want Whittaker to catch the lie about her location; he was probably already wondering about her suspicious behavior. But she wasn't going to tell him about the Psychic Consortium. Somehow, she didn't think he'd be terribly open-minded. Open-mouthed maybe, but not open-minded.

Since she had some time before he arrived, she took out her compact from her bag and retouched her makeup. And refused to analyze why she was freshening up before seeing him.

Any evidence of primping was secreted away before he pulled up in his unmarked sedan. She stepped off the curb and began to grab the handle, but stopped when he slid out of the car and hurried over to her side. She managed not to roll her eyes when he held the door open for her and shut it as well.

Admittedly, it was far more pleasant sitting in the front seat rather than the backseat ride she had the last time she rode in a police car. And after he slid inside, she had to admit the view was far better up front, as well. She glanced to her side as discreetly as she could to admire his profile as he pulled back into traffic.

She was so distracted trying to be discreet that it took her a few moments to realize that he was circling around the streets, peering out his window at the local area.

"What are you looking for?"

"I'm trying to figure out where you really were when you called." He kept peering at the stores and restaurants in the area.

"You're what?" Cassie was ready to protest until he turned the corner onto 36th Street. She did her best not to look at the Psychic Consortium.

"There are no truck loading zones on 34th Street. There are some in this section, but I can't figure out why you were so reluctant to let me know where you were." He stopped the car and glanced around. "After all, you wouldn't be hiding a shopping trip for purses, or roses or...no way."

He turned to her in disbelief. "Tell me you weren't at the psychic."

She obeyed his order and didn't tell him. Unfortunately, her blush gave her away.

"You went to a psychic? About the murders?" Whittaker leaned his head back on the headrest. "Jesus, I know we haven't found the murderer, but give us a break. I really don't think a psychic is going to know more than we do."

"It's not that..." She changed the subject. "Look, why don't we go somewhere and you can ask me what you wanted to ask me? Then I'll explain what I was doing. Maybe."

"Fine. In fact, I'm hungry, are you? Alfonzo's has some good pizza, if you like that."

"I could get something to eat." She looked over at his navy blue suit. "But, I think both of us are overdressed for Alfonzo's. How about Golden West Café? It's only a few blocks from here. I'm more appropriately dressed for that than you are, but their food is phenomenal, especially if you like Mexican."

"I like Mexican."

Cassie was reaching for the door handle when she noticed that Whittaker was out of the car and sprinting for her side. She waited, bemused, until he opened her door. "Wow, you really do take this damsel in distress thing seriously."

He smiled crookedly, so that only one dimple showed. She felt lightheaded. She had a serious weakness for dimples.

"No, that's just lessons from my mother," Whittaker answered.

"Yoo-hoo! Cassie!"

The bright alto trill brought the flaming heat back to Cassie's cheeks as she turned.

Whittaker was already staring at the woman and her...entourage. Linda had Dorian in a large, strange looking backpack. George was stowed in a bag she had up front, and Houdini perched on her shoulder, wearing a harness and leash.

Furiously ignoring Whittaker low whistle of disbelief, Cassie demonstrated her manners as well as she thanked Linda again for her time. She didn't thank the birds.

Then she hurried down the street towards Golden West Café.

Whittaker caught up with her at the entrance and reached forward to open the door. She ended up walking into his arm when he suddenly stopped and stared inside. The shock of contact with him turned to amusement when she saw the expression on his face.

With his hand still on the door, he turned and stared at her. "You're kidding, right?"

"What? It's a good restaurant."

"Yes, but it's…it's…" He waved his free hand around while he struggled to find the correct word. "Frou-frou."

"It's eclectic," she said firmly as she moved his hand and opened the door before striding through. "And the food is really good." Knowing the true path to a cop's heart, she added, "As is the coffee."

Whittaker reluctantly followed her inside. Waiting at the host stand, he stared at the surroundings. Clutter seemed to be the décor. Random objects and art pieces hung haphazardly on the walls, and old bikes, baby carriages, and ancient appliances littered the room. Chipped plaster walls showed the brick underneath, as well as layers and layers of previous paint colors.

"Eclectic?" As they followed their host, thin as a heroin addict, to the table, Whittaker thought the place looked more like a pawn shop than a diner. He pulled out a seat for Ms. Ellis, since the host hadn't bothered to, before taking a seat on the other side.

"It is eclectic," she said, a cute note of petulance in her voice. "It's not as Baltimore as Café Hon, but it does have its own flair."

He stopped staring at the restaurant and focused intently on her. "Just like that woman we just met outside the Psychic Consortium."

She disappeared behind a menu so quickly he nearly laughed.

"So, I'd recommend any of the Southwest dishes, they're always good," she said.

He smirked at her distraction technique but let it go. They were both quiet for a moment as they studied the menu. After he made his two decisions, he put down the menu.

The stare worked on her as well as it worked on suspects. He saw it all the time. No eye contact. Fidgeting. And she was squirming so uncomfortably he almost considered pointing her towards the ladies room.

She flipped the pages of the menu back and forth. "Look, I'll explain that a little later. Besides, you called me. Don't you have a question for me? Do you have a lead?"

He debated on whether or not to let her change the topic when the waiter came back over to take their order. After she ordered *huevos rancheros* and a coffee, he gave the first of his choices. "I'll have a coffee and the chorizo burrito."

"I'm sorry sir," said the waiter. "We're out of chorizo."

He let out a long-suffering sigh "Of course you're out of chorizo. Then, I'll have the green chile cheeseburger."

"Why weren't you surprised when they said they were out of chorizo?" Ms. Ellis asked when the waiter had left to turn in their orders. She looked cute, the way her nose sort of wrinkled when she was asking a question.

He shrugged. "It's my superpower."

"Superpower?"

This time an eyebrow made a delicate arch over one of her eyes. Had he ever noticed the shape of a woman's eyebrows before? He reached for the plastic container of sweeteners to distract himself.

"Yeah, restaurants are always out of my first choice. My friends finally decided it's my superpower. I think it's a curse, but they tell me I just haven't figured out how to properly manipulate it yet." He arranged all the packets by color, then slid it back into the center of the table. "I'm used to it now, so when I look over the menu, I always make sure to have a second choice ready."

She laughed. "Well, then why don't you just ask for your second choice first then?"

"That doesn't work. You can't fool the superpower gods." He said it so seriously, she laughed again, as he'd wanted. But as much as he liked her laugh and wanted to hear it again, it wasn't his purpose today. "Not that I really believe in that or anything like that. Or psychics."

She sighed and reached for the now properly arranged sweetener holder. He hoped she wasn't going to mess them up again. Instead, she just slid the container back and forth.

"You're not going to drop it, are you?"

He shook his head.

"Can't we at least talk about why you called me first?" she pleaded.

He relented, for the moment. "Fine, we'll delay that conversation. We wanted to ask you who would have gotten your novel prior to its release. After all, the first murder took place before your book was released to the public."

"So then you think my book has something to do with these murders?"

"It might have something to do with the timing, Ms. Ellis. So—"

She interrupted him. "Look, can we drop the Ms. Ellis stuff? After all, I know about your superpower, we should be able to be more informal. Why don't you try saying Cassie? And I'll try James? Jim? Jimmy—"

"Definitely not Jimmy," he cut in, hustling out his darkest, most threatening glower to offset her sudden impudent grin. "Don't even think about it. James would be fine though, if you like."

His threatening cop face did nothing to dispel the mischievous expression this time.

"Maybe I should just use your last name? That's the tradition between cops, right, Whittaker?"

"That would be fine, too." If she wanted him to treat her like another cop. With the way his thoughts were starting to stray, it might be a good idea. "Anyway, now that we've sorted out that thorny issue, the timing of the murders is interesting."

Now this, he noted, wiped any lightness from her features.

"Your book came out yesterday, the same day as Solange's murder and three days after Seth's murder. So if we assume the killer is using you as the connection to these people—"

She interrupted him again. "Does that mean you don't think I'm the killer?"

It was his turn to sigh. "Ms. Ellis…Cassie, you know I can't answer that. You're as aware as I am that we haven't confirmed your alibi."

She returned the sweetener holder, moved her water glass aside, and leaned across the table. Whittaker fought to keep his eyes on her face, since her new angle offered an intriguing glimpse down her shirt. Not that he was looking there.

"True, but hopefully you'd realize I'd be clever enough to have one if I had killed these people."

Even though he didn't think she had done it, he couldn't resist arching one eyebrow in derision. "Or arrogant enough not to bother."

She straightened, her hands gripping the edge of the tables so tightly her knuckles went white.

"You do think I did it. I can't believe you think I actually—"

"Cassie," he interrupted firmly. "Do you really think I have dinner with people whom I suspect of murder?"

"Perhaps you're being clever. Figuring that in this informal setting, it's an easy way to disarm me and get more information."

"If I thought someone was guilty, I'd get it out of them officially in interview."

She released her death grip on the table and took a deep breath. "True. True. It's not like anything I might say here is permissible anyway, you haven't read me my rights. No, wait, that doesn't matter, does it? If I volunteer information outside of an official arrest, it can still be included."

Damn. He was glad that most of the people he interviewed didn't have her knowledge. "Correct. Anyway, who would receive the book before it's actually released? That's my question. It could lower the number of suspects."

"That might help, but there are so many people involved in printing the book. There's the agent, the main editor at the publishing company, the book editors, the typesetters, the printers." She ticked them off on her hand. "Plus there are all the people to whom we sent ARCs."

Arks? Whittaker thought. *What the hell?* "Arks? As in Noah and all those animals? Two by two?"

She smiled. "No, as in Advanced Reader Copies," she clarified. "Although I tried to keep quiet about the release, since I didn't want to jinx it, I know Aaron sent ARCs out. He wanted to get some good reviews for the back cover, so he sent it out to reviewers, his clients, and other book type people. He e-mailed me the list of who he sent it to, so I can forward it."

"Did it work? Did you get good reviews?"

"Some, yes. And it generated publicity for the book."

He could see pride and enthusiasm shining in her eyes before the animation stilled.

"Now these murders are going to cause even more publicity," she said.

"Has anyone commented on that?"

"Aaron has." She looked over at him. "But not seriously, James. And that was just when Seth was murdered. He won't say that now that Solange died. She was my friend. Sort of. And he knew her."

"Did he?" Whittaker said, his interest piqued. He knew he didn't like that man. Not that it was jealousy like Freeman claimed. Just because Kaufman spent so much time with Cassie, that didn't bother him.

"They met once when he and I were having dinner together."

"You had dinner with him?" He winced inwardly at the accusation in his voice. Especially since she caught it and looked at him curiously.

"Sure. Aaron often conducted business over meals. Mainly for the tax write-off, I suppose. Anyway, Solange came over, I'm sure with the intention of finding out if he was my boyfriend. If he had been, she'd have done her best to steal him from me. I told you about the animosity between us."

"Yes, I know."

"I really regret it all now," Cassie said and stared at the floor. "It was all so stupid."

Incredibly stupid, Cassie thought. Their petty rivalry was stupid. *Nothing like death to teach you what's important.* She had thought her mother's death was horrible, but the suddenness and violence of murder made these deaths worse. Was Aaron to blame?

"Do you suspect Aaron?" she asked. Conversation stopped as the server brought their food. She considered the possibilities as the steaming plates were placed in front of them. Aaron would qualify as someone she knew, and someone who might think that the killing was necessary. He'd look at it as a marketing effort.

"Do you?" he countered after the server topped up their water glasses and left them in peace.

She picked up her fork, trying to interpret his facial expressions. "Honestly, I don't think he has the balls to do it."

It didn't produce the reaction she expected. She couldn't decide if he suddenly had to burp or smother a laugh. Since he reached for his coffee cup, she suspected the latter.

"You may be right about that," he said with one final cough. "Anyway, if you can send me the list of everyone who received those…ARCs, I'd appreciate it. And now that we covered that, what's up with you and the psychic? Do you actually believe in that stuff?"

She took a bite of her food to delay the conversation a moment more. "No, not really. I just, well, I wanted to do something. I know you and Detective Freeman are working hard, but I knew these people. And somehow, I feel at fault."

"It's not your fault, Cassie."

"It's related to me, it has to be. You think that. I think that. So does the Psychic Consortium."

"And who, exactly, are the members of this Psychic Consortium?"

She admired his ability to remain inscrutable asking the question, but somehow, she didn't think he'd be able to maintain that façade when she told him the answer. "Well, Linda Kowalski is the, um, head of the Psychic Consortium."

"Linda Kowalski. She's another one of Mr. Kaufman's authors, right?"

"Yes, and she writes mysteries where her main character is a psychic and uses her superpower—and not one like yours—to solve crimes."

"I wish it could work that way. They could just tell me how the crime took place, who did what to whom. Not that it would be admissible in court." He leaned back and smiled widely.

Cassie's stomach clenched as the dimples deepened. Not just because of the dimples themselves, but because Whittaker must have a good sense of humor under that stern exterior. And she found that more attractive than anything on the outside.

"I'd love to see Judge Howitzer get a case like that. He'd throw it out of his court."

"Well, it doesn't look like real psychics—if that's not an oxymoron—give that much information anyway. They…um, the predictions they gave were rather vague."

"Of course. That way they can later interpret them to say they were right."

"Well, I don't think Dorian, Houdini, and George really think that way." Cassie smiled at him and paused, trying to build up the tension before the big reveal. "They're birds."

He stopped with his hamburger halfway to his mouth. "I beg your pardon?"

"Birds."

"As in?" He set down the burger and flapped his arms.

She laughed. "Precisely."

He leaned forward, moving his tie to the side so it didn't drag on the plate. "So, the other members of the Consortium are birds that predict the future?"

Cassie waited to take a bite before answering him. In retrospect, away from Linda and her birds, it did seem ridiculous. "They are. They're all parrots, I think, and can talk. Dorian is amazing, actually. If you just heard him and didn't see him, you wouldn't realize it was a parrot speaking." She hadn't.

"And what did these Psychic Birdbrains say?"

She frowned at him over another forkful of *huevos rancheros*. "Be nice or I won't tell you."

He rolled his eyes. "Fine, what did the Psychic Consortium tell you?"

"Hey, these birds have a history of making predictions. And yes, some are really vague, like saying that there is a matter of national security right before 9/11. But some were pretty specific."

"Really?" Whittaker asked as he picked up his burger. "Like what?"

"Well, Houdini predicted an F-5 tornado. Dorian predicted the 2007 California wildfires and Hurricane Katrina."

"So they're meteorologist birds?"

"James." She had to defend the birds, Dorian especially. He really was a smart and beautiful bird. "He said about the fires that 'You have to move all those people out of there' and 'It's a fire, and all fires are bad' right before the fires started." She frowned at him as she saw a spark of humor light his eyes.

"It's a fire, and all fires are bad?" he repeated.

"Yes, and before an F-5 level tornado hit Greensburg back in 2007, Houdini asked Linda something like if anyone had ever seen an F-5." She frowned more as Whittaker placed a hand in front of his mouth, obviously trying to hide a smile. "Before Hurricane Katrina, Dorian said that you could be a meteorologist all your life and never see anything like this. That it would be a disaster of epic proportions. And Katrina definitely was... What's so funny?"

Whittaker laughed outright this time, and not even the dimples lessened her annoyance.

"It would be the perfect storm."

She set down her fork with a clatter. "What would be the perfect storm?"

"That's the end of the quote. 'You could be a meteorologist all your life and never see something like this. It would be a disaster of epic proportions. It would be...the perfect storm.'" He smiled at her. "It's from the movie of the same name."

"It's a movie quote?"

"They all are." He laughed again. "'It's a fire, mister, and all fires are bad,' is from *The Towering Inferno*, 1974. The quote, 'None of you has ever seen an F-5' is from *Twister*. Not sure what the national security line was from, that could be from anywhere. These birds must have been exposed to lots of movies. What did they tell you?"

She thought back. "Um, they said, 'Can't take no pleasure in killing. There's just some things you gotta do.' That's what Dorian said."

"'Don't mean you have to like it.'"

She slumped down in the chair. "Yes, that's what Houdini said. Where's that from?"

"*Texas Chainsaw Massacre*, 1974."

"Why do you know all this?" Cassie asked, flinging her hands up.

"I like disaster movies."

"What about, 'What do we say to them?' and the answer, 'Welcome to California?'"

"*War of the Worlds*, 1953. Good movie."

She grumbled to herself. "Great. Just great."

"Still, they must be smart birds if they can quote movies like that," he said. "Anyway, now you look cranky. Let's talk about something else. What story are you working on now?"

She liked that they were talking about something other than the case now, it made this feel less like an interrogation and more like two normal people having dinner. She wished it were a date.

"The third book in the Marty McCallister mysteries. *The Merlot Murders.* You might be able to tell that I like alliteration." She paused to see if he understood that term.

"Aren't all of us attracted to alliteration?"

She grinned at his cleverness. "Absolutely. Anyway, I've struggled for a while to figure out how to get the poison into the wine. Cork is rather porous, so that helped. But I was afraid most needles would break or the hole would show in the cork. Michelle suggested using one of those wine openers with the CO_2 cartridge."

She noticed he waited until she finished her food before he flagged down the waiter. Yes, his mother must have trained him right.

"I've seen those wine openers, but never used one. Seems rather high tech to me. I prefer the regular waiter's corkscrews."

"You like wine?" Cassie asked. Oh, she was doomed. "I would have thought beer more appropriate."

"I like beer too. It goes better with donuts, which all cops must like as well," he said dryly.

Cassie cocked her head to the side and smiled. She really liked his low-key sense of humor.

When the bill came, he managed to grab it before she did, immediately handing over his credit card. "I've got it, Cassie."

She wondered if he was getting the bill because he was being a gentleman, or was he doing so because it was a business expense and he could get reimbursed by work. She knew she was starting to think of him as more than a cop, but had no idea what was going on in his mind. She snorted to herself, did any woman ever know what was going on in a man's mind?

But she considered him as he leaned over and signed the check, the light glowing in his brown hair. Was he only thinking of her in terms of these murders? Did he think of her as a potential resource? A potential suspect?

A potential girlfriend?

She got up slowly, not wanting the evening to end. She cheered up when she realized they still had to go to the impound lot. Not that an impound lot was the ideal setting for their first date. But it would give them more time together.

chapter 15

Thanks to the city's budget cuts, there was even more together time in store for Cassie and Whittaker. The darkness of the impound lot wasn't just due to its location under the Jones Falls Expressway. It was locked up tight for the night.

"Shit, they closed early." Cassie glanced over at Whittaker, worried what he might think of her cursing. Since he seemed more amused than perturbed, she figured he heard much worse than that at the police station. "I guess I need to do the damsel in distress thing a bit longer. Can you drive me home?"

"My pleasure."

Was it? she wondered as he drove back to her house. She knew she enjoyed being with him, but did he consider spending time with her just part of the job? She wished she could figure out how he felt towards her. And not whether he thought she was guilty. She was fairly certain he didn't.

Which reminded her: they both had more important things to worry about than a burgeoning attraction.

She slid past him as he held her car door open. "Do you want to come in? I can print out that e-mail from Aaron. Get you the list of people who received the book early."

She thought she detected a faint expression of unease as he glanced around the area, but he followed her up the stairs to the stoop of her rowhouse. As she stuck the key into the lock, a fresh wave of panic hit her.

Oh God, the house. She never had finished cleaning up from the search. Oh well. She turned the key.

"Come on in, excuse the mess," she said, as Donner ran up to her, mewling pitifully. "I could blame it on the crime scene crew, but the clutter is mostly my fault."

The presence of a new person didn't seem to bother Donner as much as his culinary needs did. She hurried back to the kitchen to feed him. That filled up the initial uncomfortable time as she realized that she and Whittaker were alone. "Let me go print out the information from Aaron," she said and escaped upstairs.

She found the e-mail, then ran to the bathroom while it was printing. She sighed as she glanced in the mirror. As always, her hair was a mess; it never behaved on humid days. Which in Baltimore, meant the entire summer.

She went back down and noticed he had taken off his suit jacket and neatly folded it over the arm of the sofa. "Can I get you anything? Coffee, tea?" *Or me,* she finished the pattern in her head, then squashed the thought. It wasn't appropriate.

Walking back to her kitchen to see what else she had to offer, Cassie called out, "I also have orange juice, milk. Oh, and of course, I have wine." She straightened, holding a bottle of her favorite German white. "I could show you the high-tech wine opener."

That appeared to pique his interest. "And show me the way you can poison the wine?"

"I'd be happy to." Dropping the printed e-mail on the counter, she opened a drawer and grabbed the wine opener. She quickly ran through the method. "Then using a turkey baster bulb, you can force the liquid into the bottle."

"And the hole's not noticeable? I'm disturbed it's that easy."

"It shows a bit. But only if you look really carefully. Honestly, cork already has small holes in it, so you might think it's just normal wear and tear." She smiled at him. "So, would you like some wine, or are you still on the job?"

"Since Riesling is my favorite white wine, I'd love a glass."

Even more things in common, she thought with pleasure as she popped the CO_2 cartridge back into the opener. "Let me grab some glasses and you can use the nifty wine opener."

"So I just press down on the button?" he asked.

"Yes. Just a quick press. The pressure from the carbon dioxide ejects the cork." She reached into the cabinet for glasses.

"Nothing's happening."

"Nothing's happening?" She turned around and noticed he was now firmly holding down on the button. She gasped. "Let go before it—"

A geyser of liquid erupted from the bottle.

Cassie had one moment to admire the splash, spray, and sparkle of the fountain of wine before it went everywhere. On her, on Whittaker, on the cabinets, the counters, the floor. Donner squeaked in protest and ran out of the kitchen as wine landed on him.

"Explodes," she finished weakly.

Here was an interesting spatter pattern, she thought as she watched Riesling run down her walls. Grabbing the paper towel roll, she started mopping up what must have been over half the bottle of wine, starting with herself.

Whittaker snatched some towels to help clean up, refusing to look at her.

Which was good. She wasn't certain she could maintain if they had made eye contact. As is, her stomach hurt from the effort of holding back. In silence, they wiped down the walls, floor, and cabinets. She sent a silent prayer of thanks that she had moved her laptop upstairs.

But once the wine had been wiped up, she couldn't take it any longer. "I'm sorry, James, but I have to laugh."

And she slid right down to the floor and broke, almost howling in laughter. She couldn't help it. Whittaker always seemed so careful, so precise. And now this…

She hiccuped loudly and tried to catch her breath. Seeing him standing there red-faced and with an expression of chagrin just started her off again. It took a while before she was able to stop and stand up. One final giggle escaped before she noticed his shirt.

"You're soaked!"

He glanced down with a rueful smile. "Appears so."

"Why don't you take it off?" At his narrowed eyes, she rolled her own. "And I'll wash it, Detective Whittaker. I'm not trying to hit on you." *Unfortunately.*

"That's not necessary. To wash my shirt, that is."

"How about if I at least dry it? I can loan you a shirt in the meantime." At his frown, she laughed again. "Right, you're not wearing girl clothes. Just let me just have it."

He hesitated for a second, then unbuttoned his shirt and handed it to her.

As she took it from his hands, their fingers brushed, and an electric shock pulsed through her arm. She had thought the phrase about "sparks flying" was cliché, but now she wasn't so sure. Staring into his eyes, she was certain the feeling wasn't one-sided. After one humming moment, they both looked away.

Cassie distracted herself from the current that was pulsing in the air and headed to the small door off of her kitchen. She ducked her head as she went down to the dug-out basement. She tossed the shirt into a dryer with a fabric sheet, hoping that would take some of the wine smell out, and thought about Whittaker.

He seemed attracted to her. However, knowing how proper he acted, she bet he was considering how it would look if he pursued anything. After all, she was connected to two current cases he was investigating. Although she didn't believe the General Orders stated anything against outside relationships with witnesses, he would still worry what people thought. Considering his reaction to Golden West Cafe, and outside her house, he seemed very concerned about appearances.

When she got back upstairs, he had finished pouring what was left of the wine. He had moved into the living room and was petting Donner, who seemed extremely content with the caresses. She took advantage of Whittaker's momentary distraction to admire the stretch of the white T-shirt across his broad shoulders before crossing over.

"I've got it in the dryer; it should only be about twenty minutes or so." She took the glass he handed her. "Maybe we can talk about non-murder things."

He raised an eyebrow. She was already beginning to think that habit of his was incredibly sexy. "Like what?"

"Well, do you like sports? Football, baseball?" She walked back to the sofa and settled down, tucking her legs under her and spreading her skirt around.

He settled back into the cushions of the armchair. "Well, I'm born and bred in Baltimore, so naturally, I'm an Orioles fan."

"Even if they can't manage to put together a .500 season?" She grinned to take some of the sting away; the O's were her team, too.

"Yes, even if they can't manage to put together a .500 season. I keep thinking this will be the year, and then they just crash and burn. But I keep the faith anyway. How about you?"

"Also an O's fan even though I was born in Atlanta. My grandfather keeps trying to convince me that I'm a Braves fan. But since I hate the Braves only a little less than I hate the Yankees, I don't see that happening any time soon."

"You were born in Atlanta? You don't sound like a southerner."

"My mother is, well, she was. She died when I was ten." She accepted Whittaker's condolences, which sounded sincere. She figured he had a lot of practice stating he was sorry for someone's loss. "But she's originally from Alabama. My dad's from around here, but wanted to go to college in a new part of the country, see something new. They met at Auburn University where they both were studying education. After they graduated, they taught school in Atlanta for a few years, but my father never fit in down there."

"I've heard it's hard for outsiders to feel welcomed." Whittaker scratched Donner when the cat jumped into his lap.

"Seems like it was that way for my dad. That's why he convinced my mother to move up here. I don't think my Grandmother Julia has forgiven him yet. And once…once my mother died, well, Grandmother wanted me to move down there, even talked about fighting him for custody. But there was no way I was going to leave my father."

She sipped her wine to wet her throat. Even now, it was hard to talk about her mother's death. "How about you, what's your family situation?"

"My family?"

She heard the discomfort in his voice. Had she been too forward? "I'm sorry, I don't mean to pry or anything."

He shrugged. "It's okay, you're not prying. Besides, you shared personal information with me, now and during interview. It's probably time to even out that score. What would you like to know?"

"Well, you said you were born here?"

"Yup. Right here in Balamer, hon." She laughed at his authentic-sounding Baltimore accent. Then he cleared his throat and spoke in a more serious voice.

"I was born in Maryland General Hospital on July 21st, just about thirty years ago."

Two years older than she was, Cassie realized. That was a good age difference. "Coming up on your big three-oh, huh?"

He shrugged. Men never seemed to worry about their ages as much as women did.

"Are your parents from around here too?"

"Yes."

The short answer surprised her. "What do they do?"

"My mom's an administrative assistant. My father works as a bartender."

"Really? I would have pegged you as a second or third generation cop."

She saw his fingers tighten around the stem of the wineglass, but all he did was raise it to his lips, drain the last mouthful, and set it down with a deliberate click on the coffee table.

"Well, you're right, actually. My grandfather was a cop. My dad was a cop, then he retired and became a bartender."

She was taken aback by the sudden forced quality to his words, almost like he was working hard at sounding casual. What happened between him and his father to make him so tense?

"And do your parents live in this area?" She kept her voice light and conversational; she didn't want him to close off from her.

He visibly relaxed when she didn't pursue the topic. "Yeah, they both still live in this area, although they're no longer together. They divorced when I was eighteen."

It was her turn to offer condolences. "I'm sorry."

"Yeah, well, it happens. I was actually at the academy at the time, so I didn't have to watch it or anything. My sister Chloe wasn't so lucky. She was still at home, so she had to deal with it. Even if she didn't have to hear it."

She wondered what he meant by that. Before she could ask, he continued.

"She's deaf," he explained. "She told me it was one time where she really appreciated it, since she didn't have to hear them argue."

"She's deaf?" she repeated. Then, putting down her wine, she lifted her hands and signed to him. *Do you know American Sign Language?*

He laughed before he signed back. *Yes, family learned ASL when we learned Chloe was deaf.*

He spelled out Chloe, then put his hand in the sign for the letter "C" and rubbed his cheek. Cassie figured that must be the name sign for his sister.

The time went quickly as they signed back and forth. She learned his sister was ten years younger than he was and that she attended Gallaudet University. They also exchanged each other's name signs. His was the letter "J" signed next to his eyes, for his unique gray eyes. Cassie's, not surprisingly, was the letter C signed next to her hair. He laughed when she indicated that she and Michelle had learned ASL just as another way to talk, especially in class.

Since they were being so quiet signing back and forth, it was easy to hear the buzz of the dryer. Reluctantly, she went and got his shirt.

She handed it to him, being careful not to touch this time. After he shrugged into the shirt, she watched in fascination as his dexterous fingers ran down his body, closing buttons. She stood there, imagining those fingers of his sliding down her own body, cleverly pushing her buttons. Enjoying that mental image, it took her a few moments to realize he was talking to her.

"I said, can you do me a favor?"

"Of course, what do you need?"

"Since you seem to be connected to these murders, I worry about your safety. Have you ever taken any self-defense courses?"

"No, but do you really think that's necessary? I don't think the killer is going to go after me, just my contacts." She took a moment to consider it. Maybe the killer was saving her for last. "Unless I'm the climax of the story. The final murder."

"That thought occurred to me, as well. And regardless, it won't hurt for you to be prepared. I know someone who teaches RAD class. Have you ever heard of it?" He walked over to his suit jacket. She was sad to see him putting on more clothes, the reverse had been more pleasant.

She shook her heard.

"It stands for Rape Aggression Defense class, but it teaches a woman how to defend herself from any aggressive action. In fact, my sister has taken the class a number of times, so that she can feel secure walking around. People often think they can take advantage of a deaf person. Chloe will prove them wrong if they ever try to take her on."

Could be interesting. And would be great research. "It sounds good. I've never taken self defense."

"I know the instructor at Anne Arundel Community College, June Erlensen. You should take her course, she's good. A former co-worker of mine. RAD classes are often taught by cops."

"Hmm...I like the idea. In fact, I'll ask Linda to join me. She'd probably enjoy the research of it as much as I would. Plus, I think she's lonely."

"The Bird Lady?"

She frowned at him, but didn't notice any responding sign of guilt. "She's a nice woman. And don't discount the birds. Maybe they'll solve the murder before you do."

"Now that's competition I never expected to have. Gives me yet another reason to solve these murders. Another reason." He gave her a long look as he emphasized his words. "Lock up behind me."

She leaned up against the door and smiled widely. He was concerned about her safety, that must mean something, right? Then again, he was a cop, sworn to protect and serve. Maybe that's all this was.

But what did he mean about "yet another reason to solve the murders"? She knew what she wanted him to mean, that he'd be free to date her then. Is that how he meant it?

She rushed to the phone to call Michelle and analyze the evening.

Check ARC list

MONDAY 10 JULY 09:27:12

chapter 16

He forced his face into blandness and his stride to a saunter as he entered the bullpen the next morning, expecting Freeman to be on him like white on rice about his meeting with Cassie.

But his partner merely said good morning. He didn't even glance up from his paperwork.

Whittaker relaxed and crouched down to turn on his computer.

"Did you see that pretty Ms. Ellis yesterday?"

He jerked up, banging his head into the bottom of the already banged up metal desk. Rubbing the spot of impact, he tried for casual. "Why do you ask?"

Freeman's grin was huge and knowing. "Why do I ask? Oh, I don't know, because you had left here with the intention of seeing her, returning her book, and asking her who might have gotten the book early? Then I didn't see or hear from you again. And since I'm your partner in this investigation, I figured maybe you should share what happened last night." He laced his hands behind his head and leaned back, propping his feet on the desk. The grin went wider. "*Everything* that happened."

He scowled at his partner. "Nothing happened, Freeman. You know I would never break the rules."

Freeman's grin vanished as he settled his feet back down. "Boy, no one is comparing you to your father. They're not going to judge you if you started a relationship with her. She didn't kill anyone, other than in fiction."

Whittaker kept his voice low. "No, but we can't prove that. I'm not starting on that path. And I'm not going to have anyone say that I did."

"Whittaker..." Freeman paused, shook his head, then let out a long sigh. "Okay, fine, nothing happened. Did she say anything useful?"

Whittaker was glad his partner dropped the conversation. It had nothing to do with Cassie. He just didn't want to talk about his father. Ever. But he could talk about the case.

"She provided an e-mail from her agent. It lists who received the books prior to the public release." He fished the wrinkled paper from his briefcase and slid it across to Freeman.

The older man picked up the sheet gingerly, using only two fingers. "What the hell spilled on this?" He sniffed suspiciously at the paper.

Whittaker was saved from answering when the phone rang. Gratefully, he snatched it up. At the voice on the other end, he glanced over at Freeman. "Um, hello, Ms. Ellis."

"Uh-oh, we're back to Ms. Ellis, are we?"

A musical laugh floated over the connection. Whittaker quickly clamped the receiver more firmly to his ear so the sound didn't leak out. All he needed was for Freeman to hear Cassie laughing like that and his partner would tease him mercilessly.

"Now, we don't need to be that formal, do we, *Jimmy*?" she went on. "I thought we were past that...Jimbo."

He grimaced and swiveled his chair to turn his back on his grinning partner. "Fine, Cassie, you win. How can I help you?"

"Actually, you already have. First, I wanted to thank you for taking me to the impound lot last night, even though they were closed. Thank God they were open when I biked there this morning. I don't want to talk about how much it cost."

"I don't blame you."

"Also, I wanted to thank you for e-mailing me the contact information for June Erlensen. I already called and signed up for the RAD class. It starts tomorrow afternoon, so the timing is perfect."

"I'm glad to hear that. I always think it's a good idea for women to take the class."

"Oh, definitely. And this day class is geared to help older women protect themselves, so it's perfect for Linda. It should be beneficial for both of us. I've done some research on the class—"

"Research. Of course you have," he interrupted with a chuckle.

"Okay, so I research everything. But that website showed some demo videos and it looked very effective. I can't wait to take the class and kick some butt."

"Well, don't practice on innocent bystanders, okay?" He turned back around. Tucking the phone between his ear and shoulder, he started pulling out the rest of the paperwork from his briefcase. "I'd hate to arrest you."

He winced. That wasn't the best thing to say to someone he'd already pulled into interview twice. He was relieved when she laughed again.

"I won't," she said. "Wouldn't want you to handcuff me."

That created an interesting mental image. Whittaker cleared his throat and reminded himself he was at work, and people were starting to stare. Of course they were, he thought darkly, with Freeman chuckling like a fool and waving at everyone around him to take notice. *I'm going to kill you,* he mouthed at his partner.

Aloud, he said, "I'll talk to you later if we find out anything regarding the information you provided last night."

The sigh that came over the line was so deep he had no trouble visualizing the eye roll that went with it.

"Uh-oh, we're getting all formal again. Fine, Detective Whittaker, I look forward to anything you may discover. And if I think of anything else, I'll be sure to contact you."

As he hung up the phone, he fixed Freeman with his nastiest, meanest glare. "Don't. Say. Anything."

"Whi—"

"Ah-ah!" Whittaker held up a hand. "Don't."

"Fine, but—"

"Not another word, Freeman." Whittaker turned his snarl on the room at large and the smirking faces turned in his direction. "There's nothing to see here, people. Move along and go about your jobs." He ignored the snickers from the other detectives. Whose idea was an open bullpen anyway?

His partner gently cleared his throat.

"Can I say something about the list?"

"The list?" Whittaker relaxed a little. "What? Do you see something?"

"Well, there seems to be some overlap between Cassie's day planner and this list. I thought she said she hadn't told anyone about the book until last week."

Whittaker came around the desks to look over Freeman's shoulder. His partner had circled six names. "She didn't. But her agent did, for publicity. These people on the list received the ARCs—Advanced Reader

Copies," he explained for his partner's benefit, "two months prior to the book release."

"That would give someone plenty of time to plan a murder or two." Freeman tapped the list with the end of his pen. "Hmm, we had planned on interviewing these six again today anyway, since they were in the planner. We didn't get a vibe from them before, so I'll take Officer Payne and do the interviews while you research these other people. You're better on the computer. Make me a copy of the list…a non-sticky one, please."

Whittaker stood at the copier and glanced around the bullpen. Someone had something hot, he thought as Wertz slam down his phone in excitement. He watched as Wertz and Garcia grabbed their jackets before running for the door. He flattened himself against the wall to let them race past.

Wondering what case had such urgency, he glanced at the board at their caseload.

Then he cursed his stupidity and cleared the jam out of the feeder. He was an idiot for trying to use it on the sticky ARC list. He flattened out the ARC list and laid it directly on the glass. Finally getting two copies, he ran the wine-covered paper through the shredder, hoping that was the end of that screw-up. Stupid fancy corkscrew.

After handing a copy to Freeman, he settled in for a long search session at his computer. Instead, he started thinking about Cassie. Last night had been…intriguing. He couldn't deny his attraction to her, at least not physically. When she had said she wasn't hitting on him, he had been rather disappointed.

Although he didn't know what he would do if she did hit on him. He knew that neither he nor Freeman believed that Cassie was guilty of these murders. But until they could prove her innocence, other cops—or worse, his higher-ups—might suspect her. Maybe even think he was covering up for her.

He'd never do that, he thought, curling his fingers on the keyboard. He'd never cover up a crime for anyone, no matter how physically attracted he was. Although he suspected his attraction to Cassie was becoming more than just physical. He had a good time talking to her, spending time with her, getting to know more about her.

Okay, the wine episode had sucked. While she had found it amusing, it would be a while before he could laugh at it.

He had enjoyed her reaction though. She had a lovely laugh, even when it was at his expense. And he liked her energy…and her intelligence and curiosity about everything around her. Plus, he appreciated her tact.

He was certain she had caught his reluctance to talk about his dad, and she must have suppressed her own curiosity to let the topic go.

He sighed. It was time for him to let this topic go and focus on what he was really supposed to be doing. He glanced at the list and started entering names into the search engine.

Years of training allowed him to concentrate on what he was reading and ignore the constant chatter and noise around him. He did look up an hour later, when Wertz and Garcia came back in, flushed with success. He applauded along with others as they marked off a case that was just about to go into the cold file.

Taking a moment to get a refill on his coffee, he congratulated them on their victory. Then he sat back down and hoped for a one of his own.

The ARCs had gone out to a number of people who were well placed in the publishing world. Some of the names—or at least who they worked for—Whittaker recognized without benefit of Google. He was impressed despite himself. Aaron Kaufman might be a self-absorbed jerk, but he sure did his job well.

He decided, for now, to concentrate on those on the list who were less than five hours away. He doubted someone would come from Seattle to murder two people, especially not with a three-day gap in between. He would expect the killings to have been timed closer together if someone came to town specifically to commit murder.

Unless…there was some type of publishing conference going on…

To his dismay, he discovered a National Library Association conference going on at the Baltimore Convention Center that week.

Shit, never mind eliminating anyone off these lists. He made a note to check registration against all the names. For now, he went back to the Internet.

Every person listed had blogs and he spent a lot of time reading them. Interestingly enough, a number of the people posted their review of Cassie's book that very morning or the day before. And the blog entries all included links to *The Baltimore Dispatch* review and their coverage of the murders.

Great, he thought, *the murder coverage and Cassie's involvement went viral.*

He said the same to Freeman when he and Payne came back in from interviews.

Freeman wrinkled his brow and glanced at Officer Payne. "Viral? Like the flu?"

"No, more like funny videos." At Freeman's blank look, Payne pointed at the computers. "You know, when someone e-mails all of their friends about this cat eating broccoli, then those twenty people forward the video to all their friends, who forwards it to all their friends. And it gets posted everywhere online too. Anyway, do you need me to help recap what we found out in the interview, Detective Freeman? Or should I begin to call those contacts?"

"I got it. Thanks for your help." Freeman took the notes and papers the young officer handed over and tossed them on his desk. "Going viral. Huh. Why is it there are all these new sites and terms on the Internet, but nothing that helps us?"

"What would you like to see?" Whittaker asked. "Something like FaceCrook, where criminals log in and post their crime status? Or how about a site for prisoners to network together? We'll call it ClinkedIn."

Freeman didn't get it, but Payne almost snorted up his coffee.

"Tell me what you found out during your interviews."

"Well, I let the rookie here get some experience dealing with the press, since we had to go visit Christine Schmidt again. He took lead, and it was easier this time, since we weren't trying to hide the connection to Ms. Ellis. I guess we're improving her reputation again. She said she was at a book conference at the convention center all day—"

"The National Library Association conference," Whittaker cut in.

"Yeah! How'd you know that?"

Whittaker folded his arms and leaned back in his chair. "I know everything, Freeman."

Freeman scowled at the computer. "Anyway, genius, Ms. Schmidt gave us contact information for a few people who would have seen her there. Payne's contacting those people. Right, Payne?"

Payne gave a quick salute from where he sat, already on the phone.

"I love rookies. Anyway, I suppose she could make it there and back, but it would be risky. We've requested security camera tapes, but of course they want a warrant before they give them to us. Ms. Schmidt stated she hadn't met nor heard of Solange Gavreau until Saturday, when she heard about the murder on the news. On a more interesting note, Ms. Ellis' medical experts, Liam Brody and Paul Larson, are each other's alibis again. Hey, where'd you get dessert?" Freeman stopped abruptly when Garcia walked by with a plateful of key lime pie.

Garcia pointed towards the common area and hastily swallowed. "Morris brought it back from his honeymoon."

The rest of the detectives in the area swarmed out of their chairs.

Freeman started to get up, but Whittaker shook his head. He wanted to hear the rest of this.

His partner looked wistfully towards the back of the room. "Fine. But it's your fault if I miss pie. So, Larson claims he had dinner at Brody's house. Evidently their wives are friends too, and went out for a girl's weekend. Brody confirmed the same thing independently when I posed the same question to him. And both of them knew of Solange Gavreau before this Saturday, since Ms. Ellis had mentioned her to them."

There was an interesting possibility, Whittaker thought. "We hadn't considered two people working in conjunction. It might make sense. One could follow the vic, the other could follow Ms. Ellis to make sure that she doesn't have a solid alibi."

"Or both follow the vic and one plays lookout. Both of them are instructors at a local university, as well as being paramedics, and both used the university as their whereabouts for Montgomery's murder. I confirmed that they had been there during the day, and thought the timing would be rather tight to get to Montgomery's location if they had snuck out between classes. Besides, neither of them sounded guilty, but I could be wrong there. But how would either of them get Cassie's day planner?"

Whittaker grabbed the folder and flipped through the pages. "Well, perhaps when she saw Larson, on Tuesday, the day before the first murder. She listed a Fourth of July party at his house that day."

"And Brody could've been there too, since he and Larson are friends. If I had to pick one, by the way, I'd head towards Larson, based on our conversation. He seemed rather fond of Ms. Ellis, perhaps overly so. Praised her a lot, said she was like a daughter to him."

"Like a normal type of interest or more like fanatically obsessed?"

Freeman shrugged. "Seemed normal, but who knows."

"Interesting. Let me call Cassie…Ms. Ellis." Whittaker grabbed the phone, thankful that Freeman had booked immediately toward the pie and hadn't caught his slip-up.

She answered, but only said, "Wait a minute!"

He waited, listening to the click of computer keys for a full two minutes. Finally, she came back with an absent "Sorry? What?"

"Am I interrupting, Ms. Ellis?"

"What?" she repeated. "Oh, no, not really. Let me clue into reality again, I was just writing. You're calling me Ms. Ellis, so this must be something official. Is there news?"

"Not news, per se. I just have a few questions. First of all, you told us that you hadn't sent out any copies of the ARCs to your friends and family prior to Wednesday, right?" He opened his notebook to the correct section and prepared to jot down her answers.

"That's correct, but as you can see, my agent sent some out to reviewers, to make sure there was some advanced marketing on the book."

"And to some of your contacts?"

"Oh. Yes, to some of them. I wanted to make sure that my medical experts, in particular, saw the book before it was in final production. That way they could correct any mistakes I had made. Why? Do you suspect Paul or Liam?"

Why wasn't he surprised that she had jumped to that conclusion? "Should I?"

"No! God, no. I mean, I suppose both of them are…cold isn't the right word. They both have a dark sense of humor; comes from being emergency responders. So they joke about death, a lot, but I don't see them going off and killing someone. If I stretch my imagination, and I'm good at that, maybe Liam would be willing to kill Seth—no, Donner, you have to get down—oh!"

Whittaker listened, puzzled, as strange sounds like rustling paper, clicks, snaps, and muffled curses came over the line.

"Sorry about that." Cassie came back on a little breathlessly and picked right up where she'd left off. "—since Seth caused the sort of trauma that Liam worked hard to eliminate as a firefighter. But to then kill Solange? No way, for either of them. Definitely not Paul, he's got a weak spot for women."

Whittaker noted that down. "And one for you?"

He liked that she never just answered a question, she always took time to consider it fully.

"He's not physically attracted to me, if that's what you think. It's more he's adopted me. Plus he keeps trying to set me up with his son. Invited me to his Fourth of July party, things like—And that's another reason you're wondering, isn't it?" She sounded irritated. "Since perhaps he could've gotten the day planner there? Or Liam, for that matter, he was at the party as well."

"I'll ask again," said Whittaker. "Do you remember the last time you saw the day planner?"

The sigh she made must have been right against the transceiver, for it sounded like a sudden burst of static.

"Aaron and I determined that I had it Monday at his office. That would be the last time I can recall seeing it."

He wrote that down and noted to himself that she had chosen to talk about the case with her agent.

"Do you often see Aaron?"

He could hear Cassie ask "What?" at the same time that his partner exclaimed "What? Where the hell did that come from?" out of a pie-filled mouth.

Whittaker winced, that was not one of the questions he had planned to ask. "I meant, do you often see Paul and Liam?"

"No, not really. I met them when I took a CPR course and they were the instructors. I went up to them afterward and asked more questions, like I always do. Then, when I was working on *Mailbox Murders,* I met with them for lunch now and then to discuss those murders in detail. They gave me some great—although graphic and disgusting—ideas."

"And since then?"

"I haven't seen them recently, other than the Fourth. I called Paul a few times though."

Whittaker grabbed his copy of *Mailbox Murders* and paged to the back. "And you thanked both of them in the book?"

"I did. I thanked all my resources."

"That's good to know. Thank you very much for your assistance, Ms. Ellis."

He heard her laugh at his formality, then a quick snicker. He braced himself for her next teasing.

"It was my pleasure, Jamie-kins."

He cringed anyway. Hanging up, he froze in terror when he saw Freeman laughing hysterically. Had he overheard?

"What's so funny?" he demanded.

Tears running down his face, Freeman pointed at the computer. "A cat eating broccoli. I gotta send this to my friends."

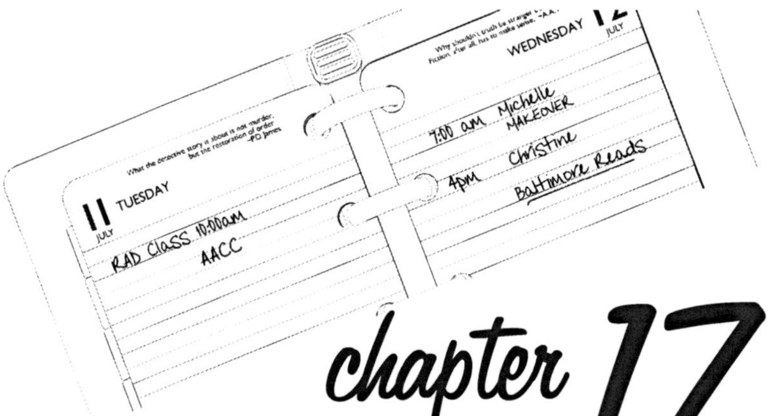

chapter 17

Cassie punched as hard as she could, knocking her opponent onto the ground. Before she could follow through with other moves, his partner moved in and stopped her.

"Very good, Cassie. Your turn, Linda."

Cassie had to admit, the RAD class was very beneficial. It gave her some exercise, some socialization with other women, and a whole lot of confidence.

And all that after one class.

She turned to watch Linda. It amused her to see such a serious expression of determination on the sweet, grandmotherly face as the older woman punched the instructor's mitt. Determined, hell. Even in her current getup of a bright green shirt and yellow leggings, Linda was fierce.

She must have dressed to match George the budgie, Cassie thought. Next to such intense color, her collegiate T-shirt and gray leggings made her feel dull and drab.

But her outfit hadn't affected her learning. She'd picked up a lot in a short time. How important it was to remain watchful, and how to alert others if approached by aggressive strangers. How to yell, not scream. How to escalate her defense in response to the stranger's attack. And how to disable the opponent and escape safely.

"Wow, you guys are awesome." June, a hard-edged female cop with short, choppy curls and a tightly muscled body, walked to the front of the room after each student had a chance to fight against her and her fellow instructor. She dropped the punching bag she carried. "You're all laying down some hard throws and punches. I wouldn't want to mess with you."

Cassie felt empowered. She had never felt graceful, in part because Michelle excelled at every sport while she was only good at bicycling. But these moves felt good. The more she practiced them, the more force she used, the more powerful she felt.

At the end of the class, June called them together. "Thank you for coming. You were all great. Don't forget that."

Cassie felt great. She glanced around at the faces of the other women, mostly older retirees: tired, flushed, some with their makeup smudged from sweat. But all looked different than they had at the beginning of the class.

"Now, remember, and this is important." June's face and tone turned serious. Her gaze caught and held Cassie's for a moment, then moved on to every woman in the group. "These techniques work because the opponent isn't expecting you to resist and doesn't know the techniques you'll use to escape. I'm not saying that your husband, father, co-worker, or friend is a rapist, but they might tell someone else, who might tell someone else who is. So please don't share these techniques with any men. That's it! Have a great rest of the day, ladies!"

Linda bent down to grab her purse and backpack and said to Cassie, "That's not a problem for me. No men in my life to tell, unless you count Dorian and Houdini."

Cassie didn't respond as she thought about the man she was starting to want in her life. She wished she knew for sure what he thought of her.

"Hmm…I'm not hearing a 'me too.'"

How did he think of her? She thought he'd enjoyed spending time with her the other night, and not because it might help him with the cases. They seemed to be interested in the same things, and it was easy to talk to him.

Of course, she'd thought that before with men, especially those she had a lot in common with, and ended up just buddies. She didn't want to be just buddies with Whittaker. But was she just attracted to him because he was a cop, since she had developed a thing for cops lately? Or was it more?

A sharp tap on her shoulder made her jump. "Who…what? Huh?"

"Is there a man in your life?" Linda adjusted the straps of her bags over her shoulders.

"Well, yeah, of course. There's my dad." Cassie tucked her hair behind her ear and plastered what she hoped was a bright, innocent expression on her face. At least the color there could be excused to exertion this time.

Linda waggled an admonishing finger at her. "I don't think so. That look on your face just a bit ago was not you thinking about your father."

"No, it was me thinking of a question I wanted to ask June. For my books. You'd probably be interested too, right?"

Cassie hoped she had successfully changed the topic as they walked over to the instructor, who was packing the gear they'd used in class into a large duffel bag. "June, can I ask a question?"

June straightened. "Sure, Cassie. What is it?"

"These techniques are really good, but what if the attacker has a weapon? Like a gun or a knife? I know that's probably advanced, but I was just wondering for my research."

Cassie was already planning how she could use what she'd learned tonight for her Marty McAllister books. Especially for the book she was working on right now, in which she planned to have Marty face an attacker with a knife.

"Good idea," Linda agreed. "I could use it for my main character as well."

"That's right, you're the two authors. I'm all for getting the facts accurate in books, even fiction. Hey, Vince!" June called over to the tall redhead, who had been helping pack up the gear.

Cassie felt sorry for him. He'd had to take the brunt of their attacks the entire evening by playing the bad guy.

"Vince will help me demonstrate, won't you? Get out your notebooks, ladies," said June, giving her assistant an evil smile. Cassie watched avidly as June demonstrated how to take the attacker by surprise and how to twist the body just right to disarm their opponent.

"I wish I brought a video camera," muttered Linda.

Cassie nodded. It would be handy to replay this when she was writing an action scene. "The other thing I wanted to know is…Vince is a man. And he's learned these techniques—"

Vince, still stretched out on the mat, started to laugh. "Thanks for noticing, Cassie. And yes, I do know these techniques. But trust me, with June swearing to hunt me down and make me suffer—I'm not crazy enough to tell a soul," he said, sitting up to rub his shins with one hand and his ribcage with the other. "Besides, I'm a police officer. I know all sorts of defensive techniques."

A police officer? Cassie thought, taking a closer look at the man. Yet she wasn't falling all over him with lust and attraction. He was cute, and funny, but she didn't feel anything for him like she did for Whittaker.

Thanking the instructors, Cassie and Linda headed out.

"Thanks for coming with me," Cassie told Linda as they emerged into the humid Maryland afternoon. A dark smear of storm clouds lined the horizon to the west.

"Thanks for asking me." Linda hitched the straps of her backpack a little higher. "So, what man is in your life? I don't have to be psychic to know you were hiding something."

Cassie had been hoping her new friend had forgotten her slip of the tongue. No such luck. "It's not that. Look, why don't we go get coffee…no, no coffee. You don't want to get coffee with me. People die when they have coffee with me."

"I'm not worried about that, dear. And you shouldn't blame yourself for some psychopath's actions."

"Why don't we go to McDonald's for lunch, and I'll let you know there."

"That's fine, dear. The one in Severna Park?"

Cassie nodded. "Yes."

"I'll see you there."

* * *

By the time Cassie got to McDonald's, she felt calm and composed. She'd used the time on the short drive to think about what she wanted to say. That was, once she argued herself out of not saying anything at all. She needed to talk to someone. And Linda seemed like the kind of person who would listen without being judgmental and maybe, just maybe, help her sort out her confused thoughts, emotions, and growing attraction to one James Whittaker.

Linda was already inside the air-conditioned interior and smiled a greeting as Cassie let the heavy glass door shut out the sticky afternoon.

"Put that wallet away," said Cassie as she saw Linda withdraw a small, embroidered wallet from her purse. "It's my treat. You were nice enough to give me a free reading."

Linda tucked her wallet back into her purse and smiled in agreement. Cassie paid, and after collecting their order, led the way to a table in the back, away from the hot slant of afternoon sun that seared most of the main seating area.

"So, what were you thinking about on the drive over?" Linda ripped the paper covering from her straw.

Cassie wished she didn't have such an expressive face, blaming that instead of any psychic abilities on Linda's part.

"It's not a big deal," Cassie snapped, then regretted it since the denial made it look like it was, and Linda looked hurt. "Sorry. Honestly, I was just thinking of Detective Whittaker. He's assigned to the murders, as you know, and I've seen him a lot since my day planner got me involved in those cases. Well, I see him and Detective Freeman, of course."

"I can totally understand thinking about Detective Whittaker. He looked very intelligent and serious when I saw him on the news. Although he's even better looking in person."

"Yes, he is," Cassie said, nibbling on a french fry. "An intelligent cop, I mean," she added hastily, fresh heat flooding not only her face, but her entire body.

"Of course," Linda said. "And since I can see you're not ready to talk about Whittaker, let's talk about the murders instead. Have the police had any luck solving them?" She dug into her salad.

"No, no luck solving the murders so far. I can't figure out why someone would kill Seth…or Solange." Cassie blinked back tears. It was interesting what the finality of death did to her feelings towards her former classmate.

"Really?"

That question put her back up as she prepared to leap to Solange's defense. "What do you mean really? Are you saying—"

Linda raised a hand. "Wait, Cassie, I'm not saying anything negative about your friend, more about you not being able to think of a reason. You're a murder mystery author; I'm sure you can find some motive."

That was a good point, Cassie thought. "Yes, of course I can think of some motive. I've had multiple conversations with the detectives about that. But I can't believe anyone with any of those motives would really do such horrible things. I know I write about people who have no social conscience, who destroy a life without a second thought…but I don't know anyone like that in real life."

"And I'm sure it's frustrating to you that you can't solve this particular crime. I mean, you can't write the ending and sum everything up."

Cassie picked up a napkin and shredded it into smaller and smaller pieces. "Yes…nor can I point the detective to the right place to find the clues."

"And since this 'story', let's say, is already written, you can't delete a scene, go back, and rewrite it."

Cassie swallowed past the lump in her throat and nodded again. If she could, she'd at least go back and be nicer to Solange.

"But you can't," Linda continued gently. "You can't change the past. And you can't blame yourself for what happened either, Cassie. You aren't the omnipotent, omniscient author of the real world, dear. People chose their own actions, not you."

Cassie closed her eyes. "I know…I do know that. But I want to do something to help, anything."

"Like what, solve the mystery?"

Her hands stilled. "That's an idea."

Linda set down her fork. "Cassie, I was joking."

"I'm not. We write whodunits for a living, so we should be able to figure out what steps to take, right?"

"Well, my stories won't provide us much instruction. After all, in my novels, we'd have a psychic who would be able to sense certain things about the crime and provide assistance. Neither I, nor the birds, were able to help too much there. I don't think this is a good idea, young lady. You should leave this to the detectives. They have the real skills needed to solve these murders."

"Not necessarily. After all, you and I both chose to have the protagonist in our stories be a regular person and not a police officer, right?"

"Right. But I do it because the reader can relate to the regular person more than a cop."

"And you also do it because civilians can do things a cop can't. They don't have to worry as much about procedure. And boy, does Detective Whittaker ever think about proper procedure." Too bad she kept thinking improper things about him. Cassie took a sip of soda and flushed those thoughts out of her mind.

"Yes, for a good reason."

"Right, cause there's all these rules of collecting evidence when you're a cop. Not so much for civilians. Plus people are often more forthcoming to a regular person than a cop. Besides, now that I've had some self-defense training, I can take care of myself."

Linda frowned. "That remains to be seen. And remember, one of the main points of our lesson today was not to put yourself in a dangerous situation. The instructor said that a number of times."

Cassie finished her food and pitched the trash in the receptacle. She stood up, firm in her resolution. Like her self-defense training, her decision to investigate made her feel powerful.

"Don't worry. I'm not going to do anything dangerous."

* * *

This wasn't dangerous, she thought as she drove through the quiet neighborhood of single homes. Paul was her friend. Therefore, it wasn't a bad idea for her to go to the paramedic's house and talk to him. Of course, she was here to interrogate—to interview him regarding two murders that he may have committed.

Well, she didn't really think he had anything to do with them. But Whittaker did. She figured that's why he had asked so many questions about Paul and Liam.

But why would either of them have committed murder? What would be the motive?

What did she know about Paul Larson? He was very protective of her, even fatherly. So perhaps he thought eliminating these two people was protecting her. He hadn't liked her spending time with Seth Montgomery. Neither had Liam. Her medical experts had often ganged up on her and lectured her about visiting a convicted criminal.

So, with that motive, Cassie could visualize what happened as she automatically followed the GPS commands to get to Paul's house.

> Paul decided to take matters in his own hands. If Cassie wasn't going to listen, he'd just go and eliminate the problem.
>
> Looking at the stolen day planner, he found Seth's address. He found the rundown house easily enough. Likewise, it was simple to break in. He found an ideal spot to hide and laid in wait.
>
> When Seth Montgomery walked in, Paul popped up from his hiding place, and gave the slimy arsonist one warning.
>
> "I know you've been meeting with Cassie. I want you to stay away from her."
>
> Seth sneered at the man, underestimating him. "I ain't seen Cassie in weeks."
>
> "Liar!" Paul yelled, holding out the day planner. "I see here that you met her today."
>
> Seth took the planner from Paul, frowned, and glanced down at it.
>
> While he was distracted, *probably trying to read*, Paul sneered to himself, he pulled the trigger.
>
> "That's your last appointment with Cassie," he said, and walked away, proud that he had protected his naive young friend from a bad influence.

She stopped at a red light and mulled it over. It was a possible scene. She knew Paul had fired guns before. He'd been in the Army and worked as a medical tech for years before he went civilian. Still, it just wasn't in keeping with Paul's character.

Especially if he had also killed Solange. Paul worshipped women. But…she had told him about Solange, had complained about her, if truth be told. So perhaps again, he was trying to protect her from a bad influence.

Once again, she started to visualize murder, then came to a sharp stop both in her mind and on the street as she started to go through the red light. She smiled apologetically at the driver who had honked at her.

When the light turned green, she went back to imagining. This time she had an even clearer picture of the scene, having been on site herself.

> "Look, bitch," Paul said.

Wait, Paul would never say that to a woman. Then again, if he was about to shoot one, he could probably curse at her.

> "Look, bitch," Paul said. "You've been cruel to Cassie one too many times."
>
> Solange stammered out an apology, reverting back to her native French in her panic. But Paul wasn't hearing it.
>
> "Women like you never change," he said and raised the gun.
>
> When Solange screamed and ran, he coolly discharged the contents of the clip into her back...

Cassie shuddered as she pulled up to the large brick house. Maybe this wasn't such a good idea. No, Paul wouldn't have done any of that. But if he had, she wanted to catch him. Stop him.

She walked up the flagstone path, knocked on the door, and fought the urge to flee.

"Cassie!" Obviously pleased to see her, Paul waved an arm and quickly ushered her into his house. "Come in. What are you doing in my neighborhood?"

She tried to return his greeting. Then turned and saw Mary, Paul's wife, standing silhouetted in the kitchen with a knife in her hand. Cassie sucked in a breath. Would Mary have been in on it too? She let out that breath when Mary stepped forward, an apron around her plump frame.

"It's so good to see you," the woman said, pleasure shining in her brown eyes. "Paul was just talking about you."

"Was he?" Cassie tried to ask casually. "Oh. Well, I was just driving through the area and thought I'd stop by."

"Do you have some more questions for me?" Paul asked eagerly. He always appeared to enjoy her questions, the more graphic the better.

Mary shook her head, then reached up one hand to pat her bun back into place. "If you do, I'm going to finish cooking dinner. Will you stay?"

"No, but thank you. I have some questions for Paul, so I'll just ask him and get out of your way, if that's okay."

"Of course. Paul, you go sit down with Cassie. I'll bring you both some lemonade and cookies." She turned around and walked back into the kitchen.

Cassie followed the silver-haired man into the family room and immediately felt more comfortable. Well-worn sofas, pretty fabrics, and family pictures made the space relaxing and homey.

She loved this house, the feeling of it. Paul and Mary had raised three children in this house and still entertained them and their grandchildren on plenty of occasions. Cassie had been invited to a number of those events since Paul wanted to set her up with his son, John. She hoped eventually John would admit to his father that he was gay so Paul would stop his matchmaking efforts.

Paul took the nearby recliner and stretched out his long body. She chose to sit on the couch since it was closer to the door. "It was good seeing you at the Fourth of July party. I can't believe you didn't say a word then that the book release was so soon. I've been waiting for you to say when it was coming out."

"Well, I didn't want to tell anyone about it, didn't want to jinx it." She smiled her thanks at Mary when she brought in the cookies and lemonade.

Paul picked up an oatmeal raisin cookie and nibbled on it. "So, what brings you here? More questions on murder?"

She hesitated. "Well, yes, but not fictional this time."

"I assume you're talking about Seth Montgomery's murder and your college friend's death," he said slowly.

She nodded and grabbed the lemonade sitting in front of Paul, just in case. "I am. I'm, well, I'm concerned, of course. About their deaths, and worried about others that I've used for my research, like you and Liam."

Paul reached for the other lemonade and took a sip. "Do the police think the killer is targeting your contacts?"

"It's a possibility," she admitted. "After all, I was the last to see both of them."

He grinned. "Should I be worried that you're visiting me, then?"

"Paul! Please don't joke about it. I'm worried."

He sobered up and rubbed a hand over his chin. "Don't you worry, Cassie. I'm careful."

That's what worried her. She casually set her lemonade, without drinking, on the oak side table. "Anyway, I was thinking, with your experience as a paramedic, seeing murder scenes like this, you might have a good perspective about what's happening."

"Well, Cassie, I think someone is shooting people."

"Paul," she admonished. "This isn't the time for your sick sense of humor."

"Okay, so maybe I know more than that."

Her entire body tensed up. "You do?"

"I started to look up the report from the first call after the detectives came to talk to me after Montgomery's death. The report was still in the bin and hadn't been sent for storage. But…I didn't read it all. I felt guilty when I started to read it, so I put it down. I knew better. It was just hard to resist. I was worried for you. I know you."

"And you knew them," she said, then immediately regretted it. Was she showing too much of her hand?

He peered at her from above his bifocals. "No. I didn't really know them. Just what you told me. Anyway, the report was pretty standard anyway. There's probably nothing in there that the police didn't tell you. He was killed in his living room. They even noted how filthy his place was. He had been shot two times, once in the chest and once in the abdomen. They pronounced him DOA…well, technically the Medical Examiner did that when he arrived, but it was rather obvious to the paramedics."

"I'm sure it was." Cassie swallowed and bit her lower lip. "It was…it was obvious with Solange, too. That she was dead. I was…I was actually there when Solange was killed. Well, not *there* there. Just in the parking garage. I called 9-1-1." She twisted her hands in her lap and knotted her fingers. "I thought about doing CPR, but it was too late…she was obviously dead."

"I can understand you not wanting to do CPR on her if she was visibly wounded," said Paul with gentle sympathy.

Cassie shuddered. "Oh, she was visibly wounded all right."

"Give me a second." Standing up, he headed out of the room and upstairs.

Cassie froze. Had she said something she shouldn't have? Was he going for the gun? Should she call the police?

She jumped as something pressed up against her neck. Turning slowly, she laughed when she realized it was the family cat. Trying to calm herself, she gave the Siamese a few strokes and prepared to run if needed.

But when Paul came down, he was just carrying some papers. Handing them to her, he sat back down in the recliner. "These are pamphlets from the National Center for the Victims of Crime. It's for the family and friends of murder victims. I know you weren't that close to Solange, and definitely not to Seth, but I thought you'd still benefit from talking to someone about these murders."

Cassie saw the caring on his face, heard it in his voice. And knew she had been right, Paul would never kill anyone. She sighed in relief.

"Thank you, Paul. But I think what will make me feel better is when the killer is caught. Do you have any ideas of who it could be?" She leaned down and tucked the pamphlet in her purse.

"Well, it had occurred to me, for a second at least, that it was you."

"Me?" She jerked back upright and caused the cat to bolt from the room. "You thought I did it?"

"Well, you have to admit, Cassie, you are a bit obsessed with murder. And you like your research. I thought—just for a moment, mind you—that perhaps you had taken your research a bit too far. But then I remembered how squeamish you'd get at some of our descriptions of murder and accident scenes. And of course, you're much too nice a person to commit cold-blooded murder."

"Thanks," she said, and leaned back on the cushions. She wanted to pout, but since she had suspected Paul of the same thing, she had no right.

He started laughing. "And you thought the same of me, didn't you? No worries, Cassie. I haven't committed murder either. I wouldn't. Come on, I've dedicated my life to saving lives, I would never take one."

"Yes, I realized that as well. I only thought it for a moment." She reached for her lemonade and took a big swallow before snatching a cookie.

"I wish I could help, Cassie. I spoke with the detectives after each time, but I doubt I was able to help. Detective Whittaker and Freeman even came to my work again today and talked to me for about an hour. Still, I didn't have any more information to give them."

"What did they ask you?" She wanted to smack herself. Of course, after that conversation he had with her yesterday, Detective Whittaker would have interviewed Paul again.

"Whether I knew the two victims. Whether I had seen your day planner, or had seen anyone go near your purse the day of the party."

"Had you?"

He shook his head. "No. I had read in the report that a day planner was found at the first murder scene, which I admitted to the detectives. I hadn't known it was yours then though."

"I'm glad you admitted it to them. And no, before you ask, I neither know how the day planner got there nor where I had seen it last."

"Cassie, do me a favor. You told me to be careful, now I'm going to ask the same of you. If the killer is using you as the nexus point for his murders, you might be in danger. Especially if you do what you just did."

"What I just did?"

He folded his arms in front of his chest. "If you thought, even for a moment, that I was the killer, what the hell are you doing coming over here?"

She flushed. "Yes, well, I suppose that wasn't the best idea."

"Promise me you won't do anything like that again, young lady," he said as Mary came in to announce that dinner was ready. Invited once again to eat, Cassie declined and said her goodbyes.

She hoped he wouldn't realize that she never did promise.

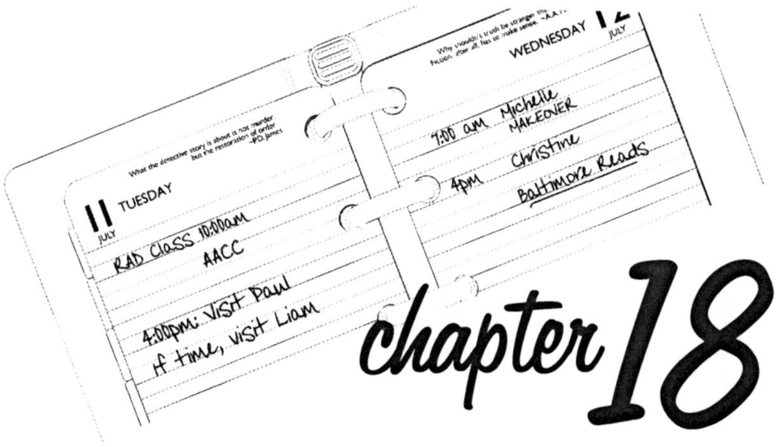

chapter 18

Cassie was so preoccupied from her meeting with Paul, it took her a while to realize the car she kept seeing in her rear view mirror was the same dark blue sedan.

Before fear could choke her, she recognized the vehicle. More importantly, she recognized the figure behind the wheel.

Whittaker.

When they both stopped for a red light, she glanced back in the mirror. He had both hands gripped around the steering wheel, lips pressed together, and he glared out of cold eyes. He was pissed. At her?

She parked her car between two of her neighbors' and got out to wait for him.

He closed the car door so carefully and deliberately she could tell he had barely stopped himself from slamming it. She didn't need to stretch her imagination to visualize a small, furious Chesapeake Bay thunderstorm raging over his head.

He stalked over. "Why were you at Larson's?" he demanded.

Oh yeah, he was angry at her. She decided to meet his heat with ice.

"Visiting." With a sharp pivot, she turned her back on him and strolled up the steps. She ignored him when he held her storm door open for her.

Cassie turned the key and entered, nearly stepping on Donner, who yowled as if she had come down on his tail. "I'm sorry, Donner." Scooping up her cat, she walked to the kitchen to attend to his needs. Poor kitty. She was neglecting him.

"Why?"

He'd followed her into the kitchen. She straightened from filling Donner's food bowl, bag of cat chow in her hand. She deliberately took her time folding down the top and applying the bag clip.

Whittaker stood with his hands on his hips, glaring at her. "Tell me why you went there."

She put the kibble away and mimicked his stance and glare. "Tell me why you were there."

"Doing my job. What the hell were you doing?"

"I told you, I was visiting." Cassie pushed past him and went into the living room. She plopped down on her green couch and put her feet up on the coffee table.

"Visiting him? The day after I asked you questions about him? I didn't admit we were considering him just so you could go and risk yourself by poking around. For God's sake, what the hell were you thinking?"

He didn't yell, he didn't even raise his voice. He didn't need to, not with that powerful cop glare on his face.

She looked away and studied her fingernails. "I was thinking that I wanted to find out if he had anything to do with Seth's murder. Or Solange's."

"And what? You thought you'd just saunter in and find out?" He paced back and forth in her living room; his stride too long for the narrow space.

"I have to do something, James. I'd prefer not to lose any more friends, and we're no closer to finding out who the hell is doing this."

He stopped then and turned. "*We? We're* no closer? There is no *we*, Cassie. You shouldn't be investigating these murders. You're a civilian, for God's sake."

"And I'm the civilian who's responsible for these murders."

"The hell you are!"

"The hell I'm not," she said mildly. "Look, I'm not saying it's my fault that people are getting murdered, but I do feel some responsibility. I wanted to do something. I know Paul, so I'd be able to see in his eyes if he was guilty of something."

"And if he was, I'm sure he wouldn't want you to know. You put yourself at risk."

"Oh please, it's Paul. He'd never hurt me."

Whittaker threw up his hands in disgust. "You suspected he may have killed two people, but don't think he'll hurt you? That makes sense."

"I can take care of myself." She stood up and walked towards the kitchen. She wanted some water.

Whittaker grabbed her arm. "What? You've taken one RAD class and suddenly you're a self-defense expert?"

With an abrupt twist of her arm, just as she had learned in class, she broke free of his grasp. "I got free of you, didn't I?"

Her cocky feeling lessened when his eyes darkened and he took a quick step towards her.

"I wasn't holding you that hard."

Cassie didn't even have time to gasp before finding herself backed into the wall, Whittaker's hands tight on both arms. The solid weight of his body pressed hard into her.

"Now get free," he said.

There were things she had been told in RAD class, techniques specifically designed to get her out of this position. But she couldn't think of any. All she could think was how excruciatingly aware she was of each contact point between his body and hers. All she could do was stare into his stormy gray eyes as the anger drained out and was replaced by another powerful emotion.

This close, it was impossible not to see, or feel, his internal struggle for control. Or the exact moment when he lost the battle and lowered his head to hers.

It was instantly hot. Instantly mind-numbing.

Cassie reveled in it. She had never felt like this. She had read descriptions in the romance books: the heat, the fireworks going off, the complete loss of feeling in the legs. She hadn't believed any of it, assumed they were over the top. Until now.

The descriptions didn't do it justice.

She almost tumbled when he suddenly released her. Bracing a hand on the stair rail, she tried to catch her breath.

Whittaker raked a hand through his hair. "No, we're not supposed to do this. A police officer shouldn't get involved with a suspicious character—"

Even through the rapid beat of her heart, his words got through and knocked her back to her senses. "I'm still a suspect? You think I did it? That *I* killed these people?

Before she could lose her temper, he stepped back to her. He kissed her again, hard and brief.

"No, I don't think that," he said, leaning against the wall. "But I can't eliminate you from the list either. I don't think you did it, Cassie. Nor does Freeman. But I can't say to my superiors that no, you aren't a suspicious character because my gut tells me that you're innocent."

"Would you get in trouble for kissing me?" she asked.

"No, not real trouble. They wouldn't write me up or anything. But people would talk."

"And?" she asked. "What's the big deal if they talk? You know I didn't do it."

"I don't want them to talk about me. They do enough of that already." He strode over to the couch and sat down.

She followed, sitting with her body angled toward him, one leg tucked beneath the other. "Why? Why do they talk about you?"

He stared down at the floor and reached out to pet Donner when he hopped up between them. "Because they compare me to my father."

"Your father? What about your father?" She suddenly put two and two together. Whittaker had seemed reluctant to talk about his father the other night, especially regarding the fact that he used to be a police officer. *Used* to be a police officer. "Does this have something to do with why he's no longer a cop?"

"It has everything to do with why he's no longer a cop," Whittaker said bitterly. "My father was a sergeant for twenty years, worked Vice and then the Drug Unit when it branched off. Did a good job of it, so I thought. He helped take down a number of drug dealers, small and big-time. He was my hero, the reason I became a cop. Then, my first year in the Academy, he got caught by IAD—Internal Affairs Division."

She didn't interrupt him to remind him that she knew what IAD stood for.

He ran a hand through his hair again, leaving it even more disheveled. "Well, now it's called the Internal Investigations Division. He'd been on the take for years. They discovered a number of unexplained bank accounts in his name. He retired a couple of days after that."

She squeezed his hand as he stopped and swallowed audibly. "Dishonorably?"

"No, they didn't have enough evidence to prosecute. But everyone knows what he did. And I refuse to have anyone think I'm like him. I'm nothing like him," he added.

"I'm sure you're not, James. At least not regarding your honorability. But I don't think it's good to be so worried about being like him that you stop yourself from doing things you want."

"Like kissing you?" He turned, glanced down at her lips. Looked away. "But if I start on that path, what's going to prevent me from breaking rules?"

"Because you know right from wrong, and would never do anything really wrong."

"You know me that well, do you?"

"Hey, we're getting to know each other thanks to whoever is killing my contacts. And as you said before, this is another reason why we need to solve these murders."

He groaned. "It's not *we*, Cassie."

"Is too. Look, Detective Whittaker, you have to use all the tools available to solve a crime, right?"

He nodded slowly, clearly wary of a trap.

"I'm a tool."

At his snort, she smacked him playfully.

"I don't mean it *that* way. The crimes are connected to me, so I should be able to help."

"Helping is okay. That's why we've brought you in for interview, hoping you could tell us something. But helping doesn't mean you go out and interview suspects. Especially on your own."

She gave a satisfied little grin. "Fine, then you can come with me to meet with Liam."

"You can't accompany me to an interview."

"I'm not asking to go along with you." She reached out and smoothed down his hair. "I'm asking you, Mr. Off-Duty Police Officer, to go along with *me* to talk to Liam Brody. Honestly, I doubt he knows anything. I'm more worried that he's going to be a victim."

"I do need to talk to Brody," he said, checking his watch. "I wasn't actually able to talk to him today other than a short phone call. He was at a day-long training until seven tonight. Should just be getting home soon. I was just watching Larson's house for a while before I headed over to his house. Until I noticed you, that is."

"Well, now we can go together. Look, I'm going to talk to Liam with or without you."

He sighed. "Then with me." He stood up and reached down a hand to her.

She gripped his hand, letting him pull her up from the couch. "Come on, let's go visit Liam Brody," she said, keeping his hand in hers as she dragged him to the door.

* * *

They had good timing. They arrived at Liam's house just as he pulled his van into the driveway.

"Now, we agreed that I would do all the talking," Cassie said as she got out of the car.

"We agreed to no such thing," Whittaker replied, already scanning the area.

Cassie inspected the layout for herself and tried to emulate Whittaker's careful surveillance. The houses here were small, but the yards were large with plenty of trees and bushes. Dusk was just settling on the area, throwing the street into shadow.

Liam had gone to his mailbox first thing and had his hand in the box when she called his name. He turned around in surprise.

"What a lovely surprise, Cassie, me darling," Liam said.

Cassie smiled. Despite the fact that his family hadn't stepped foot in Ireland for over a century, Liam loved to act like he was born and raised there. "Hello, Liam. This is Det—"

She got no further before Whittaker tackled her and Liam to the ground.

Seconds before shots rang out.

Whittaker had already gotten into a crouch, pulled out his gun, and returned fire before she even realized what was going on.

"Go," he hissed at them. "Get behind cover. Run." He grabbed his radio and called out his location and status.

The only cover, other than the pitiful mailbox Whittaker had ducked behind, was Whittaker's car. She pulled Liam up, and they retreated as quickly as possible, weaving back and forth. Cassie hoped she ran in a random pattern. She had been in the area when the Beltway Sniper had attacked, and she remembered being told to move randomly.

More shots rang out.

She actually felt the rush of air as one whizzed by her. She heard the crack as a bullet hit Whittaker's car just as Liam dived behind it. Cassie followed him and pressed her back against the car as she struggled to catch her breath. Her heartbeat sounded like a drum, pounding in her ears.

She spun around to Liam. "Are you hurt?"

He gripped his chest, but other than that, didn't seem injured. "No, just...what the hell?"

"Later." She turned again and tried to peek over the top of the car to check on Whittaker.

"Stay down!" he yelled, just as another bullet hit about a foot to the right of her.

Probably a good idea, she decided. Her red hair was as good as a bullseye for taking aim. Listening closely, she heard the rustle of bushes behind the house and the sounds of someone taking off in pursuit.

Whittaker! And he didn't have back-up.

She wanted to go after him, protect him, but realized that was a really stupid idea, since she was unarmed. Plus, she suspected he could take care of himself.

She stayed with Liam, made sure he was okay, and tried to slow her heartbeat back to normal as the sound of sirens grew closer.

Vehicles squealed to a stop and police officers poured out, armed and ready. She recognized one officer from her forays to the police station. He must have recognized her as well, since he crouched next to her.

"Any injuries?" he asked, his dark face concerned.

Cassie shook her head. "No. Officer Morris, isn't it? I'm fine. You're okay, Liam, aren't you?"

She placed a hand on the older man's back to assist him as he started to stand up.

"I'm fine," Liam said, clearing his throat. "Takes more than getting shot at to take me down. But getting shot would've done the trick. I'll have to thank your boyfriend when he gets back."

She was glad of the dusk and flashing red lights that helped camouflage the inevitable rush of heat to her face and cheeks. "He's not my boyfriend."

She listened to the chatter coming from the police radio. She could hear Whittaker giving his location as he gave pursuit. Heard the discouragement in his voice when he reported losing sight of the shooter.

Officer Morris shook his head as they heard the radio report. "Whittaker couldn't catch him? Perp must've been really fast on his feet."

Other emergency vehicles pulled up. Firefighters came over, swarming over Liam when they recognized one of their own. Cassie was glad to see Liam's normal healthy color return as he took some good-natured ribbing from his buddies.

After giving her report to Officer Morris, Cassie waited for Whittaker. She shook her head as she inspected his car. The hood had at least two bullet holes in it, including the one that had almost taken off her head. She gulped as she realized how close it had come.

When she saw Whittaker jogging back, looking all hot and sweaty, her heart rate picked up again. And it had nothing to do with almost being shot.

Officer Morris trotted over to him. Whittaker spoke to him and a few more police officers for a couple of minutes before heading back to her.

"You okay?" he asked as he checked her over from top to bottom.

"As okay as one can be after being shot at. Thank you for saving my life. And Liam's." She glanced back to where her friend was sitting on the back of an ambulance as a paramedic checked him out. "How did you know?"

He shrugged. "It felt wrong. Then I saw the gun pointing out of a bush tucked next to the house."

"So I guess Liam's eliminated as a suspect, right?"

"Since most of the shots were aimed at him, I think so." Whittaker took out a handkerchief and wiped at his forehead.

"And I'm eliminated as well, right?"

He stared at her for a good minute, enough to have butterflies swimming in her stomach. "Yes, this eliminates you too. Are you sure you're okay?"

Cassie looked down at herself. "Well, I'm probably bruised from when you tackled me, but other than that, I feel good. Really good, actually. Energetic."

"Adrenalin rush," he commented.

"I feel like I did a good job avoiding the bullets, but I suspect that it was as much luck as skill."

"Mostly luck, really," Whittaker said, smiling now.

"I thought getting shot at would feel all slo-mo and Matrixy, but it doesn't. It's fast. Really fast. I get the 'faster than a speeding bullet' reference now."

"I've never seen a civilian react as calmly and analytically to being shot at before." He shook his head in amazement.

"Have you been with many civilians when they've been shot at?"

"This would make one. But I've spoken to a number after the fact. Most of them are a little shocky."

Cassie took stock of herself again. "I don't think I'm in shock. I'm full of energy. Of course, that could be because of our kiss earlier."

He hushed her. "Shut up, Cassie. Um, Ms. Ellis."

"Whittaker!" a familiar voice called. Any trace of informality Cassie had so enjoyed vanished as Whittaker straightened and turned away from her to greet his partner.

"Getting shot at without me, Whittaker?" Freeman asked. "Did you get a good look at the shooter?"

Whittaker shook his head. "Not really. It was dark. I couldn't quite get a bead on the height, but between five-seven and five-ten, medium frame, black pants and top. Black ski mask, so I didn't see the face."

"Male or female?"

Whittaker shrugged. "Couldn't even tell you that. But damned fast on his or her feet, I'll tell you that much."

"Must be if you couldn't catch him." Freeman turned to Cassie. "And how are you this evening, Ms. Ellis?

"Also getting shot at without you." She grinned at him "You're welcome to join us the next time."

He cocked an eyebrow at her. "You seem fairly calm."

"It was fun."

Whittaker groaned while Freeman placed a comforting hand on his shoulder. "Oh God, Cassie. It's many things, but it's not fun."

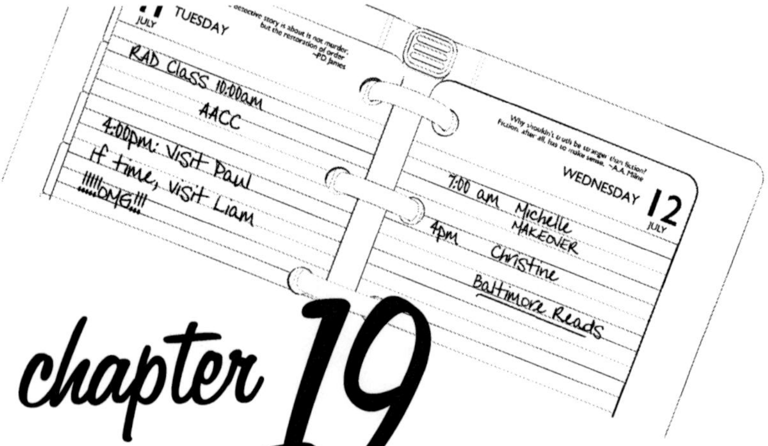

chapter 19

The rest of the night wasn't as fun.

It took hours for the police to investigate the scene and take their formal reports. Cassie had worried about questions as to why she and Whittaker were together. She watched in surprise as Whittaker smoothly explained he was conducting a follow-up interview with Liam Brody and felt bringing Cassie along would make her medical contact more forthcoming.

She had to reassure herself that Liam was really okay. And calm his wife when she came back from her book club meeting to a yard full of emergency vehicles and media vans.

Media vans! She didn't want her father to see this on the news. She pawed in her purse until she found her cell phone. "Don't worry, I'm okay," she said in lieu of a greeting.

"Oh God, Cassandra. I hate it when you start a conversation like that. What happened?"

Downplaying how close the bullets had been, she told him the details. "I'm fine, Dad. A little shook up, as is Liam. And Detective Whittaker was amazing."

She heard him sigh. "Amazing, was he? I'm glad I'm didn't lose you tonight, but it sounds like I'm still losing my girl in some ways. Falling for a detective, no less."

She glanced over at Whittaker, who was receiving reports from some uniformed police officers. "You don't have to really worry about that until this killer is caught, Dad."

"Still, why don't you both come over tonight? That way I can see for myself that you're really okay, and meet this fine gentleman."

The fine gentleman headed over her way.

"Let me call you back, Dad." She closed the phone. "Did we find out anything?"

"It's still not *we*, Cassie. And no. None of the neighbors noticed anything. They heard the shots, of course, and many of them came out to see what was going on. A couple saw the perp running by, and me behind him. But no one got a good look."

"Shoe impressions?"

"Yes, it's a medium size shoe and the indention's not too deep, so the person isn't heavy."

"But you knew that already when you said he had a medium frame. Did Crime Scene collect any casings?"

He scowled at her as he swatted away mosquitoes. "Yes, they did their job, Cassie. Do you want to take over the investigation?"

"Can I?" She grinned impudently at him.

Rolling his eyes, he gestured at her phone. "Who was on the phone?"

"My dad. Told him I was okay. And he'd like for us to come over so he can make sure of that."

"Well, I suppose I could get someone to take you over there." Whittaker scanned the area and gestured toward Officer Morris. Cassie reached out and pushed his arm back down.

"No," she said firmly. "It *is* a 'we' this time, Detective Whittaker. My dad wants to meet you." She couldn't help being amused at the expression of fear that crossed his face. He hadn't looked half as worried when bullets were flying.

"I have to write up a report on tonight's incident."

Freeman had walked up at the end of her statement. "I can take care of that, Whittaker. You go with Ms. Ellis, meet her father." He smirked. "Show him you have only the most proper of intentions."

Cassie liked Freeman. A lot. She grinned at him. "Oh, James is always proper."

"Of course. Bit of a stick up his ass, that boy."

She laughed as Whittaker shoved his hands in his pocket and shifted uncomfortably. "He does seem rather anal."

"He is. And don't forget arrogant."

"Okay, enough bonding between you two. Come on, Cassie." Whittaker stalked over to his car and held the door open for her. "See you tomorrow, Freeman."

"I was just getting started," Freeman called out.

"That's what I was afraid of," Whittaker muttered as he walked around the car.

* * *

Whittaker brooded as he navigated around the other police vehicles. He managed to be quiet for a good three minutes before he broke. "I do not have a stick up my ass."

She chuckled, but then replied seriously. "Yes, you do. One that got lodged up there when your father did what he did."

He gripped the steering wheel tightly and stared straight ahead for the next couple of blocks. Then he relaxed his hands. "I suppose. But it's there for a good reason, Cassie. I wanted to be a cop all my life, wanted to make a difference. I take pride in what I do. I don't want what my father did to reduce that."

"But you can't go through your entire life worrying what other people think either."

Easier said than done. He had always worried about others' opinions. At first, it was because he wanted to impress his father. His dad had been his hero throughout childhood and he had wanted to be just like the strong, honorable police officer. Since his father's criminal activities were exposed, Whittaker wanted to ensure he was nothing like the man.

Cassie interrupted his thoughts. "Okay, two questions. Number one, how do you know where to go?"

He glanced over at her. "Oh, I looked up your father's address when we first investigated you."

"And what, memorized it?"

"Since my friend Ian lives two blocks away, yes, I did. What's your second question?"

"Even though there is now proof positive that I'm innocent—unless I'm crazy enough to have an accomplice shoot at me—you still aren't going to feel comfortable having any type of relationship with me yet, are you?"

He was discomfited that she knew him so well already. "No. I wouldn't feel comfortable."

She slouched down in the seat. "Hmmph."

Although he thought she had the cutest pout, he struggled to come up with a way to charm her out of her sulk. They were passing the Captain James Restaurant, maybe he should ask her if she ever ate there. Then again, he still needed to go there. After all, where else can you eat crabs in a restaurant shaped like a merchant ship? Before he could even speak, she jerked upright again.

"Hey! Doesn't tonight also eliminate Mark from the suspect list?"

"Mark Griffin?"

"Yes. Because trust me, if he had wanted to hit Liam, or me, or you, he would have."

"No, that wouldn't really eliminate him. After all, you admitted your ability to avoid being shot was mostly luck. I don't think someone could deliberately miss a randomly moving target by as little of a window. Even an expert marksmen like Griffin."

"I guess you're right. Although he is really good. Oh, what stance do you use?"

He tried to keep up with her rapid change of topics. They were talking shooting, so he assumed she meant shooting stance. "Chapman."

"I'm not familiar with that one. Mark uses the Weaver stance, but he taught me Isosceles, since I don't have as much upper-body strength."

He was having a conversation about gun stances with a civilian. More importantly, a civilian he already found attractive. "It's a modified Weaver stance. Still uses the push-pull method, but the gun arm is straight instead of both bent like in Weaver. Named after Ray Chapman, who used it in competition."

"Ray Chapman? How odd, he shares the same name as the only baseball player that was killed during a major league game."

"I had noticed that as well, actually." He shook his head at her trivia knowledge, but had to test her further. "And the pitch was thrown by?"

"Carl Mays of the evil New York Yankees, 1920," she replied quickly.

And now they were talking baseball. He was definitely sunk. In general, he compartmentalized his friends. He talked to his fellow cops about murder, his male friends about baseball, and his fellow gun aficionados about guns.

Here was a woman he could talk to about all these things. And she was hot.

They talked about the current baseball season until he pulled up at the curb near her father's home.

He noticed Cassie's father watching through the window as he opened her car door. Although he didn't do it for that reason, he still hoped it earned him some brownie points. He had no idea how to prepare himself for this. What to say. How to act. He could face criminals any day, handle gun battles without blinking an eye. But, somehow, the thought of meeting the father of a girlfriend—a potential girlfriend, anyway—made him nervous.

She ran up the stairs and threw her arms around her father. Whittaker thought she did it more to comfort her father than to draw comfort for herself. He still couldn't believe how calmly she was handling being shot at. Although that was probably also due to her bright relief that they had prevented Liam from being killed.

He walked up the stairs and shook her father's hand when it was offered.

"Dad, this is Detective James Whittaker. James, this is my father, Charles Ellis."

The man had a good grip and good eye contact. Even if Cassie hadn't introduced him as her father, it was obvious. They shared the same eye and hair color, although her father's hair was going gray. He assumed she got her height from him, too.

"Come in, come in," Charles said, shooing them into the narrow living room.

Whittaker noted that Charles Ellis' home had a similar layout to Cassie's. He wondered if she had chosen her place because it was so similar to her childhood home. Living room in front, kitchen in back. Beyond that, a small covered porch and the back yard.

Whittaker sat stiffly next to Cassie when she patted the couch cushion next to her. He tried to swallow his discomfort, not of meeting her father, or of sitting next to her, but of positioning himself with his back to the front window and door.

"It's nice to meet you, Detective. I can't thank you enough for saving my daughter's life tonight."

Whittaker shifted in his seat. He hated being thanked for what he saw as doing his job. "I'm glad I was able to react in time, sir, and that Cassie and Mr. Brody were able to get to safety."

"I just wish you could've caught the bastard," Charles said as he clenched his fists in lap.

Cassie's reaction was more energetic. She punched the pillow next to her. "That makes two of us."

Three of us, Whittaker thought to himself. "Unfortunately, we weren't able to capture him tonight, but I have complete confidence that we will do so soon. I'm hoping that the frustration of missing the hit tonight will lead the killer to make a mistake."

"I just hope no one is killed when he makes that mistake," Cassie said quietly. "Can't you send protection to the other people that were mentioned in the day planner?" She turned big blue eyes, full of worry and pleading, in his direction.

"I wish we could, Cassie. Honestly, the police department doesn't have the budget. You had a lot of contacts listed."

"Well, I didn't know someone was going to use the dumb thing for his hit list. I wouldn't have written down as many names if I had." She picked up the bright yellow pillow and thumped it back on the couch.

"You couldn't have known, Cassie." Her father stood up and patted her shoulder before walking back to the kitchen.

"And we still don't know that the shootings are related to your day planner," Whittaker said. When she turned and stared at him, he struggled to hold back a laugh at the utter disbelief in her eyes. "Okay, it appears like they are related. But you should never make assumptions."

"Right. Thinking that three murder attempts in one week, all of them contacts from my day planner, are related, is an assumption," she muttered and punched the pillow again.

"I figured you would enjoy some coffee," Charles said, carrying back a tray."I thought about getting donuts as well, but that's too cliché, don't you think?" The look of mischief in his eyes reminded Whittaker of Cassie.

"I appreciate the coffee," he said, taking a mug. He noticed Charles add cream and sugar into Cassie's without asking.

Charles poured himself a cup. "It's decaf, since it's so late."

"What time is it?" Cassie asked and glanced up at the cuckoo clock on the wall. "Oh my God! It's past midnight. And Michelle is coming over early to prep me for Christine's stupid cable show."

"Now it's a stupid show, Cassie?" said her father with surprise. "You were excited to go on it before."

"That was before people started dying all around me, wasn't it?" She hugged the abused pillow tight against herself. "And before I ended up dodging bullets. Oh, and it's nothing like *The Matrix,* Dad. Not slow motion or anything."

Charles' hearty laugh made Whittaker smile. So there was at least one person in the world who could follow Cassie's mercurial changes of topic and mood.

"I wouldn't think so, Cassandra. I'm just glad you avoided those bullets. Very glad. And I'm sorry about Seth's death, about Solange. But you shouldn't let this all completely ruin this experience for you, Cassie-girl. Not many people get their book published." Pride in his daughter shone on Charles' face.

As Cassie got up to give her dad an impulsive hug, Whittaker could only think about the relationship he used to have with his own father. How happy he was to win his father's hard-earned respect the day he joined the police academy. How he enjoyed, at first, being known as Richard Whittaker's son.

Now he barely spoke to the man. That was his choice, not his father's. Whittaker didn't want his reputation to be stained by association.

Releasing her father, Cassie turned toward him. "Well, we should get going. Michelle is coming over at seven. The show's not until four. What the hell can she have planned that requires that much time?"

"Knowing Michelle, I'm sure she has plenty of plans," Charles said, grinning at her. He shifted his eyes to Whittaker. "It's nice to meet you, Detective Whittaker."

He stood up, wincing a bit at the twinge in his thigh. He should have stretched after that evening's chase. "Please call me James, sir."

"And please call me Charles. None of this 'sir' business."

Cassie snorted. "Michelle's going to be jealous."

"Jealous of who, Cassie? You? Did she want Detective Whittaker for herself?" Charles asked.

Again, Whittaker was struck by the similarities between the man and his daughter. That same devilish look, and the same ability to embarrass him. He just was glad he didn't have the same tendency to turn red as Cassie did.

An endearing blush stained her face as she playfully punched her father's arm. "Dad! No, it's that she still has to call you Mr. Ellis."

"No, she doesn't," her dad said, with a mock wince. Playing it up, he rubbed his arm. "I told her years ago she could call me Charles."

"Yeah, but she just can't get comfortable saying that. Just like I still call her parents Mr. and Mrs. Edwards. So you see? She'll be jealous that James gets to call you Charles."

Whittaker wasn't sure he understood that, since Michelle could choose what name to call Cassie's father. But, as Freeman liked to say, female logic wasn't meant for men to understand. "Just smile and nod like you understand," Freeman had said. Charles must have received the same advice somewhere along the line, he noted, since he was also smiling and nodding at his daughter.

* * *

On the drive home, Cassie managed to wait a whole minute before piping up. "I'm glad you two got along so well." Another wait, this time barely thirty seconds. "So, did you like him?"

Though he knew it wasn't the reaction she was hoping for, he had to laugh. Stopping at a red light, he turned to her. "You don't do subtle, do you, Cassie?"

"No. Why bother?" She shrugged. "So did you like him?"

"Yes, very much. His pride in you is obvious. He's observant, smart, has a good sense of humor. He reminds me of you."

When she raised her eyebrows and opened her mouth, he cut her off before she could interrupt.

"And yes, Cassie, before you ask, yes, I like you. That should have been obvious after tonight."

He drove through the now-green light and glanced over at her. Oh, Lord, did she look smug. He was so in trouble.

"Anyway," Cassie said, after three minutes of silence, "he likes you."

"Well, yeah. It helps that he thinks I saved your life."

"You did save my life," she said. "And Liam's."

He scanned the waterfront as they drove through. At this hour, the tourists were gone and only the homeless and drug addicts remained. "I'm glad I was there. I'm not so glad that you were. Will you promise me that you'll let the police investigate this crime?"

"No."

That made him pull the car over and double park on one of the narrow streets. Throwing on his hazard lights, he glared at her. "Did you just say no?"

"Yes. I mean, no. I mean, yes, I just said no." She sighed and started over. "I'm not saying I'm going to investigate, James. I'm just saying I can't promise you I won't. I don't want to make a promise I can't keep."

While he was glad she was concerned about her integrity, he was concerned about her safety. "Can you promise me to at least *try* and let the police investigate the crime?"

She smiled. "I can promise that. In fact, I'll seal that promise with a kiss." She leaned in to him.

This time it wasn't all hot and fast. He might have led the first kiss, but she definitely ruled this one. She started off slowly. Even at the initial gentle pace, he could feel the heat and energy racing between them.

Then she deepened the kiss…and it was anything but gentle.

He had her seat belt unbuckled, both hands in her hair, and had almost pulled her into his lap when the honking of a car horn interrupted them. He backed away and blinked to clear his vision. Glad to see she was breathing as hard as he was, he put the car into drive.

"Don't forget to buckle up," he reminded her. His voice was low and scruffy, but that wasn't surprising considering the dryness of his throat.

He definitely had to catch this killer, so that he could continue this relationship with Cassie without murder hanging over their heads.

* * *

Donner ran to the door the second it was opened, meowing plaintively and clawing at Cassie's already torn sweats.

"Oh, you poor thing," Cassie said. "I know. I've been starving you lately." She looked over at Whittaker. "Usually, my schedule is more regular, and I'm home most of the time. I suppose he'll have to get used to it. I'll be out a lot promoting the book."

He nodded and contemplated the best way to approach his idea. "You said Michelle was coming over tomorrow, right?"

"Yes, at seven. Way too freaking early."

He glanced at the clock. "That's only five and a half hours away. Still, I'd prefer knowing you're safe. As you said, the killer might be frustrated that he got stopped tonight."

She stopped in the middle of pouring the cat food, causing Donner to squawk in protest. "You think I'm in danger?"

"I'm not sure, but I'd be more comfortable knowing you're safe. Would you mind if I spent the night?" At her raised eyebrow, he clarified. "On the couch, Cassie."

"I don't mind if you stay here, but you don't need to stay on the couch."

Now it was his turn to raise an eyebrow. "Cassie."

She laughed. "I have a guest room. You're welcome to stay there."

He knew she had baited him and wasn't certain what it meant that he liked it. "Actually, I'd prefer to be down here. Closer to the front and back entrances. You don't have any others, do you?"

"No. I have a basement, but unless the burglar is the size of a breadbox, he won't squeeze through those windows." She glanced up the stairs. "And there are windows upstairs as well, but both have air conditioning units in them. Um, do you need anything to, well, sleep in?"

What was it with this woman offering to loan him clothes? "No, I'll just stay as is."

She sauntered over and stroked her hands down his tie. "You'll remove this, at least, won't you?"

"I will. I might even go wild and take off the jacket too." He leaned down and kissed her lightly. "You should go upstairs and stop tempting me. We both have to get up soon. I'll probably head out about six or so. Need to be in at seven and I still need to go home, shower, and change."

She smiled up at him. "Yes, if you walked in wearing the same suit as today, Freeman would have a field day."

He shuddered. "That he would."

He settled down on the not terribly comfortable couch and tried not to wonder what she wore to sleep in.

Or, what she didn't wear.

chapter 20

Cassie woke up to simultaneous pounding on her door and the ringing of her cell phone. Hearing the Beatles singing *Michelle* on the cell phone clued her in on who was calling and who was pounding.

Checking her alarm clock, she cursed before answering the phone. "Hello Michelle. You're at my front door, aren't you?"

Michelle ignored her question. "Were you still asleep? Are you okay? Can I come in?"

"Yes. Yes. And yes," she said, as she heard Michelle opening the locks downstairs. As her main cat sitter, Michelle had her own keys to the place.

She hung up the phone and saw the note Whittaker had left her. She grabbed at it and hid it behind her back when Michelle rushed into her room.

"Hey, I thought I was the late one. Since when do you have trouble being ready?" Michelle gawked at her. "Are you sure you're okay? You look exhausted."

"Late night last night."

"Late night? That sounds interesting." Michelle raised an eyebrow and turned towards the bed. "You kick around your blankets so much I can't tell if you were alone last night."

Cassie slipped behind her friend to get clothes from the dresser. "Now that you mention it, Detective Whittaker spent the night last night."

She heard her friend gasp and spin around. "Really?"

Glancing over her shoulder, she smiled as she walked to the shower. "Really. I'll tell you about it after my shower."

"Cassandra…" Michelle whined.

Cassie smirked and closed the door.

Even though she raced through her shower, it wasn't fast enough for Michelle. She had barely finished getting dressed when the bathroom door opened.

"Spill. Now."

Cassie calmly applied toothpaste to her brush and brushed her teeth.

"Cassie."

It was hard for her friend to look stern. With her petite stature, she always ended up looking like a pissed-off leprechaun. But Michelle did her best as she glared at Cassie in the mirror.

Cassie easily ignored it. To continue torturing her friend, she took her time rinsing and drying her face. Only then did she answer.

"Well, he did spend the night. But downstairs on my couch."

Michelle looked disappointed. "On the couch? What fun is that? Why'd he spend the night?"

"Let me make you breakfast and I'll tell you."

With an evil grin, Michelle agreed. "Great. Can I have an omelet?"

"Oh, shut up." Cassie took pride in her cooking ability. She could make *haute cuisine*, fancy pastries, cook any type of meat to perfection. But for some reason, she just couldn't manage an omelet. "You'll get baked eggs and like it."

"Love them, actually. But I'll love hearing about your sexy detective even more."

"He is sexy, isn't he? And fast. If not for him, I'd probably be dead."

"What?" Michelle asked as she trotted down the stairs, almost tripping when Donner raced ahead of her.

Since Whittaker's note had said he fed Donner, Cassie ignored the cat's whines and put together the baked eggs as she told Michelle of the last night's occurrences.

"Wow," Michelle said. "I guess at this point, even I—the optimist amongst us—can't say that this is coincidence. Someone's targeting your contacts."

Cassie pulled the baking dish from beneath the broiler and slipped the eggs into the heated cream and butter. She nodded as she set the timer. "I know. I called all of them last night while I was at Liam's and told them to be careful. In case the killer went after someone else after being frustrated last night."

"Be careful yourself, Cassie. How do you know the killer wasn't after you last night?"

"That doesn't make sense. How would he know I was going to be there?" Cassie countered.

Michelle stood at the sink and filled up the tea kettle. "I don't know, maybe he followed you. In any case, you were in danger…are in danger. Especially if you're playing detective."

"I wasn't playing anything, thank you very much. I'm serious about wanting this over. I don't want anyone else killed."

"I know that, sweetie." Michelle stepped over and put an arm around her. "But I don't want you killed either. You might write about murderers, and read about detectives, but you're not actually trained to go and solve crimes."

"I know, I know. I've already heard it from Linda, from Detective Whittaker, from Dad, and now you. I'm not going to do anything stupid."

"You mean you won't do anything too stupid."

Cassie laughed as the timer went off. "I'll try not to do anything too stupid, how about that? The stupidest thing I'm going to do today is go get made over." She sighed as she put on an oven mitt.

* * *

It wasn't that Cassie didn't like makeup. Or that she had an issue with someone else applying it on her. It was just that every time she had a professional do her makeup, she ended up looking like a clown…or a hooker. Occasionally both.

They had already been to Nordstrom's to pick out a new outfit. Even though Cassie had protested that she'd need to sell over five hundred books to pay for the new Tahari suit, Michelle talked her into it. Admittedly, the lime green color was perfect for her hair and skin tone. And their regular hairdresser had done a fantastic job, as usual. But the makeup artist had her worried. Michelle swore up and down this time would be different, that she had found someone phenomenal.

"So what is he, the Maestro of Makeup?" she grumbled as she got out of the car outside the large department store.

Michelle snorted. "Maestro of Makeup, that's a good one. How about the Commissar of Cosmetics?"

"Expert of Eyeshadow."

"Royalty of Rouge."

"Leader of Lipstick." They continued this game until they arrived at the makeup counter. From all the descriptors, Cassie was expecting some flamboyant persona wielding brushes full of the bright colors she hated.

She was pleasantly surprised when Mario ended up being a fiftyish, unassuming man who made up her face in discreet greens and browns. Even better, he managed to hide all signs of her late night. Looking in the mirror, she felt every bit the professional, successful author.

She smiled brightly at Michelle. "Okay, I'm ready."

* * *

She thought she was ready. But seeing all the lights and cameras surrounding the two chairs, she wasn't so certain. She realized how clever Michelle had been by scheduling the makeover. Cassie had been more worried about how ridiculous she would look rather than worrying about her first television appearance. Even if it was just a local cable show, she was nervous.

She was glad she had spent the money on the new outfit when Christine came over wearing an Armani suit in cornflower blue. The reporter gave her a cup of coffee and some warm encouragement. "Don't worry, Cassie, it'll be fine. Besides, this show doesn't get many viewers anyway."

"It might this time," Aaron put in. He had joined them at the television station and had expressed great admiration for Michelle's success with Cassie's makeover. "After all, Cassie is getting a lot of media attention now."

Cassie swiveled on her new heels and glared at him. "Aaron, this is not the time to bring that up."

"Actually, Cassie, I'll probably be bringing it up myself," Christine mumbled.

She swiveled back, bobbled, and almost fell over. Her father gripped her by the elbow to steady her. "Christine!"

The woman ducked her head in apology. "I'm sorry, Cassie. But my sponsors called this morning to make certain I'd be covering the murders. I have to do what they ask. They almost pulled the sponsorship last month, and I don't think I can get another bookstore to sponsor this show. But besides that, it's...well, it's news, Cassie."

Aaron placed his hand on Cassie's shoulder. "She's right, you know. It might be a bit uncomfortable, but she can't avoid the topic."

"We're here to talk about my book," she insisted, trying to appeal to the group. Her father and Michelle looked as upset as she felt, but they didn't say anything.

"And we will. Of course, we will." Christine was quick to soothe her. "But you're a murder mystery author. I have to discuss the fact that you're actually involved in real life murders. I'll be as delicate as I can, I promise."

Cassie huffed out a breath. "Can we at least have some topics off-limits?"

Christine bit her lip. "How about we have a signal? If there is something you can't talk about, either because it makes you too emotional or it's something confidential, just raise the index finger on your left hand."

That would have to do, Cassie thought. At least it was something, but she dreading this experience more and more.

Christine looked towards the cameraman, whom she had also introduced as the director of the show. "Anyway, two minutes until we start, Cassie. I need to talk to Eli for a minute. Excuse me."

"I'm sorry, Cassie-girl." Her father put his arm around her and pulled her close.

Michelle linked arms with Aaron. "So, tell me all about being an agent," she said, dragging him off to a corner of the room.

Cassie was grateful her friend let her have a moment with her father. She leaned into his comforting bulk. "I feel horrible, Dad. It still feels like it's my fault that Seth and Solange are dead. And now it's like people are expecting me to use their deaths to my advantage."

"I don't think most people are thinking that, Cassie. Even those who seem to be saying it." He took her by the shoulders, looked into her eyes. "Anyone who understands you knows that while you might write about murder, you'd never want anyone to die in real life."

"No." She fought back tears. "I know how devastating it is to lose someone you love. I'd never wish that for anyone else."

"Oh, Cassie."

"I just miss Mom now," she sniffled. "I wish she could be here…see that I'm published."

"She'd be so proud. She is proud of you, Cassie. And she does see it. She's still watching." He pulled her back in for a hard hug.

She held on for a minute to draw strength and then took a step back. "You're right, Dad. And I'm going to mess up my makeup. Michelle will kill me."

"Go make us proud, Cassie."

She took a deep breath and joined Christine. "Okay, I'm ready. But try and concentrate mostly on the book, please."

Christine nodded and indicated Cassie should accompany her to the armchairs and coffee table in the studio set-up. "I will. You know I loved your writing. You have such promise, Cassie."

"Maybe," Cassie muttered. "But if these murders keep happening in real life, I might stop writing."

"I hope that doesn't happen."

"So do I, Christine." She couldn't stop a jaw-popping yawn and hoped she wouldn't do that on camera.

Christine yawned right after she did. "Stop that, Cassie. Don't get me started."

"Sorry, I had a late night last night." Then she shook off her exhaustion and focused on being a smart, charming author for the next fifteen minutes.

She managed fine when Christine asked her to summarize the plot. Years of practice talking to agents had let her perfect the book pitch. It helped that Christine knew the book. Cassie had heard of other authors being interviewed by hosts who hadn't bothered to read the book. She had been told how awkward and obvious that was, and how the author had to work so much harder.

This was easy.

At least, it was. Until Christine got to the questions about the real life murders.

"So Cassie, your book is about a clever murderer. And I understand that you are dealing with one in real life."

She glanced off-screen towards her friends and family for support. "Yes, unfortunately, that is true."

"How many people have been killed so far?"

Cassie sucked in her breath. So far? Like more were to come? That was a horrible thought. "Well, I'm not sure that I can answer. I don't believe the police have definitely linked the murders yet."

With an apology in her eyes, Christine pressed the point. "But you have been questioned regarding two murders, is that correct?"

"I was questioned as a possible material witness."

"Why is that?"

Cassie hesitated. She had to be careful what to reveal. "Well, in the case of Seth Montgomery, I had met with him earlier in the day. With Sol—"

"How did the police know that you had met with Seth Montgomery?"

So maybe the woman was only a book reviewer, but she seemed to have the nose of a crime beat reporter. "Unfortunately, I can't answer that question," Cassie said firmly, hoping Christine would take the hint.

Christine only leaned closer. "And with Solange Gavreau?"

"Again, it appears I was the last person to see her alive."

"The last to see her alive," Christine said in a low, dramatic voice as she turned to face the camera. She swiveled back to Cassie and asked, "Well then, do the police view you as a suspect?"

She had to be careful. "I can't speak for the Baltimore police, Christine. I believe they are pursuing all leads."

"And these two people had something else in common, didn't they? Weren't they both resources for writing your books?"

That was a safer question. "Yes, I used Seth Montgomery's insights for my second book, *Matchbox Murders*. And Solange Gavreau was my legal expert for both books."

"And there was another murder attempt last night, wasn't there?"

Cassie winced and raised the index finger on her left hand. "That hasn't been positively connected to the previous two murders."

"But isn't it true that the intended victim of the shooting last night was another of your sources?"

Fighting the urge to squirm, she took a deep breath to gather her thoughts. "Again, I can't answer that as the intended victim's name has not been released."

"You were shown on the media coverage, Cassie. I saw you and Detective Whittaker on site."

Cassie cursed her hair and raised her left hand higher so that Christine could see the signal. "You'll need to speak to the police regarding that."

Christine finally noticed Cassie's gesture and stopped that line of questioning. "Can you tell us anything about the two initial victims, Seth Montgomery and Solange Gavreau, both of whom you saw right before they died?"

Cassie told Christine what she knew of Seth Montgomery, painting as sympathetic a picture as possible.

"Fascinating. And Solange Gavreau? I understand you were classmates in college?"

It was easier to talk about Solange. Cassie had known her for years and really, other than her competitive streak, Solange was okay. She had been smart, beautiful, and competent at her job. Cassie wondered what their relationship would have been like if they hadn't been competitors.

"Both of these people have had their lives ended tragically, ended too early by this murderer." Cassie put bitter emphasis on the last word. "For no real reason, someone has ended these lives."

"No reason? Don't the police have any idea as to the motive?"

Cassie shook her head. "They haven't shared that information with me."

"But you're a murder mystery writer and often think about murderers and motives. Don't you have any ideas?"

"Plenty. Sadly, there are many reasons why murder is committed." Cassie thought of the scenarios she had created for her novels. "Revenge, protection, greed. But still, these murders seem so cruel and cold."

She noticed the cameraman signal Christine, who swiveled around again to face the camera, smoothing out the crease in her silk skirt at the same time.

"This has been Christine Schmidt of *Baltimore Reads* speaking with Cassandra Ellis, author of *The Mailbox Murders,* and a connection to two real life Baltimore City mysteries. We will continue to watch this exciting new author and update viewers on these intriguing murders. Please tune in next week as we interview Mark Griffin, a weapons collector and author of *Choose Your Weapon.*"

Cassie jerked her head towards Christine. She hadn't realized that the woman had convinced Mark to do the show.

"Cut. That's a wrap. Great show!" a voice came from behind the camera.

Cassie jumped out of her chair and followed Christine. "You got Mark to agree to go on TV?"

Christine stopped and smiled. "I did. At least, I think I did. He took a lot of convincing, let me tell you. But as I told him, any positive coverage showing a gun collector without demonizing him is a good thing. Especially in Maryland, where we're always fighting liberal gun control laws."

"That is a good way to convince him, Christine." They walked over to Aaron, Michelle, and her father.

"I'll also be seeing him tomorrow at seven to take photos of him shooting some of his guns." Christine swept her fingers through her hair.

"On his firing range?"

At Christine's nod, Michelle pouted. "Hey, I haven't even been on Mark's range."

"I'll take you one day, Michelle. Anyway, he's got some nice guns. Make sure he shows you the Colt SSP," Cassie said, wondering if he had fixed the broken magazine.

Christine put a hand on Cassie's arm and gently turned her. "I'm sorry, by the way, for asking all those questions. Especially for how long it took me to realize you didn't want to answer the question about last night."

Her father passed her a handkerchief, and Cassie mopped at her forehead. Those lights had been hot. "It's okay, Christine. You were just doing your job."

"I'm glad you understand that, Cassie. And you did a great job handling the questions. Those on your book and on the murders."

"Thanks. I just hope the police are able to catch the murderer before anything else happens." God, she hoped that nothing else would happen.

"I'm sure. Anyway, thank you very much for coming on the show. I hope we can talk again for your future books too." She turned to Cassie's entourage. "It's nice meeting all of you, too."

Reminding herself to send Christine a thank-you card when she got home, Cassie walked into her father's embrace.

"God, that was awful," she moaned into his chest.

"No, it wasn't. You did a great job, Cassie-girl."

"It wasn't that bad, was it?" Aaron asked. "You did a good job of fielding the questions on the real-life murders."

"Did I?" She appealed to Michelle.

Michelle dragged her eyes away from Aaron and focused on Cassie. "Yes, of course."

Cassie relaxed; she knew Michelle would always be honest with her. "I was worried that some of the questions and answers made me look guilty. I wonder if the viewers are going to think I committed the murders."

Aaron shrugged. "I bet they'll still buy the book even if they do think that. In fact, that might make them more likely to buy it. A murder mystery book written by an actual murderer? It would be a great hook."

"Aaron. I'm not an actual murderer." She scowled at him.

Aaron carefully stepped over electrical cords to walk towards the exit doors. "I know that, Cassie. I'm just saying it would be a great hook if you were."

Shaking her head, she spent a few minutes with everyone outside until she couldn't stand the heat any longer. Kissing her dad and waving her thanks to Aaron, she got in Michelle's car.

On the drive back, Cassie had to check again. "Okay, I want the truth now. How did I do?"

"Huh?" Michelle asked. "Oh. You did really well, Cassie. You sounded like the bright, charming author you are when you talked about the book. I would have run out and bought it. Then you sounded like an innocent bystander when you talked about Seth and Solange."

"Good. Although it sounds like Aaron would prefer if I sounded guiltier. I can't believe he thinks this is good marketing."

"He's not that bad, Cassie. In fact..." Michelle paused.

"In fact?"

"Well, I just wanted to make sure that you aren't actually attracted to him. Are you?"

She turned towards Michelle. She tried to look her in the eyes, but Michelle kept them on the road.

"And why do you want to know that?"

"Just answer my question first."

"No, not really. I mean, he is good-looking, but I don't really want a relationship with him. Why? Are you worried you're poaching?" She tried to put a threatening expression on her face, but ended up grinning.

Michelle glanced over and looked relieved to see the grin. "I'd never want a man to come between us, Cassie. So yes, I am making sure you don't want him."

"Do you want him?"

Her best friend shrugged as she turned onto President Street. "I don't know. I definitely think he's hot. And, well, he's asked me out for tomorrow."

"Really?" Cassie drawled out.

"Really. I told him I had to check my schedule, but I just wanted to make sure it was okay with you. I think I'll just meet him for drinks after work though, just to test things out."

"Oh, it's fine with me." Honestly, she was glad to see something positive come from the horror of her book release.

chapter 21

Cassie fielded calls from friends and family all night and into the next morning. She had posted online that she would be on television, and it looked as if a lot of people had watched the show.

Even Mark had called. And her gun expert wasn't known for liking the telephone. Unfortunately, like every other call, the topic went quickly from her book to the actual murders.

"Yes, the police are still investigating," she told him, deciding not to say she was looking into them as well.

"That's good, but you need to be careful. I don't like that someone is so focused on you and keeps bringing you into these murders. What's to say they won't go after you next?"

"I'd rather they go after me instead of anyone else." She pushed Donner away from the laptop and stretched out on the bench in her eating area.

"That's a bad idea. Especially since you won't listen to me and buy a gun for protection."

"I don't want a gun in my home, Mark. You know that. But I guess I'm glad you have them, since you're one of my contacts as well."

"Oh, no need to worry about me. I can take care of myself."

She knew the ex-Marine could defend himself from any attacker. And unless the killer was stupid, he or she knew it too. She didn't worry about Mark.

"Yes, you can, and not just because of your guns. Oh, and talking about guns, I can't believe you're going on Christine's show next week."

He grunted. "Actually, I don't believe I ever agreed to go on the show. We talked about the possibility, but I never confirmed it. I'll talk to her when she comes over this afternoon to take pictures."

"I think you should do it. She was good with me yesterday, even while asking some hard questions. And it sounds like she's pro-gun, so you'd get fair treatment."

He grunted again. "She must be the only pro-gun journalist in Baltimore, then. I'll think about it. Going on television is different than getting interviewed for the paper. I can't believe I'm doing any of this. Whose idea was this damned book again?"

Her laugh turned into a yelp as she rescued her teacup from Donner's experiments on gravity. At least, she assumed that was his reason for constantly knocking things off the table.

"Guilty as charged. But it was a good idea. You've got a fascinating collection that should be shown so people can learn about guns. This way you educate, without having to deal with people."

"I like the latter part. The 'without having to deal with people' part. And I'll tell you this: I am not doing all these crazy book signings, like you are."

"I wouldn't expect you to. Oh, talking about guns, did you get that magazine for the Colt SSP repaired?"

"No, I still need to. I looked at it, and shot it some more, but it still malfunctioned on the second shot when fully—"

She cut him off when she heard a knock on her front door. "Oh, Mark, I need to go. Someone's here."

Looking through the peephole, she felt her heart beat faster. She glanced quickly in the mirror next to the door before opening it wide. She had chosen her outfit that morning with him in mind, just in case he dropped by. She thought she looked good in a loose purple tunic and black leggings. Nice, but still casual.

"Hello, James."

He was wearing a tailored suit of dark charcoal gray that deepened the hue of eyes. He was also carrying a large cardboard box in one arm. When he smiled at her, those irresistible dimples had the usual effect, and she had to put a hand on the door jamb to balance herself.

"Good afternoon, Cassie. May I come in?"

"Of course." She waved at Detective Freeman who remained in the car.

"I'm just stopping here for a few minutes. We were passing by and I wanted to give you this." He handed the box to her.

"You're giving me a gift?" She was turning to mush already and had no idea what it was.

He shrugged and shoved his hands in his pockets. "Sort of a gift."

Taking the box to the dining room table, she glanced over at him. "To congratulate me on my show yesterday?" She was fishing for compliments, she knew she was, but she didn't care. At the very least, she wanted to know if he had even watched the show.

"You did very well. Christine asked some hard questions and you fielded them."

Cassie beamed, distracted enough to forget his present. She stood locked in his gaze for a long moment and wasn't sure who leaned in first, but that didn't matter once their lips made contact. Their kiss was cut short when the cat leaped onto the dining table and swatted the box.

She laughed. "He loves boxes."

Whittaker reached over to scratch Donner. That distracted the cat long enough for Cassie to search for and find scissors. "I hope he likes what's in it, actually."

She stopped cutting through the tape and stared at him. "You got Donner a gift?"

He just smiled.

Opening the box, she removed the contents and felt like a romantic, sappy fool. He had brought Donner—and her—a present. The automatic feeder and timer would come in handy with her new schedule. Most women might not have appreciated the gift, but she was ready to swoon. He had thought of her cat. It was so sweet.

"Thank you, James." She cupped his face and kissed him. Once, then twice. Then three times for luck, a longer kiss that Whittaker broke off with a sigh.

"Sorry. I need to get going."

"I'm sure Detective Freeman will tease you enough already. Are you following a lead?"

He dropped the box on the floor and laughed when Donner jumped immediately into the center of it. "Of sorts. We're trying to track down who leaked the photos and other information to Ms. Gavreau. Right now, everyone has denied sending her any of the information. They probably still leaked it to someone else, but not directly to her."

"You think that will lead you to the murderer?"

"I don't think anything yet. I try to go into these situations without preconceptions."

"Huh. I don't do it that way." She bounced the box lid and moved her hand quickly to avoid getting whacked by claws. "Well, he likes the box. Anyway, I always envision the scenario first and try to figure out if it would work. Marty works that way as well."

"Marty is fictional, Cassie. And walking into a situation already thinking you know things is a good way to make mistakes. I don't like to make mistakes."

"No, I'm sure you don't."

When they heard the sound of a horn honking, he rolled his eyes. "Talking about mistakes, I better go before Freeman really gets annoying." He kissed her quickly and headed out.

"Thanks for the feeder, James. Donner thanks you as well."

"You're welcome." He looked down at the cat. "And you're welcome too, Donner. I guess."

"Oh, he'll appreciate it more than I will, trust me. Good luck today."

"I hope it doesn't take luck, but I do hope we find out something."

She waved again to Detective Freeman and leaned against the door jamb. "Me too."

Worried all over, she spent the next hours checking up on her contacts, but each one of them reassured her in some way that everything was all right. Well, she ended up comforting Paul's wife, Mary Larson, who was obviously worried, considering what happened to Liam Brody.

Christine sounded almost as if she'd like some newsworthy excitement to happen to her, but everyone else brushed off her concerns. She didn't bother calling Mark back since she figured he'd reached his phone quota for the day.

She shook her head while she addressed Donner, who was purring contentedly in his new box. "I guess people aren't worried until it's actually happened to them or to someone they know."

She had barely set down the phone before it rang again. Checking the readout, she grinned. "Hey, Michelle."

"Hey yourself. How's your day going?"

Cassie told her about Whittaker's gift. She wasn't surprised to hear her friend sigh in pleasure.

"Oh, he knows the way to your heart, doesn't he? That's so nice. And considerate." Michelle sighed again and cleared her throat. "So, I'm going to see if Aaron is nice or considerate. I'm meeting him at the Harryman House at four-thirty today for drinks."

"In Reisterstown? Why so far away?"

"It was his idea. Doesn't he live close to there or something?"

Cassie paged through her day planner and checked. "Yeah, he does. Same road, in fact. That doesn't sound considerate or nice. Does he think you need to be near his bedroom or something? Or is he just making sure he has a short drive home?"

"Cassie," Michelle chided. "Maybe he just likes that restaurant."

"I guess so. I wish you luck."

"I hope I get lucky," Michelle said with a laugh.

Cassie laughed with her, but she knew her friend was all talk. Michelle might talk about sex—a lot—but her friend was extremely choosy and careful.

"Well, I'm not sure I'll wish that one for you, but I hope you have a good time."

"Me too. And if not, I'll give you the standard signal, okay?"

Cassie agreed and hung up, making certain that her phone volume was turned on in case Michelle did text with the signal. Then it would be her job to call her friend and fake some type of emergency so that Michelle could leave the date early.

She turned back to her computer and tried to get into the murder frame of mind. A fictional murder frame of mind. She managed to add over two thousand words, but then got sidetracked into Internet research on how to make ricin. Even though she regularly benefited from it, Cassie was disturbed how easy it was to find things out on web. Then again, there were probably also agencies monitoring those sites.

She grinned at her computer screen. She was doomed if anyone ever did a search history on her computer. She had the oddest sites bookmarked, including the newly added step-by-step guide to making ricin.

When there was another knock on the door, her first thought was that Whittaker had returned. However, since it was only four forty-five, she doubted he was finished with his shift yet.

Running over to the door, she was surprised to see Linda, surrounded once again by portable birds. With a concerned glance at Donner—she wasn't sure how he would handle loose birds—she opened the door.

"Hello, Linda."

"Your friend's in danger, Cassie," Linda blurted out without preamble.

"What friend? Why do you think that?"

"They keep saying so."

She barely controlled the eye roll. "What? Are they saying 'Red's in danger' again?"

She winced as Houdini squawked those exact words and flapped his wings, sending Linda's white hair into disarray. She turned to check Donner and saw he had abandoned his box and was now slinking forward.

"No, Donner, don't even think it," she said.

Linda shook her head and took off the backpack containing Dorian. "Not just that, Cassie. I mean, yes, Dorian and Houdini keep stating that, but it's not *just* that."

Taking a deep breath, Cassie decided to say the hard truth. "Look, Linda, they aren't predicting the future."

Linda placed the backpack on the table and reached for the little carrier bag on her chest. "What?"

"They're quoting movies. *Twister, Texas Chainsaw Massacre, The Perfect Storm,* movies like that."

Cassie was surprised when the other woman rolled her eyes. "I know that, Cassie. Dorian and Houdini's previous owners ran a movie theater. The point is, they quote the right movie at the right time."

"You knew that?"

"Yes, but that's not important. What's important is that they are insisting that Red's friend is in danger."

Cassie reacted just in time to snag Donner before he jumped on the table. Gripping him tightly, she ran upstairs. She locked him in her room and ignored his yowls of protest.

Trotting back down the stairs, she apologized. "Sorry about that."

Again, Linda shook her head. "He's a cat, he's doing what he's supposed to do. But you need to hurry about your friend."

"Because Dorian keeps saying that I'm in danger? Presuming I'm Red, that is."

"They're saying that your friend is in danger."

Cassie started to shake her head in denial, but she couldn't help but wonder which friend could be in danger. She glanced up at the clock.

"Oh, God, Michelle."

Her best friend.

Michelle was a resource. She had edited the book. And she was currently out with Aaron, who was one of the few people Cassie had considered would actually have a motive. The more her books sold, the more he'd get from his percentage.

He had said that he would do anything to market her book...would he go that far?

She could picture the scene perfectly. When she met with him on the Monday before the first murder, he grabbed her day planner out of her purse. He knew when Seth would be out, thanks to the appointment listed in her planner.

> Breaking in to the arsonist's home, the agent laid in wait for Seth Montgomery to return. He practically drooled, thinking of all the publicity that would follow Cassie Ellis and her book. Maybe he'd even get to handle the movie rights. He'd have it made.
>
> When the front door scraped open and a belch announced the arrival of his victim, he jumped up from behind the couch...

The pictures she had seen indicated that the gunshots had come from that angle.

> "Who the hell are you?" Seth demanded, although he was sweating in fright.
>
> The agent remained silent. Throwing down the day planner, Aaron unloaded two shots into Seth, a chilly look in his hard brown eyes.

Then he waited a few days, having gotten Solange's address from her day planner. Cassie's imagination easily wrote the next scene…

> Those same cold brown eyes watched the beautiful lawyer leave her office for her coffee house meeting. He smirked. Getting Solange to call Cassie and arrange a meeting had been almost too easy. It just took one phone call. Of course the blonde couldn't resist any opportunity to bait the author.
>
> Following at a discreet distance, he parked a row over in the parking garage. It shouldn't take long. Not long at all. He pulled out his smartphone and amused himself with Tetris as he waited for his victim to return.
>
> When the unsuspecting Frenchwoman walked back to the car alone, he gripped the gun tightly and readied himself for his big moment.
>
> When she finally got to her Mercedes, Aaron slipped out of his silver BMW and walked towards her.
>
> "Solange," he called out.
>
> She looked over and saw a handsome man standing by an expensive car. Flirting instinctively, she gave him a catlike smile.
>
> The smile then turned to fear as the dashing stranger pulled out a gun.
>
> She screamed and turned around as he shot—

"Cassie?" Linda gripped her tightly by the arm.

Cassie focused on the older woman as fear slammed through her.

"Oh, God, Michelle is in danger." She grabbed her cell phone and her keys and raced out of the house, leaving Linda inside.

She called as soon as she was in the car. "Answer, answer, answer," she chanted.

Michelle didn't answer. Obviously, she would've turned off the ringer if she went on a date.

Cassie hung up and called Whittaker.

"Michelle's in danger!" she blurted out when he picked up. "Meet me at the Harryman House."

"What? That's in Reisterstown, Cassie. Out of the city."

"I know. Just meet me there."

She hung up and threw the phone on the passenger seat as she concentrated on driving out of town. Right before she exited the interstate, the phone chimed the arrival of a text message. She grabbed for it and fumbled, just catching a glimpse of the readout before it fell to the floor. Michelle!

"Oh God, she needs help." Cassie sped down Main Street, double parked outside the restaurant, and raced inside.

And almost ran head-on into her best friend.

Michelle was coming out of the ladies' room in the lobby, safe and sound.

Cassie gripped her by the arms. "Are you okay?"

Michelle arched an eyebrow. "I'm bored out of my mind, but other than that, I'm okay. You didn't return my signal text."

Cassie backed up and ran a hand through her hair. "That's what the text was about?"

"Yes, I needed to get out of there, Cassie. It was horrible. The man talked about himself the entire time. Bragged about himself, really. I thought you were psychic when I noticed you had called me right before I got out the phone to text you."

Cassie shook her head as the panic cleared. "Oh God, psychic is the problem. Serves me right for believing a bird."

She was about to explain it when Whittaker raced in to the lobby.

"What's going on, Cassie? Freeman is parking your car, you left the keys inside."

Cassie hung her head in shame. "I, well, I was worried that Michelle was the next target."

"Me?" Michelle looked at her in shock. "I'm not a resource."

"That's what I thought too. But then I realized you're my editor. You're in my acknowledgments."

Michelle stared at her. "Well, shit, I never thought I was in danger." Then she smacked Cassie on the shoulder. "Wait, you thought Aaron was the murderer? And you let me date him?"

"Well, I didn't suspect him until today. Did you suspect him, James?"

Whittaker clicked his phone closed. "He's in the clear. You should've just asked me."

"Why is he in the clear? He has a motive." Then she shut up as the man himself walked through the lobby. "Hello, Aaron."

He looked at the group quizzically and turned to Michelle. "I thought you said you had to help Cassie."

"I do," she said smoothly. "That's why Cassie is here, so I can help her. Thank you again for the drinks, Aaron."

Aaron took the hint and kept walking.

After he left, Cassie turned back to Whittaker. "So, why don't you suspect him?"

Whittaker's lips twitched, cluing her in that he was fighting a smile. "Because he has an unassailable alibi for the first murder."

"What alibi?"

When he refused to answer, she folded her arms and glared at him. "Look, I want to know why I shouldn't suspect him."

Whittaker shook his head but evidently couldn't hold back the smile any longer. When Michelle nudged her, Cassie glanced over to see Michelle staring at Whittaker, a silly grin on her lips. Michelle had a weakness for dimples, too.

"Detective Whittaker." Cassie tried to hold back the whine, but now she really wanted to know.

"Okay, okay. He was at the emergency room."

"That's an unassailable alibi? Maybe he went there on purpose for cover."

Whittaker's smile got wider. "No. I made sure to check the records and well, it definitely was an emergency."

Michelle cocked her head. "And what was the emergency?"

"Nothing. Really." He grinned. "Okay, he just needed stitches. He cut himself."

Since Whittaker was refusing to look at them now, Cassie knew there was more. "How?"

"Shaving."

Since the how wasn't the funny part, she kept asking questions. "Where?"

That's when he started laughing, but he still wouldn't answer. Cassie's frustration grew when Michelle joined in with insane giggles.

"What?" She poked a finger in Michelle's ribs. "How do you know what's so funny?"

Michelle struggled to take a deep breath. "Think about it, Cassie. Where would a man really hate to be cut, and it might be embarrassing if he was shaving there?"

It took her a moment, but she got it. By the time she stopped laughing, Cassie was wishing for a bathroom. She snorted as she realized something. "That's why you reacted that night, at Golden West, when I said he didn't have the balls for it."

Still laughing, Whittaker nodded his head.

Cassie leaned against the wall and sulked. "I can't believe I fell for Linda's predictions again."

"The Psychic Birdbrains again?" Whittaker asked, sobering. "Cassie, I told you they're just quoting movies."

"I know, I know. I just jumped to conclusions."

She was glad when he just smiled and held back the *"I told you so."*

"Anyway, I'm sorry I wasted your time, Detective Whittaker. And sorry that your date was a waste of time as well, Michelle."

"Well, that's why I always start with just drinks, just in case." Michelle smiled at the detective. "Maybe you can join Cassie for drinks, Detective, since you're already here."

He flicked a glance at his watch. "Actually, we've got a few other things to check out. Maybe later, Cassie." He kissed her on the cheek. "Nice seeing you, Michelle."

Cassie watched him leave, and realized her friend was staring at him. She gave her a playful push when she noticed just where Michelle's eyes had wandered. "Stop it. I saw him first."

"Now I see why you aren't attracted to Aaron, and I don't mean because Aaron's a bore. The cop is hot."

"He is, isn't he?"

"Have you cooked for him yet? You should cook for him. Invite him now," Michelle hissed when Whittaker jogged back in.

She wondered what he wanted until he handed her the keys to her car. She bit her lower lip and felt stupid all over again.

"It's parked in the lot behind the restaurant."

Cassie took her best friend's advice. "Look, are you getting off any time soon?" She nudged Michelle when she snorted, obviously taking that comment in a perverted way.

"I might. Depends on what we find out."

"Well, if it's not too late, I'd be happy to cook for you."

His eyes brightened at the offer.

Cassie figured if the idea of dinner made him so happy, then her friends were right when they said the way to a man's heart is through his stomach.

"She's a great cook," Michelle put in, earning another nudge.

"I'd love to have a home-cooked meal, can't say I do much of that at home. I'll call you as soon as I know anything. Might be late though."

"I don't mind late."

Now she had to figure out what to cook.

* * *

Back in the car, she thought that she should cook Parrots *à la* King. She still couldn't believe she had fallen for that psychic bird bullshit.

Still, she called Linda and tried to be nice.

"Did you find your friend?" the older woman asked immediately.

"I did, and she was just fine, Linda. I really think that Dorian and Houdini are just quoting some random movie this time."

"It wasn't Dorian or Houdini, Cassie. It was George."

"George?" Cassie asked absently as she put the key in the ignition. "I didn't think she even talked."

"She does, but only rarely predicts. And she's still chirping 'Red's friend danger' over and over again."

"I don't know, Linda. My friend is fine..." Cassie paused as she realized that Michelle wasn't her only friend meeting someone that evening. "Oh God, I'll call you back."

chapter 22

Mark.

Who was meeting Christine Schmidt.

The same Christine who was benefiting from the publicity of the murders with greater readership and more viewers.

Giving her motive.

The same Christine who was pro-gun and had sounded knowledgeable talking about firearms.

Giving her means.

And the same Christine who was meeting Mark today.

And now she had an opportunity.

Cassie's heart began to race as she pulled out her phone again and dialed Mark, cursing when he didn't answer. *Don't panic,* she told herself.

She turned the key in the ignition, stepped on the gas, and cursed as the car surged and moaned. She cursed again and released the emergency brake.

Okay, starting now, don't panic.

She still had time, right? Flicking a glance at the dashboard clock, she saw it was fifteen minutes until six. She had time. Christine said they were meeting at seven.

But Mark said the meeting was this afternoon. Wouldn't he have said evening if they were meeting at seven? Obviously, Christine had lied to establish an alibi.

Thinking about alibis, she used her phone's voice feature to call Whittaker.

"What about Christine?" she blurted as soon as he picked up. "What about her alibis for the murders?"

"Why do you want to know?" he asked suspiciously.

"Just answer."

"She was on phone calls around the approximate time of the first murder. We contacted the authors, and they had spoken with her around that time, calling her on her work number."

"So? She could have forwarded her calls." Once again, she was racing down Main Street, this time in the opposite direction."What about the second murder?"

"She was at a conference at the Convention Center."

She cursed when the traffic light turned red. Glancing around, she gunned the motor and went through. "She could've left at any time, it's not like they take attendance."

"We're looking into that, Cassie."

"You suspect her as well."

"We're looking into things. I told you not to go into situations with assumptions."

She veered left and gripped the steering wheel tightly as her tires protested the fast turn. "The first murder took place the day before her blog about me, the second the day before the *Dispatch* article, the third shooting—"

"Yes, we've realized that already."

She gritted her teeth at his incredibly patient tone. Now was not the time to be patient and thorough.

"She's a marathon runner. That's why she was able to outrun you."

"I hadn't known that, but wait a damn minute, Cassie. We're looking into it. In fact, we're on the way to the *Dispatch* headquarters now."

"She's not there. She's with Mark, at his home. She told me they were meeting at seven, but he said this afternoon. He's one of my contacts."

She heard him suck in a breath. "Let me call you back."

She tried calling Mark several more times as she sped towards the outskirts of Finksburg. She went three more miles and said five Hail Marys before Whittaker called her back.

"Okay, Freeman and I are on the way to Mark's home, as are the Carroll County police. Stay out of it, Cassie."

She turned onto the road that led to Mark's house. "I'm almost there."

"You're what?" She heard him mutter to Freeman. "Listen, don't do anything stupid, let us handle—"

"He's my friend, James."

"Just wait for us there, damn it. We're five minutes away. Stay in the car. That's an order!"

She could hear the desperation in his voice but hit the call disconnect button. Her heart was beating rapidly and not because of her breakneck speed. She tried to focus on the road as she roared past the rural scenery, but couldn't stop imagining what was happening at Mark's house.

They'd be in his backyard on his outdoor range, she thought. Mark had built the range himself, using a tall hill as a berm to contain the bullets downrange. He'd built wooden benches to hold the guns and ammunition, and smaller berms of dirt for rifle practice.

If Mark was still demonstrating the guns, they'd both be wearing ear protectors. Hopefully they were just wearing regular earplugs for outdoor shooting. That might make it easier to sneak up on them.

But how did Christine plan on killing Mark when he was armed? And why did she lie about the time? Thinking back, Cassie realized that the reporter had deliberately told Cassie, in front of others, that she was meeting Mark at seven.

Cassie took a corner too fast, wheels screeching and gravel flying as she fought the steering wheel for control. She turned into the skid and slowed down. It wouldn't help Mark if she died on the drive to his house.

She had to be prepared and figure out Christine's plans. The woman wasn't stupid; the success of the other murders had demonstrated her cleverness. So what was she doing?

Cassie took a shocked breath as Christine's plan became clear in her mind. It was exactly what she would write if this were the villain in a book.

Christine would set it up as a suicide. She would make it look as if Mark killed himself, probably with the gun used for the other murders. Then she'd claim she just happened to find his body when she arrived at seven. And make sure she had some type of proof that she had still been driving up earlier, like a gas receipt or something.

When Cassie checked the clock, she saw it was barely six. She said a silent prayer that she was in time as she raced up Mark's long driveway. Cassie made sure to block Christine's blue Audi from any easy escape.

She remembered to take her keys, but didn't even bother to close her door as she slid out and ran for the house. Then she froze as she heard gunshots.

It sounded like rhythmic firing, so she suspected it was Mark demoing a gun. She turned towards the sound.

Then she stilled and wondered if she should wait for Whittaker.

But she only paused for a moment. Mark was a friend. And it was her own fault that he was even meeting with Christine in the first place. Stomach churning, she ran behind the house.

The range was a good three hundred yards from the house, past a small stand of trees. She tried to move stealthily as she approached the range, but her ragged breathing sounded so loud to her ears that she figured it would be a sure giveaway to anyone, even if they had on ear protectors.

Running again, she tried to figure out what to do. Without a gun, she was only armed with her wits. And as fast as her thoughts were whirling right now, she wasn't sure that was going to help at all.

About one hundred feet away, she stopped to take stock and peek around a tree.

Mark was shooting one of his guns, his focus on the target. Sunlight glinting off shiny steel allowed her to identify the Colt SSP. The treacherous Christine was standing about ten feet away, perpendicular to downrange, a camera lifted to her face. Cassie took a quick breath of relief.

When Mark stopped shooting, the reporter lowered the camera and took a few steps toward him. He turned to the bench, picked up and loaded the second magazine. And Cassie watched in mute horror as Christine reached into the camera bag, pulled out a stun gun, and pressed it against Mark's back.

Cassie hurled herself forward, desperate to do something.

As Mark fell backward, the reporter struck him hard in the neck before catching him. Using her body, Christine eased him down to lean against the bunker, then turned and looked up.

Shit! Cassie knew she had been spotted when Christine jerked, let Mark crash to the ground, and dropped something from her right hand. A syringe!

The reporter reached into her bag again. This time, she pulled out a gun.

Cassie ran for a tree to avoid the rapid gunshots. She pressed her body against the rough bark, then pressed even tighter when a shot caromed off of her tree, sending wood flying.

Relief flooded through her when she heard emergency sirens and slamming doors. She wasn't sure if the other woman could hear the sounds—her own ears were ringing from the incredibly loud gunfire—but Christine cursed loudly.

"You called the police?" she snarled.

"Of course I did." Cassie yelled. "What did you think I would do?"

"Enjoy your celebrity, of course. We've both benefited from this. You got sales, I got followers. People are finally reading the book review section of the paper. The *Dispatch* was about to cancel it."

Cassie peeked around the tree. If she wasn't actually here, looking at the reporter, she never would have visualized this scene. It was just too bizarre to imagine.

Christine had propped up Mark next to her, a look of malice transforming her face to grotesque and hateful. She held the gun, two-handed now, Cassie noted.

Cassie could hear the footsteps running towards them. Unfortunately, it looked like Christine could see them coming.

The homicidal woman took a firmer hold on the gun and shouted. "Tell them to stay back!"

"Stay back," Cassie yelled to the police behind her. She recognized Whittaker and Freeman, who were crouching, guns at the ready, about two hundred feet back. "She's got Mark!"

Whittaker took a cautious step forward.

Christine fired. Cassie watched in fear as Whittaker dove behind a tree. She wanted to count the shots that had been fired, but had no idea what gun Christine had or how many rounds the magazine held. Besides, she wasn't feeling lucky.

Whittaker held his position and called out. "This is the police! Stop your firing and put down the weapon."

"Forget it!" Christine screamed. "I have a hostage. I won't hesitate to shoot him." She glanced down at the body next to her.

Cassie figured Christine was regretting the fact that Mark was unconscious. She could have used a conscious hostage, forced him in front of her while she backed up and fled the scene. But there was no way she was dragging a six-foot-tall, two-hundred-and-fifty pound man with her to escape.

Cassie could see the panic in the woman's eyes as she tried to figure out how to get out of there. And she could see the anger that all of the careful planning had been destroyed.

When one of the Carroll County policeman advanced forward, Christine shot two more times, then cursed when the slide locked back. Everyone rushed forward.

Christine threw down the empty gun and reached for the SSP that had fallen on the ground. She fired once. The bullet ricocheted off a tree next to Cassie. She darted behind the last tree before the clearing.

"That one was a warning. The next one goes into the old man." Christine crouched down again and held Mark in front of her for cover.

Cassie pressed her back to the tree and tried to get Whittaker's attention. After all, she knew the gun Christine was using. She knew it contained the second magazine, since Mark had already fired the first one.

The second magazine always malfunctioned.

Catching Whittaker's eye, she signed to him. *Gun jams.*

This time, she didn't care if she used the word "jam" incorrectly. As it was, she had to finger spell the word out.

She caught a quick head shake from him before she turned back around to look at Christine.

"Put down the gun, Ms. Schmidt," he called out.

Cassie tried to peer around the tree to see if she could tell if the gun had malfunctioned or not. It always malfunctioned after that first shot. Mark had said.

Still, Christine could clear the misfeed and keep firing. Cassie would have to be fast if she wanted to disarm the crazy woman. Maybe she should wait.

She looked back at the cops behind her and saw the tension and readiness to act in all of them.

And looking forward, she saw the desperation on Christine's face as the reporter realized she wasn't getting out of this scenario.

"Oh, screw this!" Christine shouted and pivoted towards Mark. "I'm just gonna shoot him anyway."

Praying that the gun had jammed, Cassie made up her mind and raced forward.

This time everything was in slow motion. She heard Whittaker call her name, saw Mark crumpled on the ground, and watched as Christine jerked the gun towards her and pulled the trigger.

Mark had once told her the worst sounds in the world were a click when you expected a bang, and a bang when you expected a click.

He was right, especially about the latter part. Cassie had expected a click.

There was a bang.

And a sharp, searing pain tore through her left shoulder.

At least her momentum carried her into a full speed tackle. Cassie fell on top of the other woman and knocked her down. The gun bounced out of the Christine's hand. She pushed at Cassie, twisted her body, and reached for the gun. Cassie wanted to go for it, but the shock was so intense she could barely move. She could barely breathe.

She closed her eyes in relief when she saw Whittaker grab the gun. And felt a vindictive joy when Freeman flipped Christine over, face in the dirt, and handcuffed her.

Whittaker rushed over. "What the hell? What were you doing? What were you thinking?" he yelled. He helped her sit up before shrugging off his jacket and pressing the sleeve against her gunshot wound.

She glanced down at her shoulder. It was bleeding badly, but didn't hurt much. More of a burning. She suspected that was due to the numbing effects of shock.

She guessed it was going to hurt a lot more, really soon.

"It was supposed to jam. Malfunction," she mumbled. "It always jams. Malfunctions."

"You counted on it jamming? Are you crazy?" He kept the pressure firm with one hand and brushed her hair out of her face with the other.

"But it always does. Mark said." She pointed at Mark with her good arm, relieved to see him sitting up with some assistance from a Carroll County police officer.

The older man looked over at the sound of his name. "What?"

"Right, Mark?" Cassie said, feeling woozy. "That gun jams, right?"

She had been right. Her shoulder was starting to really hurt as her body protested this violation.

"Malfunctions, Cassie," Mark said automatically. He stared at the gun next to Whittaker. "But only if I load it full. I only put in ten bullets for this picture demo. Why?" He finally noticed her shoulder. "You got shot?"

She glanced down to confirm it again. "Looks like it."

Tired of the current topic of conversation, she decided to pass out.

epilogue

Five hours later, Cassie tried to reassure her father that she was fine. Again.

"I'm okay, Dad. Really." She smoothed down the hospital blanket. "They gave me really good drugs."

"That's not funny, Cassandra." His face twisted up and his eyebrows came together, but instead of the scowl he'd been attempting to fix on her, the expression dissolved into relief and concern. He took her hand in both of his and sighed.

"I'm sorry. But I'm really okay. It was only my shoulder." A shoulder that hurt like hell, even with the drugs.

"Only your shoulder," Michelle muttered. "You were shot, Cassie."

"I know." Cassie decided to keep to herself the thought of how it was good research. But it would be. The impact. The sting. The adrenalin. The blood. She knew she'd be able to accurately describe a gunshot wound when she wrote about it again. That was one reason she wanted to go through childbirth as well, so she'd be able to describe it correctly. After all, they always said, *"Write what you know."*

"She was lucky it was only in the shoulder, and even luckier that I was using full metal jacket ammo so that it just went in and out," Mark said from his wheelchair.

He had already grumbled about being stuck in the hospital overnight, but his doctors had insisted. He managed to somehow bulldoze over his nurses to visit Cassie. "Assuming the gun would malfunction." He shook his head, then grimaced in pain.

"Watch that head of yours, Mark," Cassie said. "And trust me, I've already told myself how stupid I was. I'm not making assumptions any more. At least not about loaded weapons."

Mark sighed. "I've already told you the Four Rules of Gun Safety. Number One is to always assume a gun is loaded. I guess I'll have to give you a subset of rule one, to assume that a loaded gun is perfectly capable of shooting you."

She pouted. "I said I won't make any more assumptions like that."

"I hope you keep to that, Cassie," Whittaker said from the doorway. "But I suspect you won't."

He walked in the room. Cassie thought he looked sexy in his shirt and slacks.

"I just want to point out that I trained her better than this, Detective Whittaker," Mark insisted. "She knows better than to assume a gun will malfunction."

"I think she was just worried about you, Mr. Griffin," Whittaker said.

"I suppose you're right." Mark stared at the floor. "And I guess I should be thanking you, Cassie, for coming to the rescue."

Cassie suspected he was embarrassed and annoyed that someone had gotten the drop on him. "Well, since it's my fault that she was even going after you, we'll consider ourselves even."

"I need to get Mark back to his room," Michelle said brightly. "I promised his nurse I wouldn't let him stay long. Mr. Ellis, would you care to join me?"

Her father headed out with Michelle and Mark, but looked back at the remaining occupants before exiting. Cassie smiled at her best friend and silently thanked her for arranging some alone time for her and Whittaker.

Whittaker stepped up to the bed and took her hand in his. "How are you doing, honey?"

She was glad they had removed the noisy monitors, since her heart rate picked up at the new term. She could deal with "honey." It was better than "babe" or "baby", two monikers that she had always considered patronizing.

Still, as much as she appreciated his concern and the endearment, there was something more important that she wanted from him.

"Did you get her confession?"

"We did. Of course we did." He let her hand go and pulled over a chair. "We had her dead to rights, after all, with the murder weapon on her person and an attempted murder victim by her side. Besides, she wanted to talk about it. She's looking for glory from these murders."

"Which was one motive I think I skipped when I was hypothesizing," Cassie said.

"Well, I missed that one too. Should have realized it since the murders generated so much press. But we only looked at the effect on you, and didn't realize it was benefiting the media as well."

"So she really killed two people, and tried for a third, and a fourth, in order to boost her column's popularity? Her show's popularity?"

He took her hand again, rubbed it gently with his thumb. "Yes. She confessed it all. Said she hopes to get a book deal out of it. She probably will."

"God, I hope not. That would be disgusting."

"It would be." He paused, seemed to come to a decision. "Evidently, one time she was talking to you about your research for your book, and you mentioned how interesting it would be if a murder author did some real research."

Cassie laid back on the pillow and closed her eyes. "God, I remember that conversation. She said that book would get plenty of media attention in that scenario. But we were joking. At least, I was joking," she finished quietly.

"Don't blame yourself, Cassie. Most people in that situation would be joking. It's not your fault it gave her the idea to go off and commit murder."

She took a sip of water from the cup by her bed and tried to listen to his logic. But she knew she'd always feel somewhat responsible for the deaths of Seth and Solange.

"I assume she took my day planner when she interviewed me on Tuesday."

Whittaker nodded.

"She must be crazy."

"Since I think anyone who commits cold-blooded murder is crazy, I agree. But she's fine to stand trial. She's not legally insane. She knows right from wrong, just doesn't care. Or more, she doesn't care if she hurts others to get what she wants."

"I can't understand people like that. I mean, I write about them. But I don't understand them."

He nodded again. "Most people don't. Shouldn't. But Christine figures she has a right to take people's lives, as long as she gets ahead. She had it all planned out from the beginning. She knew she'd end with Mark."

"Since she'd get even more media attention since he had a book coming out too," she said flatly. A book that had been her idea.

"Yes. And she planned to frame him for the murders by having it appear that he had killed himself with the murder weapon. Since he was such a loner, she figured he wouldn't have alibis for the times of the murders."

Cassie reached for the remote to turn off the television mounted on the wall. Although it was muted, she recognized Mark's house on the news. She'd rather hear it direct from Whittaker than on the news.

He glanced up when the screen flashed off, then continued. "She'd even purchased a flask with his initials and filled it with some of his own whiskey. She stole the whiskey when she told him she needed to use the restroom. She was going to pour it in him to imply he had a drinking problem."

"She had planned this out, hadn't she?"

"She had," Whittaker answered. "She also altered her TASER so it wouldn't release the evidence markers that commercial units spread around when they're fired. She was clever."

"Not a bad plan. But wouldn't the autopsy have shown the drugs? The syringe marks?"

"Again, she had thought that through. And researched. She was going to have the syringe mark covered by the angle of the gunshot. The drug she used was fast acting and fast dissolving, and she had an hour before she was going to show up and 'find' his body."

"And go somewhere in that hour to show that she was driving to his home when the murder happened, right?"

When Whittaker nodded, she couldn't take any pleasure in knowing she was right. She kicked her feet out from under the covers and stared at the pink polish on her toes.

"Right, and that's why she made certain to tell you, in front of Aaron, Michelle, your father, and her cameraman, that she was meeting him at seven. The meeting was really set for five thirty. Since he was such a recluse, she didn't think he'd tell anyone what time they were meeting. Then his time of death would be earlier and you'd all be able to back her up that her meeting was at seven. You were smart to pick up on that."

"She really did plan it, didn't she?"

He caressed her hand again. "She did. She likes her research, like…"

"Like I do," Cassie said.

He winced. "Yes. Not that I think you would ever use your research this way."

"You did too. When you first picked me up you did."

"I picked you up? I suppose that's a nicer way to explain how we met then the real story. I picked you up at Corks."

He smiled slowly at that. Her heart skipped a beat, and not due to any of the drugs she was on.

"Did you ever suspect me?"

He shook his head. "Not since you got out your notebook and started taking notes in interview. I've never seen a guilty individual do that."

"Hmm." She was happy that he had never thought she was a killer. And contemplated making the villain in her book start taking notes in the same situation.

"Cassie?" Whittaker brushed her cheek to get her attention.

She looked over at him, started to smile, but stopped when he looked serious. "What?"

"Ms. Gavreau…Solange—wasn't supposed to be the second victim."

"No? Who was?"

He ignored the question. "Solange was a last minute choice. Mike Arnold, Christine's contact at the news desk, was also Solange's friend. He was the one who sent the pictures to her, after he got them from a source who worked at the station—a source who will no longer be working there."

She smiled at his forceful tone.

"Evidently, when Solange planned to meet you, she called Mike to let him know she was meeting you. Gave him the when and where. Solange thought Mike would want to interview you or something. Mike wasn't interested in doing that, but he called Christine at the convention center in case she was interested."

He stopped when a nurse came in to check Cassie's IV and take her dinner order.

It gave her time to consider. "So what, Christine figured that since she was close by, she could whip in and out without anyone noticing?"

"Yes, plus she knew that since you'd yet again be the last person to see the victim, it would cause you to be called into interview again."

"Setting me up?"

"No, just trying to get you more media attention. She really does think you should be grateful."

She shook her head in disbelief.

"Freeman and I were actually already onto her this afternoon. We had finally gotten a warrant to look at the convention center's cameras and saw that she had left during the time of the murder. We were on the way to pick her up when you called about Michelle.

"And talking about Michelle." He paused. "She was originally going to be the second victim. Since you had mentioned her in your dedication."

She wheezed out all the air in her chest. The loss of her best friend would have been horrendous. She covered her mouth with her hands and fought back tears. "Oh, God. Oh, God."

"It didn't happen, Cassie." He brushed her hair out of her face.

"I know." She took a few halting breaths. "But remember, I'm an author. I've got a good imagination. I can picture her in Solange's place in that horrible garage. And I can think how I'd feel. I'd be devastated. I feel horrible enough about Solange, even about Seth. But losing Michelle—having it be my fault—would have been…been…" Words failed her.

"It wouldn't have been your fault, Cassie. It's not your fault. Christine's the guilty one."

"I guess." She took some deep breaths. "I know. You're right."

"Damn straight," he said with a smile. "About time you figured that out."

She laughed, appreciating his effort to lighten up the mood as she brushed away the remaining tears. She reached out and grabbed his hand this time.

"I'm so thankful to you, to Freeman, the Carroll County police, everyone. So glad we managed to get to Mark in time."

He shifted in his chair.

Cassie smiled at him. For all his confidence, even occasional arrogance, Whittaker really didn't seem to take praise very well.

Another thought struck her. "I guess I should call Linda; tell her that the birds were right."

"Oh, come on." He rolled his eyes. "You really think that birds can predict the future?"

She shrugged, then wished she hadn't when her shoulder throbbed. "I'm just saying George was right, my friend was in danger."

"So were you, Cassie. I can't believe you ran towards a loaded gun. I was ready to take a shot at Christine when you ran across my line of sight. I thought you were crazy."

"It was supposed to malfunction." Somehow, she suspected she wouldn't live this one down for a while. Then she shook her head at her thoughts. At least she'd live. "At least it ended well."

Whittaker raised his eyebrows, then sent a pointed glance to her shoulder.

"Okay, *kind* of well. But Christine's in jail, Mark's alive, and I wasn't hurt that badly. That's what's important."

"Yes, those things are important."

He leaned closer, reached for her other hand, and rested their joined hands in her lap. Looked deep into her eyes.

"And we've moved past an important point in our relationship, right?"

She was thrilled to hear him say they had a relationship. "What point is that? Not having to hide it since the cases are closed?"

"That, too. But I mean more that we've gotten the hard stuff out of the way. You've already given me a heart attack, already been shot. You won't do that again, right?" He watched her carefully with those smoky eyes.

She just smiled. "I'll have to find other trouble."

THE END

About

Cathy Wiley, Author

CATHY WILEY IS HAPPIEST when plotting stories in her head or on the computer, or when she's delving into research.

She draws upon her experience in the hospitality business to show the lighter, quirkier side of people and upon her own morbid mind to show the darker side.

In her free time, she enjoys scuba diving, dancing, wine, food, and reading. She lives outside of Baltimore, Maryland, with two very spoiled cats.

Visit her website at www.cathywiley.com. She would greatly enjoy getting e-mail from her fans. She can be reached at cathy_wiley@zapstone.com

You can also visit her website at:

www.cathywiley.com
or follow her on Facebook and Twitter.

Zapstone Productions LLC

Publishers of unique, quality voices in fiction

A small independent publisher with offices in Minnesota and Maryland. Visit **www.zapstone.com** for more information, sneak previews, and upcoming titles.

More Cassandra Ellis...

Dead to Writes

Cassandra Ellis is a soon-to-be published author, days away from achieving her lifetime goal. But before she can celebrate, before she can even have her first book signing, she's brought in to Baltimore City Police Headquarters for questioning in connection to a real-life murder. She was the last person to see the victim alive, and her day planner was found next to the body. Cassie must use all the skills she developed as a mystery writer—plus the help of a hot homicide detective and a team of psychic parrots—to crack the case.

Two Wrongs Don't Make a Write

Author Cassie Ellis just wants to meet his father, even though her boyfriend, Detective James Whittaker, thinks it's a really bad idea. Cassie knows that Whittaker has avoided talking to, even seeing his father, ever since the elder Whittaker was discovered taking bribes and retired from the police force in shame. But now Whittaker's father is accused of murdering the individuals that had exposed his past crimes. Cassie must take action, not only to clear the already tarnished reputation of the father of the man she loves, but to mend the void between them.

Write of Passage

Author Cassie Ellis thought she'd enjoy a nice relaxing cruise with her friends and take a break from writing. Her boyfriend, Detective James Whittaker, was hoping for a little romance. But after Cassie finds a dead body on the balcony and it seems like everyone they meet on the ship had a motive to kill the victim, their cruise starts to feel more like *Murder on the Orient Express* than *The Love Boat.* (Release date TBA)

CPSIA information can be obtained at www.ICGtesting.com
Printed in the USA
LVOW050054180612

286535LV00001B/112/P

9 780971 543331